Roberta Latow has been a
Springfield, Massachussetts and N
has also been an international interior designer
USA, Europe, Africa and the Middle East, travelling
extensively to acquire arts, artefacts and handicrafts.
Her sense of adventure and her experiences on her
travels have enriched her writing; her fascination with
heroic men and women; how and why they create the
lives they do for themselves; the romantic and erotic
core within – all these themes are endlessly interesting
to her, and form the subjects and backgrounds of her
novels.

'Latow's writing is vibrant and vital. Her characters
are much more than caricatures and she describes
them in such a distinctive, dynamic way that you can't
help but be swept along by them. Latow is a pleasure
to read.' *Books* magazine

Also by Roberta Latow

Secret Souls

Roberta Latow

HEADLINE

First published in 1996
by HEADLINE BOOK PUBLISHING

First published in paperback in 1997
by HEADLINE BOOK PUBLISHING

10 9 8 7 6 5 4 3 2 1

ISBN 0 7472 5306 4

Printed and bound in Great Britain by
Cox & Wyman Ltd, Reading, Berks

HEADLINE BOOK PUBLISHING
A division of Hodder Headline PLC
338 Euston Road
London NW1 3BH

For
Iris and Joseph Faratzi
in gratitude

Label me not coward,
For I have no fear of my passions,
Erotic pleasures or sensuous dreams.
They are the perfume of my soul,
The essence of my life.

The Epic of Artimadon

ON THE ISLAND OF CRETE,
IRAKLION and LIVAKIA

1994

Chapter 1

When he entered the nearly deserted restaurant Chadwick was sitting alone at a table where she had a spectacular view of the sea crashing up against a tumble of huge jagged rock formations. On occasion it would take aim, hit the window with a splash and the salt water would run down the glass.

It was as if all the lights of the world had been turned on or the sun had burst through the roof of the small ancient building that had once been a place of worship, a mosque. Everything seemed suddenly to brighten and come alive. He was a man whose very presence made things pulsate, the adrenaline run.

The Cretan proprietor of the Rhadamanthys smiling broadly and waving his arms, rushed forward to shake the newcomer's hand, greet him with a bone-crushing bear hug. Not satisfied, he kissed him: a short, sharp kiss hard on the lips, then roughly pushed him away. He slapped the man affectionately on the cheek. Arms round each other, the two men walked to a table across the room from her, the restaurateur announcing loudly the man's arrival to the hovering waiters and the cooks somewhere out of sight in the recesses of the building.

Three men and a woman, all short, plump and dark, and

smothered in huge white aprons stained with cooking, rushed from the kitchen to greet the man. Chadwick could barely keep her eyes from drifting to the handsome intruder who looked more like the Greek god Poseidon risen from the sea than another diner at the Rhadamanthys. Out had come the bottle of wine and the stubby thick glasses. They sat, all of them, laughing, drinking, and talking food: special dishes they were going to make for him and his friends.

No, he was not alone as she was. Here was a man who had never in his entire life been alone. There was something in his physiognomy that expressed that.

Just looking at him made her feel good, so alive. This was no man with a tenuous hold on life. He held it tight in both his hands. Life was an adventure and he was a pleasure seeker, one who loved women, all things exciting and sensuous. With his laughter, his smile, his sexy good looks, generosity of spirit, he was a man who played with the world. How she would have liked to be a part of his world.

It was difficult not to steal the odd glance nor to wonder what his friends would be like. She knew one thing for certain: at least one of them would be a woman, his, beautiful, and they would have sex before the day was out. He was that kind of man. She would be a special kind of lady, his kind of woman.

While sipping her wine she looked over the rim of the glass and caught him looking at her. How often had he done that? Only for a second did their eyes meet; she recognised lust and looked away with a heart racing with carnal desire. She smiled, felt warm all over, but never looked his way again. Instead she concentrated on the delicious food set in front of her, the view, and eavesdropped on the conversation and laughter that drifted her way.

Chadwick never minded dining alone, in fact she quite liked it. But this stranger made her suddenly aware of how alone she must look to him. It was a strange sensation, one she had never known, being caught out in her aloneness. She wanted to shout across the room to him, 'Alone but not lonely'. How fanciful! She couldn't help but smile. What fun being fanciful. Another new sensation. Thirty-four years old and only just discovering life and the different worlds it encompassed.

Chadwick raised her chin and shook her head ever so slightly to shake her hair away from her face, then briefly ran her fingers through it, a lifelong habit. Hannibal had often told her it was a sensuous act that never failed to draw his attention, excite his lust. Hannibal! He would be with her always, all the days of her life. She sighed as the memory of his words burned bright for a split second. She raised her hand for attention and finally caught a waiter's eye. Her Greek was good, he was impressed as all Greeks were when a foreigner spoke their language as well as she did.

The second small carafe of house wine arrived at her table and her glass was filled before the waiter returned to sit with Poseidon and the others. Yes, by now she thought of him as that god of the sea, it amused her to think of him as a man of myth, a creature from the depths.

This, her first day, had been just wonderful and now this stranger bursting with sensual life seemed only to add to it. Chadwick felt incredibly happy, at ease with herself and life in general. It felt good to be back in Crete again and to have made her pilgrimage here to Iraklion. She had dreamed of her return for such a long time. She had fallen in love with the island and its people when she and Hannibal had made a trip there. It had inspired her to perfect her University Greek and to work on something she had been dithering with for too many years. Those were some of the happiest years of their life together, when they returned from Crete and she worked on her *History of the Life and Work of El Greco*.

She drained her glass. How surprised she had been at the book's success, the way she had taken the art book world by storm by writing the definitive work on the Spanish Mannerist painter who had been born more than four hundred years earlier, here in Iraklion, when Crete had been a possession of the Republic of Venice. Not Hannibal. He had always believed in her abilities; her success had been his success, no man could have been more proud and pleased with his wife.

Another dull thud against the window as spray from a breaking wave hit the glass and ran down the window. What a stroke of luck to have remembered the name of this restaurant given to her by an archaeologist friend who had been in Crete on a dig for two years. She stole another glance at Poseidon. This time she was more brave and allowed her gaze to linger. What, she wondered, must it be like to be made love to by a god, or even a man who lived and loved like one? Yes, there was something to be said for being fanciful. She gave a little giggle, feeling young and very foolish.

Chadwick was forking a slice of crisp and golden deep fried courgette to her lips when she felt his gaze upon her. She looked over the fork and their eyes met. They told her he thought she was lovely and luscious, as delectable as the morsel on her fork. That look however did not say, 'I want you.' It was one of admiration rather than flirtation. She didn't mind; in fact, being admired by a god would do just nicely.

Very nearly two hours had passed since his arrival had created a buzz of life, and still Chadwick lingered over her food and fantasised about the life the man across the room led. She was quite looking forward to the arrival of his friends. She thought they might somehow complete a picture of what this charismatic figure's world was all about. This way of life she would have liked, for even a brief moment, to be a part of.

How easy it was to slip into the Greek rhythm of life: long lazy lunches and afternoon siestas, racing around like a mad man or lazing like a lounge lizard, the laughter, sun and the sea. Chadwick was lingering over her wine and a third demitasse cup of strong, black and thickly sweet coffee when his friends arrived. Chadwick saw them before the man did. The woman had the kind of sensuous beauty that Chadwick had expected a woman of his to have.

The woman was only a few feet away from him when he saw her and rose from his chair, as did the two men sitting with him. The way he looked at her ... no man had ever looked at Chadwick with such passion, lust shimmering like translucent waves of heat. Chadwick's heart raced. The woman said only a few words to him. Chadwick could only catch: 'Going there was like a last lament for Arnold. It's done, it's over. Please, let's live.'

The look in her eyes was for him alone when she said, 'Let's live.' Chadwick placed her hand over her heart and closed her eyes for a moment, so touched was she by this woman who could love as Chadwick had never loved. 'Let's live' seemed to have new, different, more thrilling connotations. Chadwick had been happy, she had been in love, but where had she been? Certainly not where this man and woman had been, nor where they were going.

Chadwick was mesmerised by the couple. She heard his name for the first time: Max. Her Poseidon was immediately transformed from a god to a man, and Chadwick liked him even better. Max swept the woman into his arms and held her there. He whispered something in her ear. Chadwick's heart was racing. Every fibre of her being hungered for the love emanating from this couple as Max caressed his lady's hair, her shoulders, and taking first one of her hands in his and then the other, kissed her fingers.

At last, with an arm round her waist, he stepped away from their embrace and shook hands with the man who had accompanied her. After enthusiastic greetings for Max's guests from the men he had been sitting with, the three customers sat down. The proprietor and his staff left the table, as obviously impressed by the couple's passion for each other as Chadwick was. She could tell that by the tongue clicking (Greek admiration), the raised arm and wrist rotating, a cupped hand caressing the air (Greek wonderment) as they rushed about bringing food and more drink to the table.

Now Chadwick heard the woman's name: D'Arcy. *Max and D'Arcy.* As a couple they were like thunder roaring in the sun. Now, for the first time, Chadwick took more than a glancing interest in the man who had arrived with D'Arcy. He was incredibly good-looking, certainly as much so as Max but in a different way. He too was a big man, well over six feet, broad-shouldered, dark and rugged-looking.

Yet there was something sensitive, a certain sensual warmth, in a face that was Greek of the Classical period. She had seen that face depicted in paintings and sculpture in museums all over the world. Greek male beauty: the perfect nose, wide-set eyes, bone structure, sexy, succulent lips. He had the aristocratic looks of a young Marlon Brando, that same unbounded sexuality.

His black curly hair was worn long enough to curl at the collar of his jacket. The man's dark eyes – marvellous for being ever so slightly hooded, their expression sultry and with a definite lusty twinkle in them – excited her interest in him further. He had a moustache; she had never known a man with a bushy moustache. Chadwick found it very macho and surprisingly attractive, possibly more because of the deep winsome dimples in his cheeks, the smile that was broad and laughing and showed his very white teeth.

He was dressed in a well-tailored dark suit, white shirt and a handsome tie of black ribbed silk. He looked important, official even. It therefore surprised her that he had hardly taken his chair when he loosened his tie and slid it from round his neck to fold it neatly and place it in his jacket pocket with one hand as he opened several buttons of his shirt with the other. He seemed now to be even more attractive to Chadwick. She imagined most women wanted him. He was a strong man with a real hard core of male beauty, sex appeal, the sort of erotic looks and style to which a great many women would like to submit.

He sensed her gaze upon him. Their eyes met for only a brief moment but in that time she understood by the way he looked at her that he was a man who enjoyed women

9

enormously, taking over their bodies and their souls. She liked his Greekness, that Cretan temperament she saw in his every gesture, and yet there was too something quite elegant and polished about him. She mused on the many foreign women who had wanted and had him, what it would be like to be one of those women. And now came the fun, imagining who, what he was, how he lived, loved, what his wife was like, if he did indeed have a wife, children. Chadwick often created imaginary lives for strangers. That was how she got to know them for a few minutes.

Another splash against the window distracted her for a moment. The rivulets of salt spray running down the glass sparkled in the hot sun. Chadwick followed one of them with the tip of her finger. It was an unusually hot sun for late-October in Crete, perfect weather because as hot as it was there was autumn in the air, a clear, fresh crispness. She could not have asked for a better day. Through the window, she watched the sea crash up against the rock formations, a mere fifty feet away, and enjoyed its power and its force. The excitement of the sea contrasted with the quiet, steady warmth caressing her: the sun beating through the glass, the sound of the laughter of beautiful strangers from across the room. She had been happy, content in her life, many times and for long periods. Even as her mind drifted away from the here and now to remember, she was aware of experiencing something new and better in her life than she had ever known.

Max de Bonn was intrigued by the elegant woman at the far side of the room. She was sensuous, a very great beauty who seemed remote from, although hungry for, love. And she was alone. He had been watching her for some time before Manoussos and D'Arcy had arrived. The flirtation that had gone on between them had been pathetic by Max's standards, but then he had an excuse. He was distracted: trying to get a feast together for the woman he loved and was committed to. Two very new sensations for him. Under ordinary circumstances he would by now have captured the beautiful stranger's heart as well as her fancy and they would be only hours away from sexual oblivion. Too bad Max was so much in love with D'Arcy. What a shame to let such a delicious woman vanish without a trace from his life.

But all was not yet lost. Since Manoussos and D'Arcy's arrival, the woman seemed, if no longer flirtatious with Max, interested in Manoussos. Her glances at him were no longer stolen as they had been with Max. Her interest in his friend peaked when she had been merely curious about Max. He was an old hand at recognising a woman's desires, he was not a man to miscalculate how far a lady would go for a man she wanted. This remote beauty across the room would go to the limit, even beyond, for Manoussos. Max was amused. Always the tease, he wasted no time. 'D'Arcy, don't you find that woman dining alone intriguing?'

'I hadn't thought about it, but now that you mention it, yes, incredibly beautiful and intriguing. She looks to be a woman who has been loved but hardly touched, strange for someone so sexually vibrant. It's as if she has been encased in a crystal clear casket. She's like the beauty waiting to be released by a kiss from her prince.'

'Then you find her fascinating, much the same as I do. The way she looks at you, Manoussos, I think you're in with a chance there,' teased Max.

D'Arcy leaned closer to Manoussos and gave him a sisterly kiss on the cheek. 'Max is right, Manoussos. She wants you. She might just steal you away from us and keep you for her pleasure for the rest of her life. Now how would you like that?'

Joke as his friends might with him, from the moment Manoussos had entered the restaurant and had seen her, he'd been attracted to her. Yes, her mere presence: a great beauty sitting alone in a near-deserted restaurant off the beaten track was intriguing, but she had instantly been more than that. He had sensed her sublime sexuality, sensual danger. Here was a woman who was an adventure in ecstasy of the body, the heart and the mind. His libido craved a woman like this one, and how many more men before him would have had her? Not many, he thought. A policeman's instinct, or was it that she looked to Manoussos too discerning for promiscuity? Oh, yes, he would have her, he had no doubt about that. That was not his ego talking, rather the manner in which she looked at him.

There was something else about her besides and it had to do with the incredible good looks of this tall, slender yet voluptuous woman with raven black hair, fair skin and seductive grey eyes, large and almond-shaped. It had to do with her being much more than a beautiful woman – an aura of fire and ice and secrets, many secrets, engrained in the soul. It was all there in her face: beautiful for its stunning bone structure, a pointed chin with the bare hint of a cleft in it, a sultry, simmering sexuality. Here was a woman who had seduced men from the day she was born. How they must have abused her for stirring their lust for her! He had been watching her every movement and gesture, half as a policeman and the rest as any man who wanted her sexually, ready to take possession of her elegant perfection. She was like a goddess come to dwell on earth.

Manoussos was a man who thrived on sex with exciting, sexually liberated foreign women. He had had many, they chased after him hard. Infatuations, mild and short-lived, yes, he had had more than his share. Manoussos had fallen in love only once, and never quite out again, with D'Arcy, when they were children. They grew up together, became first loves and lovers, and had for years conducted sexual liaisons together when it suited them. They and everyone else knew they would love each other always, and so their separations were painless. Other lovers had caused them no anxieties because they had always known what they had together had never been quite enough for either one of them. Now across a sea of empty tables Manoussos felt tremendous excitement because here was a dangerous but thrilling woman who could capture his heart entirely.

After D'Arcy's having danced away from a sexual encounter for many years because she never wanted to be another notch on Max's sexual belt, which she surely would have been then, Max and D'Arcy had fallen in love. That had been less than a fortnight ago, and since then they had been together in love rather than lust night and day. Suddenly, sitting at that table with D'Arcy, Max realised this was their time; they were ready to vanish together into the sexual life they both craved. It was evident that D'Arcy was wanting him in the same carnal way as he wanted her. Their exploration of love and passion without sexual congress, something they had been steeped in for the last few weeks, was over for them. Suddenly there was little excitement about lunch and lingering over food.

From across the room, Chadwick watched Max abruptly scrape back his chair, rise and leave the table. There seemed to be a dreadful fuss between Max and the proprietor and then Max whispered something in the man's ear. Immediately he was all smiles and hugs and waving arms. She was a lady alone watching a scene that changed abruptly: watching turned to wonder as Max and the taverna keeper walked past Max's table and friends and across the room to her.

Strangely she didn't feel embarrassed when Max gazed directly into her eyes and smiled while the taverna keeper made excuses: 'I hope it doesn't offend you, madam, our approaching you like this?'

She didn't answer. Nor did she smile. Imperiously, and yet sweetly, she nodded her head and with a hand gestured to them to take a seat. Max was even more dazzled by her.

'This is my good friend Max de Bonn,' offered the restaurateur.

Max raised her hand and lowered his head to place a kiss upon it, then sat down. The Rhadamanthys's proprietor made excuses and left.

Max at his most charming and seductive. Manoussos and D'Arcy were amused – puzzled but amused. This was Max doing what they had seen him do hundreds of times, picking up a lady. D'Arcy felt no jealousy, but rather curiosity. She and Manoussos were laughing at Max's audacity: quite suddenly jumping up and leaving them to flirt with a stranger. 'What's going on, Manoussos?' she asked as the food that had only just arrived was swept away, leaving them with forks poised in the air.

But before he could answer D'Arcy, Max was on his feet kissing the stranger's hand again and walking back to them. The woman was smiling now and her face was flushed, an extra light in her eyes. Max had been very quick. He could not have been away from his table and friends for more than three or four minutes.

'You weren't jealous and you trusted me?' he asked D'Arcy.

'Next you'll be telling me you did it for me,' she teased, but admitted that she had not been the former and did the latter.

Max pulled her up from her chair and into his arms before he kissed her full on the mouth and with great passion told her, 'For that I'm going to make you the happiest woman alive for the rest of your life.' Then he turned to Manoussos and said, 'Her name is Chadwick Chase and she would like to invite you to lunch, so D'Arcy and I can run away with ours and slip into the land of erotic delights. Eros calls to us, old boy. You don't mind, do you? A beautiful woman and finding your way back to Livakia alone ... do you think you can manage?'

Manoussos stroked his moustache by smoothing it down with his thumb and forefinger, a habit when he was contemplating something or when he was pleased. When pleased, it invariably brought a hint of a smile to his lips and his dimples appeared to give him an even more handsome and boyish look. 'I have to say one thing about you, Max, you sure know how to take care of your friends. No, of course I don't mind, though had you told me what was on your mind, I could very well have managed that invitation myself.'

'But what are friends for?' Max retorted before smiles crossed the faces of the two womanisers who had been the closest of friends for so many years.

Manoussos rose from his chair and he and D'Arcy exchanged several words and kissed before she and Max walked away, a trail of waiters following them with baskets of food, the sumptuous feast Max had earlier ordered for them. Without a moment's hesitation, Manoussos walked towards the woman waiting for him.

'You have invited me to lunch. That was gracious of you, especially since you have already had yours. May I sit down?'

Chadwick was awe-struck by the man standing in front of her. It was lust. She was physically attracted to him as she had never been to any man before. She felt quite marvellous, not at all embarrassed that her attraction to him was obvious. His desire for her was no less overwhelming. It showed in his eyes, the way he looked at her. They were making love to each other, were hungry for sex to take them over. They were each other's destiny. That realisation sent a shivery thrill through her, it was visible and he didn't miss it. She raised her chin and tossed her hair away from her face, running her fingers through it.

What would it be like having sex with a man as big and bold and sexy as this? The very thought of his sex, of glorious thrustings ... what bliss, that rapture she had been waiting for for so long. Here was a man she could love, who felt no guilt about sharing a sexual act with her. The very thought brought tears of deep emotion to her eyes. She fought them back and smiled at him. 'Yes, please do, Manoussos. I think your friend has done me a great favour.'

He liked her voice, it was husky and she spoke softly, in a sort of loud whisper; there was something mysterious and promising in that voice. The way she spoke was

16

breathlessly sexy. There was something enigmatic about Chadwick Chase; like the great Sphinx of Ghiza in Egypt, her beauty and her secrets drew men to her. He drew back a chair and sat down opposite her. 'He has done us a favour, Chadwick.' And reaching across the table, he took her hand in his, kissed it, and did not let it go.

She closed her eyes for a moment and swallowed her emotions. Chadwick was struggling hard to maintain some composure. Manoussos saw that and more, not nervousness, more an innocence, inexperience, a certain vulnerability. This lovely creature had never ever lusted for a man as she lusted for him. Had she ever taken on a stranger, or been so bold with a man as she was being with him now? he wondered. A woman as sensual, as erotic and hungry for all things sexual as she appeared to be must have done. But this was different, and Manoussos sensed it because love was involved.

In an instant his overwhelming attraction to Chadwick had somehow knocked Manoussos off balance. He had nothing by which to measure her. She was unique and he was falling in love. He tried to regain his own composure and find a way of relating to this woman by whom he was captivated. Enchanted by a woman to whom he had only said a few words, and those inane – he couldn't help but laugh at himself.

This seemed to bring them both back to some kind of reality. He let go of her hand and raised his to get the waiter's attention. Turning back to Chadwick he told her, 'I'm famished, and I will have lunch. Max ran away to make love to D'Arcy and gobble up the feast he had ordered for us. And you? Can you manage a second lunch or at least toy with one, just to please me?'

It was ridiculous, but all she said was, 'Incredibly, I am suddenly ravenous,' and he was thrilled.

He rattled off several of the restaurant's specialities to the waiter hovering over them. Just as the man was rushing off to fill the order Chadwick stopped him, surprising Manoussos with her excellent Greek when she asked the man to bring an order of the aromatic buttery rice infused with cardamom, cinnamon, and sprinkled with almonds and sultanas. Then, turning her attention back to Manoussos but still speaking in Greek, she told him, 'That's the dish that brought me here to this restaurant, that and the deep dish casserole of roasted red and yellow peppers, aubergine and caramelised onions. A friend recommended this place and those dishes. I find the rice irresistible.'

'Your Greek is astonishingly good.'

He was delighted with her. She had intended for him to be impressed by her linguistic skills, not out of vanity but more that there should be no obstacle between them. The language barrier gone, he gave her the opportunity to rid them both of another that might have existed when he remarked, 'Not learned, I hope, by speaking with a Greek husband or lover?'

'University. A passion for Classical Greece, El Greco and Crete. There is no husband, no lover.'

His smile was broad and open and he pulled down on his moustache with his forefinger before he told her, 'There is no wife, no lover.'

The silence that followed was deafening for its very importance to the lives of Chadwick and Manoussos. Each of them aware of it, could do little but reassure the other that something momentous was happening to them. It was Chadwick who offered her hand to Manoussos. He took it in his and held it, stroked it, as they gazed into each other's eyes, their hearts and souls.

So many questions lovers have for each other in those first hours together. There was no doubt in the mind of either Manoussos or Chadwick that they would be lovers. Yet there was silence between them. Just being together seemed far more important than mere words, histories past or present. A lifetime in love and togetherness would take care of those things. At a moment like this, what did they matter anyway?

Instead they dined and were able, slowly, to overcome the silence that had overtaken them. That hush that seemed so right, so very important to them. It was Manoussos who broke it when he told Chadwick, 'Life is indeed miraculous. Who could have known that this was going to happen to us today?'

That seemed to say it all. They were together and it felt to them as if they had been waiting for each other all of their lives. Throughout lunch they spoke as young lovers always speak, of the wonder and beauty of every little thing: the weather, the food, their chance meeting, what had brought her to Iraklion and the restaurant that day, his friends. Chadwick was enchanted by Max and D'Arcy and their love story; the way they and the other foreigners lived and loved in the small village of Livakia, *his* village, on the west coast of the island, over the rough and wild Levka Ori mountain range.

It sounded to Chadwick like a paradise for pleasure seekers. She wanted to be there, be one of them, live at the peak of existence. Be the free spirit and the adventurer that she had seen instantly in Max when he had walked through the door of the restaurant. Be loved and full of sensual splendour in the same way D'Arcy was. Be embraced by Manoussos who saw in her their joint destiny. These were fearless people who knew what it was to be alive, hold the world in one hand and make it spin for them. They made the greatest of efforts to live and work and be happy. Here were lives and ways of living completely foreign to her, and they appealed to Chadwick as her new *today*. All she had to do was reach out and take Manoussos's hand and leave all her *yesterdays* behind her.

Water crashed against the window pane and ran down the glass. It somehow brought her out of her thoughts. She watched it for only a few seconds then, taking a deep breath, rose from her chair. Manoussos followed suit. Chadwick walked round the table to stand in front of him. He took both her hands in his.

'Are you sure about this, Chadwick? You must be, because for my part I already know there will be no turning back. We know nothing about each other or our lives and I am already more deeply involved than I ever imagined I could be with anyone. We can stop now and no one will get hurt. We should, unless you feel the same as I do. We mustn't use each other, not even for one night of sexual extravaganza. As much as I would like that, want that, we're much more.'

There was a firmness in his voice, a certainty in his words, and an underlying passion. This was not a man with whom to toy. He was honest and true and as hard as he was soft, a sensual and hyper-sexual being who was reaching out to her in love. She raised their hands to her lips and kissed his, sucked the smooth tawny skin into her mouth and bit into the flesh on the back of his hand before she turned it over, licked and kissed the palm. That kiss had sealed their fate. They were sharply aware of that as Manoussos pulled her into his arms.

Manoussos and Chadwick were standing on a wooden dock several miles down the coast from the restaurant. Manoussos knew the place. It was owned by a friend of Max's who leased it out by the day to yacht owners who wanted a safe harbour while visiting Knossos. He recognised the three-masted schooner, *Black Narcissus*. It was owned by one of the Athenian Greek ship owners who, off season, rented it out with its crew of eight. It was an ideal spot known for its deep harbour and the yachts that would tie up there for several hours, sometimes days. A deserted place of infinite beauty with its scrubby bushes, old twisted and gnarled olive trees and buff-coloured cliffs, plunging steeply to the sea. Manoussos had been there many times with Max when he sailed his fishing *caique* over to this side of the island from Livakia.

Manoussos watched this woman, this mysterious beauty, as she spoke with the captain of the boat. Until then he had not had time to be objective enough to study Chadwick. How well dressed she was in her beige suede skirt; the waist-length jacket trimmed in inch-wide bands of glossy black patent leather she wore over her shoulders to reveal a low-cut silk-knit jumper. A narrow black silk scarf was tied in a minute bow at the side of her long slender neck. At the table he had been unaware of the long, finely shaped legs, the elegantly slim feet shod in flat-heeled black alligator shoes, the chicness of the large black patent leather shoulder bag she carried with such style over her shoulder.

How luscious and lovely she was, this lady with the

voluptuous body of an intensely sexual woman and a face that still had the bloom of a young girl. Standing there on the weather-worn wooden dock, surrounded by the rocky terrain, she looked that lethal combination so attractive to men: the child-seductress and the woman. A siren, as in Greek myth – the woman living on a rocky isle to which she lures unwary seafarers with enchanting music – came to mind. The sound of her voice, that something in her eyes, the way she used her body, that was her song. Chadwick was a dangerously fascinating woman, a temptress tempting pursuit. He had known that the moment he saw her and that was what he had fallen in love with: the danger of loving her – and other things. The magnificent rewards he would reap seeking his pleasure with her, the deep sense of delight from knowing that he could make her happy as she had never been before. For that a man might risk a great deal, possibly even his life.

All that he sensed instinctively and therefore nothing about Chadwick could be a surprise. It would be a matter of knowing her as she unfolded herself, or not, to him. He didn't mind if she kept her secrets, and had no doubt that she did harbour secrets she revealed to no one. You had only to look at her once to know that. It was Manoussos's nature and the nature of his work to take things at face value and deal with them, even love.

At the moment when they rose from the table and he took her in his arms, their lust for each other demanded somewhere to go, a place to be alone in, to make love, to have glorious sex. Max had even made provision for that: the restaurant bill had been paid and a note left for Manoussos telling him where the key was to a small romantic house Max owned down the coast. Manoussos had been relieved because he wanted nothing tawdry such as a hotel room for a few hours of sex for their first time together. When Chadwick rejected Max's house in preference to taking him to where she was staying, it made no difference to Manoussos. But the point did come home to him that she had taken over this liaison.

All she had said in the taxi was that she had a wonderful place for them to go. He was more amused than surprised when he saw where that place was. She had rented the *Black Narcissus* to sail from Athens to Crete. Manoussos listened to Chadwick explaining to the captain of the schooner that she had a guest and that he and the crew could keep the taxi and take some time off in town, in fact, she insisted. It was to no avail. The captain was quite unbending. The crew could go off for a few hours but the captain never left his vessel unattended when someone was on board. Manoussos knew, as Chadwick did not, that she would get nowhere trying to change the man's mind. It was time to step in and settle things. He opened the taxi door and stepped on to the dock.

The moment that Dimitri Cronos saw Manoussos walking towards him, his face broke into a smile. The two men had known each other for years, he had even assisted Manoussos once in entrapping a smuggler of antiquities. The two men hugged each other in greeting. Then the captain turned to Chadwick and told her, 'You should have said your guest was to be Manoussos Stavrolakis. I have no problem leaving the schooner with him on board.'

The two men exchanged news of mutual friends as they and Chadwick boarded the *Black Narcissus*. Two of the crew, obviously men who knew Manoussos, greeted him enthusiastically and joined in the conversation. Chadwick sat down in one of the deck chairs, watched and listened. This outward affection Cretan men showed for one another had always astounded her. It was rich and it was beautiful in the same way as their passion for honour and their fierce pride; they swaggered rather than walked, masters of maleness unbound.

Chadwick had hardly realised the captain and crew were gone until she saw them all happily piling into her hired taxi. Manoussos came to stand next to her. She rose from her chair and together they watched the taxi pull away, stop at the end of the dock and the captain alight to close the iron gates. They swung off roughly honed pediments carved out of the cliffs that sheltered this private piece of coast and bay. The gates and the weather-worn ancient Venetian lions capping those pediments stood guard against intruders from the outside world.

From the moment Chadwick heard the gates clang shut, the chain run through them and watched the captain snap shut the padlock, it was as if her mind had done a somersault. She felt born anew, a whole different Chadwick was surfacing and a new life was just about to begin. She turned to face Manoussos, who made no excuse for taking over the *Black Narcissus* and her life. She had after all already changed his.

Chapter 2

The autumn sun was a dull pink-orange and low in the blue cloudless sky. There was no breeze and it was incredibly still and quiet, except for the sound of the sea lapping against the boat, breaking against the cliffs, the occasional cry of a bird. It was no longer uncomfortably hot but definitely warm enough for Chadwick to feel the waning sun's rays teasing her cheeks, the tip of her nose, her chin. Sexual tension vibrated between her and Manoussos as they gazed into each other's eyes. She sensed the god Eros, Greek mythology's god of love, hovering over their lives and this place: protecting, inciting, blessing.

Chadwick slipped the jacket from her shoulders and it fell on to the deck. She pulled the silk-knit jumper up over her head and casually laid it on the chair next to her. There appeared to be no urgency in her passionate desire for sex; hers were deliberate acts to excite this man who was already the most important thing in her life. She eased her skirt down over her hips and let that too fall to the deck round her ankles. Chadwick slipped out of her shoes as she stepped over it and closer to Manoussos. She was naked except for her sexuality which she wore like a cloak of diamonds. She sparkled in the sun for him as no other woman ever had, not even D'Arcy.

Chadwick had about her a sexual luminosity, a more raunchy carnality than he could have imagined. Her breasts were high and fully rounded, much more than merely ample. The nimbus encircling her nipples was large and pale mocha in colour, shaded deeper towards the nipples which were dark, a more plummy colour altogether, and pronounced, giving her breasts a strangely depraved look. Her nakedness and particularly her breasts, like her face, held a certain quality of seductive sexuality that Manoussos found irresistible. She triggered his sexual fantasies. Breasts to caress and lick, that demanded more: to be cupped in his hands so that he could feel their weight and firm flesh overflow his fingers as surely they would from their size.

Manoussos could almost hear the slap of his hands against them. He had no doubts that *they*, as *she*, demanded sex to be hard and fierce as well as soft and loving. Her entire body was firm-fleshed and shapely, her skin like satin, scented with aromatic oils and creams. Chadwick Chase was a woman honed for erotic love making, sexual demands. The narrow waist, and just the right amount of flesh on the hips and lusciously rounded bottom, accentuated how very voluptuous she was. Her sexuality demanded: Take me, use me, for our mutual pleasure. Even her mound of Venus had been groomed to tantalise: her pubes shaved away to leave just a narrow strip of luscious, dark and silky clipped hair. From her long, slender and elegant feet, her manicured hands, to the crown of her head, here was a sexual woman, moulded and cared for, who had been taught by someone to use her sexuality for a man's as well as her own pleasure. Manoussos had had enough women to sense that about

Chadwick. Instinct told him that was her past; together they were her present.

He reached for the first button of his shirt and told her, 'I've never seen a woman more beautiful, more perfect, more mine.'

She reached out and took his hand from the button, smiled at him and told him, 'Every woman should be told that at least once in her lifetime,' and continued to undo his shirt.

Manoussos slipped out of his shoes. He tried to assist but she stopped him. 'No, please. Just stand very still, let me.' And she continued undressing him.

Manoussos felt sexual urgency: to be naked and in her arms. He wanted her hands on his flesh, her caresses, her kisses, to be licked all over by her warm moist tongue. He had found the woman to take possession of his body as no other woman ever had. He felt on the verge of laughter, tears: reactions to such intense sexual emotion, the discovery of being in love. He reached out to take a breast in his cupped hands and caress it, lower his head and lick the nimbus with his tongue and nibble on the already erect nipple. The moment he touched her naked flesh he set her aflame. He actually felt her lose herself, her body go limp. Roughly he pulled her into his arms, tilted back her head. She closed her eyes and he kissed them, and then the tip of her nose; he licked the hint of a cleft in her chin and then he bit into her lips. They opened at once and Manoussos kissed her, a deep and passionate kiss, a kiss of life, one where they flowed into each other urgently and with powerful need.

His hands roamed over her body with teasing caresses, and with one arm wrapped round her waist he lifted her off the deck and held her close to him. Briefly his fingers toyed with the narrow strip of pubic hair, before they searched between her more intimate lips. He used his long slender fingers seductively to excite her. Here were caresses that completely undid Chadwick; her body tensed and she came. Exploring, caressing fingers. She called out in passionate anguish and clung to him with her arms round his neck and sucked on his ear lobe. She wanted more, much more. To be riven by him: deep, powerful thrustings to a sexual rhythm created by their mutual lust. Once she would have hidden such sexual yearnings, from the men deliberately chosen to enhance her and Hannibal's erotic life together. Hannibal had enjoyed orchestrating those sexual games. All that was over. Here was a man whom she had deeper feelings for; a stranger who made it easy for her to express her sexual self because he held nothing of his own feelings back from her.

Clinging together thus, he carried her down to the master cabin. She turned the door handle and he kicked open the door. Her hands were trembling as she helped him to undress. She explored his body not with her hands but her mouth. She kissed his chest and his nipples, sucked on them, licked his muscular flesh, bit into one of his broad shoulders. Chadwick worked down his body. She caressed his erect and pulsating sex, licked it lovingly before she wrapped her lips round it and slowly, deftly, took him deep into her throat. Only then did she allow herself the luxury of caressing the large, loose and very sensuous sac at its base that she found so thrillingly sexy.

Chadwick's rendition of oral sex was too sublime. Manoussos was transported into an erotic world from which he knew there was no return, not at least until they were sated with sex. He was on the edge of orgasm, but: Not yet, not now, he told himself. He tried to raise her off her knees but instead she took him down to the carpet to join her. From his knees he rolled on to his back, taking her with him. He placed his hands gently on either side of her head and firmly but slowly eased himself from her warm and sensuous mouth.

Manoussos pulled her up along his body until she blanketed him with her sexuality. She wrapped her arms round his neck and teased and taunted him with a subtle, lazy pelvic rhythm of her own. Though Manoussos was lost in lust for Chadwick, he was not unaware that she was a woman born to seduce, to intrigue men. Body and soul, she was indeed the sexual siren who drew men to her and for which they were prepared to ruin themselves. Lust. Chadwick Chase was pure, irresistible lust.

He bruised her lips with his kisses as together they rolled over so that he was once again in control of this, their first sexual adventure. Together they reached that moment of passion gone wild, sex unbound. She called out as she came in a series of short but violently strong orgasms and begged him, tears in her eyes, to take her.

They were base sexual demands. Chadwick wanted to be ravaged by Manoussos. Her erotic needs were Manoussos's sexual fantasies come true. Adventurous, dangerous even, they were sexually thrilling, and more so because she and Manoussos knew that he was the man who would take Chadwick where she wanted to go, give them both the pain and the pleasure of sex and orgasm more fulfilling than either of them had ever had before.

Manoussos stroked her hair and kissed her more gently,

but never stopped inciting her lust with his caresses and explicit verbal descriptions of the sex they were about to have. She was trembling, on the edge of another orgasm, but now marginally more calm, less fearful that he was not going to answer her heart's desire. Here was his moment, they were ready for each other. Chadwick was rigid with sexual tension. Suddenly she went quiet, watching his every movement. He leaned forward and lowered his mouth to graze his lips over hers as he parted those other more intimate lips, making her ready to receive him. 'And now it really begins for us,' he told her.

Their kiss was deep and passionate and he took possession of Chadwick, slowly and with infinite joy. His impressive phallus thrilled her as he eased it slowly and in such a seductive way as to give them both the greatest pleasure in this their first intercourse. Chadwick searched for words to express how exquisite, how perfectly blissful it was, how he was transporting her into sexual nirvana. But she was lost for words, all she could do was clench her fists and try and hold back from shouting, 'Yes, oh God, yes, and more and more.' She gasped, she whimpered, as he set the pace for his thrusts, created a beat to fuck by. Manoussos was an experienced libertine, but how could Chadwick have known that? She was lost to him, wholly submitting herself so that he might master her sexually.

The pleasure he took in her orgasms as well as his own spurred her on to ask for her own sexual fantasies to be satisfied. After the first few hours they were lost to all worlds except an erotic one where egos die and sexual desire is fulfilled. Through early-evening, the night, and well into the morning, Manoussos and Chadwick died many times for each other in lust and sexual depravity only to rise again fresh and anew until sated. Finally, on returning to the real world of everyday life and some kind of normality, they found themselves committed in love.

Chadwick had always found those first few hours of morning after a night of thrilling sex embarrassingly uncomfortable. Not so this morning. She was happy, at ease with herself and Manoussos, who they were, where they had been, what they had done. Here was a new world for her: one where she was a free sexual being who had met her match. Manoussos was emotionally uncomplicated about sex with her, a man who showed the greatest joy in coming together with her.

In one night he had swept away Chadwick's years of guilt for being the sexual creature she was. Hannibal had created in her a heightened sexuality to satisfy both their voracious libidos but at the same time had laid sexual guilt upon her for their lust. He had continued to do so during all the years they had been married. It was Hannibal's inability to accept his lust and love for her, his so-called morality, that caused him to lay the blame for their sexual appetites at her feet. For years she had begged him to put them both out of their misery and give her that one and only thing that had stopped them from being complete with one another. But after their first sexual encounter, when for several days he had allowed his orgasms to caress her womb, he withdrew absolutely and only ever came over her outer vaginal lips. In all else he had given her everything, they had been each other's lives. And so she had to satisfy herself with nothing more than the taste of Hannibal.

Manoussos breathed new life into her; together they raised her level of sexual self-esteem. It was as if life had begun again for her the very moment he walked through the door of the restaurant only the afternoon before. Chadwick felt a new woman. How thrilling it was going to be, discovering herself with Manoussos. She leaned over and kissed him on the cheek.

He placed an arm round her shoulders and pulled her to him. They were in a large bed, sumptuous for the many white linen and lace-covered pillows they were lying against. 'Let's get dressed and raid the galley. Are you as famished as I am?' he asked.

'I could eat a bear.'

'But could you cook one?'

Chadwick began to laugh. 'I went to a Cordon Bleu cookery class, part of a finishing school education, but they never mentioned bear. How about eggs, an omelette, one that will make you fall in love with me that little bit more?'

Manoussos liked the teasing note in her voice, the happiness in her eyes. Here was his moment to tell her 'That's not possible, I could never love you more than I do now and will never love you less.'

'You know, I believe you.'

For several seconds they remained silent and locked in togetherness. Neither could hide their happiness, it was there shining on their faces as bright as a beacon. So this is love, he mused to himself.

It was midday when the crew returned to the *Black Narcissus* and found Manoussos and Chadwick dining in the sun on mushroom, bacon, and chicken liver omelettes, toast and marmalade, and drinking glasses of vintage Krug champagne. There was the usual boisterous Cretan meeting: shaking of hands, slaps on backs. It was difficult to miss the twinkle of envy and respect for Manoussos's having conquered Chadwick Chase, though no one dare be rude enough to say anything about it to him. They knew the power that Manoussos had and could wield if he so wanted.

It was only when the captain asked Chadwick, 'What are your plans, Kiria Chase?' that the lovers realised they had none.

It took Chadwick several awkward minutes before she answered, 'We will be staying in Crete for some length of time, making it our home base.' Only then did she dare to look directly at Manoussos. There was an enigmatic smile grazing her lips and her happiness made her lovely seductive looks even more enticing.

Manoussos went directly to Chadwick, placed an arm round her waist and drew her hard against him. 'I think this calls for a celebration.'

He began refilling their glasses with what was left of the champagne. Chadwick ordered two more bottles and glasses for the captain and crew to be brought up on deck. The crew had their drink and then went about their business on board. The captain asked Chadwick, 'What are your more immediate plans?'

Once more she looked puzzled, but then turning to Manoussos asked, 'Well, what do you think? Shall we remain moored here and take excursions by car and boat round the island?'

'That would be very nice but I'm a working man. We'll see more of each other if the *Black Narcissus* makes her home base on the other side of the island, in the port of Livakia, my village and the headquarters I work from. Dimitri knows the port well. It's deep enough for this schooner and is by far the more interesting and wild side of the island.'

'The chief is right. It's the coast that faces Libya and there are easy voyages to be made to the Mediterranean coast of that country, Egypt, Algeria and Morocco. And Livakia – well, it's a very special village even for Crete. There are always interesting people coming and going because there are a dozen or so enticing foreigners who live there in marvellous houses. It's a paradise found, not lost,' quipped the captain who was telling Chadwick more about Livakia and Manoussos than she had learned from her lover. But then she did have a vague idea what sort of people lived in Livakia: beautiful people, pleasure seekers. She had after all met Max, seen D'Arcy.

For the next half-hour the two men spoke about Livakia, some of the residents, and about a murder that had taken place, a crime of passion against one of the foreign male residents, Arnold Topper. Manoussos seemed reluctant to talk much about it and changed the subject rather abruptly. That suited Chadwick; she had no desire to come down from the heights of love to hear about murder and a crime of passion. It actually unnerved her for a moment. One look of admiration from Manoussos and she was back on an even keel again.

'And I will be able to take you out on excursions to remote mountain villages. You will adore my Crete, I have no doubt about that,' he told her and graciously kissed her hand.

'When shall we weigh anchor? Will you be sailing with us, chief?' asked the captain.

'Alas, no. I should be in Livakia as we speak, but if I might make a call, I can fix that. I'll hitch a ride in one of the surveillance 'copters for at least part of the way. If you make ready to leave here this afternoon, you should reach Livakia in time for lunch at the Kavouria tomorrow. I'll arrange it. Twelve, fifteen hours' hard sailing in a good wind should do it, shouldn't it, Dimitri?'

'I would say so, Chief.'

Turning back to Chadwick, Manoussos told her, 'No matter what, I'll be on the quay waiting for your arrival, you can be certain of that.'

Then taking her gently by the elbow he ushered her away from the captain. Manoussos stroked her hair and caressed her cheek. 'Don't be unhappy. If I could sail with you, I would, but I have important work that must be done. If it were possible I would take you along with me and then to Livakia and let the *Black Narcissus* sail round to meet us. It just isn't.'

Her smile eased his pain at having to leave her. But he could feel her anxiety about their separation. 'It's only twenty-four hours, Chadwick. Each of us has waited a lifetime for this to happen to us. What are you afraid of?'

'When you see me again you might love me less.'

'More, only more, my love,' he told her, taking her once more in his arms to reassure her that was the way it was going to be. Her anxiety seemed to vanish as quickly as it had appeared. Once more she was the seductive, mysterious beauty, engaging and dangerous.

'I think I'll hold you to that for the rest of our lives,' a now much more relaxed and smiling Chadwick told him. 'Go make your call,' she ordered.

On his return, they walked together from the boat down the long wooden dock to the iron gates, the taxi that would take Manoussos back into Iraklion slowly following behind them. For a long time after it and Manoussos had vanished down the dirt track away from her, Chadwick watched the dust settle. She stared into the most exquisite emptiness and allowed it to envelop her. She luxuriated in it. Here was the richest solitude she had ever known. How could it be that one man, the right man, could make everything poetry and beauty. The heart no longer a hunter, but a song.

Walking back to the *Black Narcissus*, Chadwick thrilled to the adventure awaiting her. She was entering Manoussos's and Max's and D'Arcy's world, she was going to live her life on their terms, for fun and pleasure and in a freedom such as they had made for themselves. She had a handsome young, uncomplicated man who loved her and her sexuality. She would live with him in Livakia, make a life there with him, for him, for her. She might even write another book. They would do up a house together, sail, swim, take long adventurous holidays. Have a child, maybe children, maybe not. It would all happen for them, evolve as it should. She was already one of the Livakian pleasure seekers, one of the beautiful people, and in love. It seemed so natural to her to be who she now was. Who she had been seemed suddenly unnatural.

She hadn't meant what little she had told Manoussos about herself to be lies, more evasions. When she had told him she had been born into a well-to-do family: conservative, strait-laced even, the youngest of three, a sister and a brother, all close in age and loving and caring for each other because their parents were dead, it had made sense to her, a sort of truth. She had had a childhood romance that led to marriage then the man died ... not exactly fabrication. All partly true, none of it real lies, she told herself. And what did it matter anyway? Manoussos hadn't questioned her. It had all been said casually in conversation; things that could, if necessary, be corrected at a later date. She liked the new identity she was creating for herself.

It didn't occur to her that she was creating, at the same time, a life of denial for herself. Why kill the momentum of happiness, contentment as she had never known, by analysing her actions? Chadwick was brimming with too much pleasure for that. 'Let's live.' D'Arcy's words to Max were now her own sentiments.

Dimitri broke into Chadwick's thoughts when she boarded the *Black Narcissus*. 'He's a good man, the chief. I thought you might like to know that.'

'I do know that, Captain.'

'I'm sorry, I didn't mean to talk out of line.'

'No, please, that's all right. What I meant was, I agree with you even though I hardly know him.'

'Too bad he couldn't have sailed with us. He's a good sailor. Almost as good as he is a policeman.'

'I don't understand. Why a policeman?'

'Well, police chief – quite a high-profile one at that. They're lucky to keep him here in Crete.'

Dimitri Cronos had astonished Chadwick, that was clear by the expression on her face. 'You didn't know? Now I'm the one who doesn't understand. Are you all right? Have I spoken out of turn?'

Chadwick was nonplussed by this news. Was fate playing some ghastly trick on her, giving her a police chief for a lover, the man she hoped to make a life with? Too cruel, too cruel. It was impossible to blank this news out of

37

her mind. She would have to deal with it, make it a part of her life. Now she would have to bury her secret deeper than ever; never must it come to light, not only her own but his happiness, *their* future, was at stake. Chadwick willed herself to calmness over this news and the colour returned to her face.

She smiled, exuded her dazzling charm, and answered Captain Dimitri. 'I'm fine, and no, you certainly did not speak out of turn.' She laughed, and her mirth brought a smile to the face of the captain of the *Black Narcissus*. 'No, I didn't know Manoussos was a chief of police, not even when you called him "Chief". I took that to mean something flattering to him, as if you were intimating he was in charge. Incredibly, I realise now we never bothered to ask much about each other.'

'He's a man of substance, well respected. Much more than just a chief of police. He's a kind of folk hero here in Crete because he fights off and catches art smugglers and saves the island's antiquities. He's a handsome, quiet, unassuming man, as hard as he is soft, courageous and brave, all the things Cretan men are known for and the things women admire. He is also the definitive detective. It was he who within days found and trapped Melina, the killer of his friend Arnold Topper. It happened in Livakia. He found her, entrapped her into a confession and brought her to justice. Even that was not enough for Manoussos Stavrolakis. The girl was fifteen years old, there were mitigating circumstances, enough to raise Manoussos's social conscience. He was here in Iraklion to visit her in prison and to arrange for her to get some sort of counselling and education so that when she gets out of prison she can begin a new and fresh life for herself. He's a man who lives by the law, in that he is unbending, but he also has a forgiving and generous heart.'

Chadwick felt sick to her stomach. 'He's a man who lives by the law, in that he is unbending.' Those words kept ringing through her head, terrifying her. She fought to keep herself in check so Captain Dimitri would not feel her sense of despair. Quite calmly she enquired of him, 'How do you know all that, about the murderer Melina, and his being at the prison today?'

'They were talking about it in town. Even now the murder trial is much talked about because it took place in Iraklion and the victim was a foreigner. It was a crime of passion, a man and a woman, and her defence was that Cretan pride demanded she behave as she did. The old Cretan vendetta raised its head: Melina had one against Arnold Topper for an insult he gave her in public – he called her a thief. I assumed you knew all that?'

'No, I didn't, and would you mind if we changed the subject?'

'Murder not your thing? Well, I can understand that.'

Chadwick wanted to walk away from him, at the very least shout at him for God's sake to be quiet on the subject, but she could do neither. She was too fragmented by the past and pressured by the present, love and lustful desire. Fortunately it was Captain Dimitri who left her to instruct the crew to make ready to sail in an hour for the old port of Chania where they would replenish supplies. She was for the moment saved.

The conference room of Chambers, Lodge, Dewy & Coggs was like the inner sanctum-cum-library of a New England eighteenth-century banking house rather than that of a twentieth-century Fifth Avenue law firm acting for New York old money: the Roosevelts, Woodwards, Milikens, Vanderbilts, that sort of clientele, with arms that extended to the Boston Mayflower clans, and the Philadelphia main liners. Hannibal Chase's financial empire and family affairs had for generations been handled by the firm. Hannibal, his children and his philanthropic trusts had always been favoured clients for they were not litigious, were conservative, honourable, and very nearly scandal free. That was up until the unexpected and strange death of sixty-seven-year-old Hannibal, when his wife Chadwick inherited his entire fortune.

Now the firm was involved with just the sort of law they preferred not to deal with. Andrew Coggs Junior, who had gone to school with Warren Chase, the only son of Hannibal from his first marriage, was sitting opposite him and his sister, Diana Chase Ogden, Hannibal's only daughter from that first marriage.

These were the two people at the hub of the problem concerning Hannibal's estate. They were contesting their father's last will and testament which had been drawn up by the firm only weeks before Hannibal's death. The firm, and especially Andrew Coggs Senior, who was a life-long friend of Hannibal Chase, believed the will to be legal and binding and that there had been no skulduggery of any sort. Andrew further believed Hannibal's widow Chadwick to be innocent of the accusations being made by Warren and Diana: that she had used undue influence over Hannibal to change his will in her favour.

Warren and Diana had been made wealthy long before Hannibal's death. Hannibal had delighted in passing over his wealth and property to his children while he was alive.

He enjoyed watching them invest their money and liked seeing the security and independence his generosity gave them. They were multi-millionaires and had been for most of their adult life, therefore there was more than just money involved in their contesting of the will. Warren and Diana had been extremely close to their father and step-mother, although she was much younger than either of them. Until their father's death they had been a close-knit family. The will alienated them from sharing in Hannibal's life-long work and his wealth. They could not bear that alienation. They saw it as an injustice inflicted upon them, something that Hannibal would never have done. Their father's sudden death, and Chadwick's behaviour since widowhood, not least their unshakable belief that the father who had loved them and remained close to them would never have willingly cut them out of his will and the last days of his life, prompted brother and sister to demand of the lawyers that a thorough private investigation into the matter take place. They wanted proof that Chadwick Chase did not manipulate her husband into changing his will; and further, that she did not murder her husband.

The fact of the matter was, as Hannibal had told Chadwick at the time, that he simply felt that he had given his children enough during his lifetime. He was adamant that Chadwick should have everything after his death so that she would be financially secure and he wanted her to use the money in any way she saw fit. He insisted, however, that she was not to give the money to his children. Much as Chadwick loved Diana and Warren, she loved and respected Hannibal more, and therefore she was prepared to obey his request, as she had obeyed all his other wishes.

The meeting assembled here in the conference room library was taking place for the sole purpose of once and for all dealing with Diana's and Warren's accusations. Accusations that Chadwick was well aware of and had chosen to deny once and then ignore in order to get on with her life. The law firm had problems with this, a conflict of interest: they represented all the parties concerned. But for the moment a moratorium had been agreed.

The firm had agreed to instigate a private investigation into the allegations in general and to represent all the parties concerned by acting in an unbiased role. If and when something was proved to be other than legal and right, at that time they would withdraw from any litigation concerning Diana's and Warren's accusations and remain strictly as family and trust lawyers only to all the parties concerned. By taking that position they would therefore avoid any possibility of becoming embroiled in a full-blown conflict of interest. The Chase children agreed to that and, for the time being, to hold off taking any further legal action to contest the will.

Chadwick was unaware of this meeting or that a private investigative team was being recruited or of any other of Warren's and Diana's actions against her. She had given strict instructions to the law firm and in particular to Andrew Coggs Senior that she did not want to know anything, not the merest detail, of any measures her step-children were taking to substantiate their ridiculous allegations. Until they had proof and were actually taking legal action against her because they did in fact have a case, she refused to be put in a defensive position. She was convinced that by not embroiling herself further, a public scandal could be avoided and in time the problems would fade away, all would be forgiven, and they would once more come together as friends and family.

Andrew Coggs Senior and the firm understood the position she was taking and in some ways agreed with her even though they would have preferred her to take an interest in what she was up against. In other ways Coggs Senior felt as she did: that she had earned the right to her newfound freedom, to be alone to grieve for Hannibal who had been her whole life, and to find a new place and new life for herself in a world where hitherto she had only known Hannibal's way of living and loving.

There was a faint knock on the door. It opened and in walked Bill Ogden, Diana's husband. The men rose from their chairs and shook hands with him and, after kissing the top of his wife's head and smiling at her, he took her hand and sat down next to her.

Diana seemed suddenly less tense, she was always more relaxed when she was with Bill. A tall, slender man, he was handsome and well-dressed as a Park Avenue doctor, a paediatrician, would be. He had a manner that was kindly, instantly winning. Dr Bill Ogden was a man very much in love with his wife. That was why he was here and the only reason. He was against the adversarial position his wife and brother-in-law were taking against Chadwick.

Bill was a positive influence in Diana's life but he could do nothing to convince her that Hannibal's love for Chadwick, and nothing more sinister than that, was what made him change his will in sole favour of his wife. Bill believed that Chadwick would never have done anything to harm Hannibal; indeed, quite the opposite, she would have laid down her life for him. Diana listened to and ignored his opinion.

Andrew Coggs Junior had always had a soft spot in his heart for Diana. He, as a good friend of Warren's, had seen a great deal of her as they were growing up. He looked at her now, happy at last with the right man. The forty-two-year-old Diana was, he believed, truly happy married to Bill who was six years younger in age, but ten years older in maturity. He therefore could not understand why she was pitting herself against Chadwick, knowing very well that she loved the step-mother who had been so good to her. They had been kind to each other, had had a close relationship until her father's death.

Diana did not look like a woman who had had several marriages and children before she met Bill Ogden, but that had been the case. Andrew had always thought those unhappy marriages had a great deal to do with her relationship with her father. Diana idolised him. She was obsessive about him and had an uneasy relationship with Hannibal. It had always been Chadwick who had smoothed out the problems between father and daughter.

Andrew, as friend and lawyer, had seen her develop from an adolescent into a volatile, spoilt woman, frighteningly beautiful, elegant, and moving in a very chic circles. Living with Bill Ogden, raising her children and being successful in her own right as a private art dealer specialising in Matisse, she was at last content with herself and her life. Of all the things Diana was or was not, paranoid and vindictive did not figure in her psychological make-up. She *did* actually believe her father's death was not a natural one, that he was too family-orientated to have discarded his only son and daughter by cutting them out of his will.

Andrew watched and listened to Warren, Bill and Diana who were talking among themselves. Warren was saying, 'Thanks for coming in on this meeting, Bill. It's especially appreciated by Diana and I. We know you disapprove of our actions but thank you for not allowing it to cause a falling out between the three of us. You've asked us to think this through carefully. We have, and Diana and I are holding to the position we've taken.'

The voice of reason. Bill, still holding his wife's hand, raised it to his lips and kissed her fingers. Carefully he replied: 'It has occurred to me that Diana never really understood the complex relationship between Hannibal and Chadwick, but you, Warren – I somehow thought you did.'

Andrew Junior leaned back in his chair and stroked his chin. Warren was very close to both Chadwick and his father. They were the most important people in his life, more so even than his own wife and children. His was an unhappy marriage that contrasted painfully with his father's, but he put up with it, was stoic about it, for the sake of his children. He never discussed his unhappy home life but Andrew as a close friend sensed it. For as long as they'd known each other, Warren had loved two people as no other: Chadwick and his father. He had never confessed that to Andrew, who had arrived at that deduction from years of knowing Warren and listening to him. Andrew was convinced that Warren had both a deep and abiding love for the luscious Chadwick and sometimes a resentment of the power she had over his father.

Warren Chase was a very wealthy man but nevertheless

shocked that the family fortune should have been left solely to Chadwick. Andrew, as both his attorney.and friend, believed that when Hannibal died, Warren lost his best friend; they were in fact each other's best friend, the two men had been confidants. Although Warren had never come straight out and said so, Andrew agreed with Bill when he'd said that only Warren understood the complex relationship between his father and Chadwick. He had been aware of what others could only surmise: that lust had governed his father's love for Chadwick. Warren in as many words had told Andrew that he had always feared for the relationship between Chadwick and Hannibal because of the sexual strain Hannibal placed upon her. Only now did Andrew wonder what that sexual strain might have been.

Warren had spent years standing in the sidelines of his father and Chadwick's life, acting as their closest friend, travelling with them, being very much a part of their marriage – and loving Chadwick, wanting her for his own. His father had loved Chadwick first as a daughter and then as a wife: Warren had loved her first as a sister and then wanted her for a wife. Resigned to the fact that Chadwick would never be his, he loved her the best way he could, from day to day, as his father's happiness. Andrew knew that to be the case since once, many years before, they had somewhat vaguely discussed it.

Andrew looked down the mahogany conference table at his friend and thought, Poor bastard. Hannibal's death has traumatised him: the loss of a father whom he loved and respected and the reality that Chadwick is now free to begin another life, a new life, with any man she chooses, that's what this is all about in the guise of suspecting an unnatural death and contesting a will. But did Diana and Warren have any idea what a can of worms they might be opening once that detective entered the room and took on this case? He doubted it.

Chapter 3

Sailing the coast of Crete, with a stopover at Chania, had all gone so well. Chadwick felt incredibly happy and excited until dusk fell and night closed in around the *Black Narcissus*, still at sea, still sailing in a good strong wind towards its destination, Livakia, and Chadwick's new life.

It is incredible what love can do, lust can conjure up. Chadwick already felt like one of the pleasure seekers, Crete her Elysian fields: the place of Greek mythology on the banks of the River Oceanus where those favoured by the gods live in eternal happiness. It seemed the most natural thing for her to be sailing round the island to Livakia, she was merely going home. She had half-expected a call to the schooner from Manoussos. To say what? He had arrived safely? He was waiting for her? He loved her, missed her, wanted her? Maybe merely to hear her voice, reassure himself of her love? Any reason would do. But no call came. She slipped back to that other world that she had left behind when she told herself, 'Hannibal would have called, and not once but several times, to say all those things.'

She pulled herself back from the past and pushed it from her mind. She realised that she was having to learn how to love a stranger as much as she had loved Hannibal. How to relate to a man as a mature woman should, without the guidance of Hannibal Chase, was the order of the day.

She rose from the settee and went to the dining room where her dinner was being served: a lobster bisque freshly made by the *Black Narcissus*'s Greek chef who had been trained by M. Robuchon in Paris. He produced for the main course a succulent dish of rabbit with a mustard sauce and served it with French green beans and candied carrots. The pudding was a pear poached in red wine and cinnamon and served with dribbles of thick white cream and a hot caramel sauce. Adonis the chef came with the rental of the schooner, and over a demitasse of delicious coffee, Chadwick wondered how she had ever lived without him or the yacht.

For some time after dinner, she listened to music and around midnight called the captain's cabin to say that she was going up on deck for some fresh air. Safety measures on board the yacht demanded the captain be notified of after-dark visits to the deck, he wanted no disappearances. It was cold on deck and after several brisk turns around it Chadwick bade the captain good night. She was in her room for only a short time when she sensed Manoussos's presence. He seemed to be everywhere and to generate a warmth she had not sensed in the stateroom before he had visited it. His scent: she actually believed that his scent was still there, on the pillows and the sheets, in the very air she breathed. She walked to the full-length pier mirror hanging on the walnut-panelled wall and looked at her reflection.

Chadwick wrapped her arms round herself and sighed. She hardly knew this vibrant, beautiful woman in the mirror. All those years when people had remarked on her erotic beauty, her seductive charm, how had she never seen it as they had seen it, as she was seeing it now? How had she not loved herself for being the woman reflected in the mirror as she did now? She unwound her arms and raised them to run her fingers through her hair, shook it out, and slowly undressed in front of the mirror. Only now did she realise that she had never really looked at herself as a beautiful lustful creature, never had she caressed her breasts before, nor enjoyed the excitement those caressings caused her. Sin of sins, the new Chadwick that Manoussos had fallen in love with was committing the one that stated, 'Thou shalt not fall in love with thyself'. That realisation, of not merely liking but loving herself, was one of the more divine moments of Chadwick's life. Now she *really* believed she had something to give her magnificent lover.

In this the same bed where Manoussos and she discovered the carnal side of their love for each other, she slept through the night naked and in a deep, dreamless sleep induced by her own caresses, several orgasms, and thrilling sexual fantasies. The sun was high in the sky and pouring delectably warm through the portholes and across the rumpled white linen-covered bed when she opened her eyes. Still naked, she stood in a spotlight of sun, warming herself by it while the *Black Narcissus* made short shrift of a rough sea. Watching the coastline unfold, Chadwick was mesmerised by the power and beauty of this, the more rugged and less commercial side of Crete.

She bathed and dressed in blue jeans, a cashmere jumper, a long double-breasted jacket of navy blue wool with bone buttons. She wore white sneakers and wound around her neck several times a white silk damask scarf. She went directly up on deck. It was a glorious morning of wind and a warming sun, an autumnal nip in the air, the sky blue and cloudless. And the Aegean Sea: today an inky dark blue sparkling in the sun, its aroma of salt water like some exotic perfume, the undulating waves sending up sprays as the *Black Narcissus* cut deftly, swiftly, through them. The thrill of adventure, new horizons, the sea and sails, new discoveries, and love waiting for her. Had she ever been happier?

It was half-past eleven, Chadwick and Captain Dimitri were in the dining room breakfasting together when the first fax from Manoussos came through. 'Where are you? Notify estimated time of arrival?' The second fax read, 'The port has been advised of your arrival and has been made ready to accommodate the *Black Narcissus*. Moor her at the port entrance below D'Arcy Montesque's hanging gardens.' The third was for Chadwick: 'And so she came to us, the daughter of Zeus, the greatest of the Greek gods, and Dione. She sprang from the foam of the sea that gathered about the severed member of Uranus when Cronos mutilated him. She was called Aphrodite and was the Greek goddess of love. Welcome home, Chadwick.'

She looked up from the fax she had just read to see a beaming Captain Dimitri who had not had the grace to give her the privacy she needed to recover from such a romantic message. 'I feel I'm living in a dream, and if that should be the case, I hope I never awaken.'

'I did tell you that Manoussos was not your ordinary policeman.'

'So you did, Captain, so you did.' And she too began to laugh.

Several hours later Chadwick was on deck in the prow of the *Black Narcissus* which was riding at full sail as she rounded the point of mountainous cliffs that plunged steeply into the sea. The wind was whipping her long luscious hair away from her face and clothes so that her stunning figure was outlined against the sea and sky. Dimitri watched her and listened to his thoughts: How right Manoussos was, and lucky, to have found this mysterious and stunningly sensual woman.

Dimitri Cronos had been smitten by her the moment she had boarded the yacht in Sounion on the mainland. He had watched her, the effect she had on him and his crew. She made him itch with desire even when Chadwick had done nothing, said nothing, deliberately to entice. Her sensuality was all there in the face, the body, the essence of her soul. He felt not so much frustrated that he would never have her as privileged that he would at least have served her well; that she was for some brief time here to grace his life.

There were so many things about her face that he would always remember. The ruby red lips and their shape, they would remain in his memory forever; the proud nose; the eyes, so large and holding secrets that intrigued him. The way she shook her hair from her face, that hint of a cleft in her chin. He tried to pull his gaze away from her face but it lingered. Dimitri had never seen her as she was now. She had somehow metamorphosed herself; become even more than she had been before they arrived in Crete. She seemed suddenly a younger woman, ready to grasp the world with both hands. That sadness that lurked behind her eyes ... he had always thought this odyssey she was on had something to do with that. He wondered if he would still know her when she had rid herself of that sadness?

She seemed to sense him and turned and waved. She looked incredibly happy. He waved back and then spun the wheel hard to starboard. Livakia slowly inched into view. Since leaving Iraklion, Chadwick had seen many white villages in many small harbours, some set on this rugged mountainous side of the island, but she had never seen anything as enchanting, beautiful, strangely ethereal and peaceful as Livakia basking in the sun.

The white houses and walls, patches of courtyard against a barren landscape of buff-coloured cliffs, the odd twenty-foot-high scrawny palm tree poking up into the sky, rose up steeply from the port, higher and higher among ruins: falling down houses, some roofless, others mere walls; tall and slender shapes running at angles into one another or standing solitary, as if having risen from the stony ground like so many contemporary sculptures. Proud and mysterious, their stories of life and passion were buried deep within their art. Livakia was a large and romantic amphitheatre of a white on white village, with no roads, only narrow donkey paths of cobblestone steps radiating out from the port.

Chadwick shielded her eyes from the sun the better to see and was able to pick out a church's bell tower several houses back from the harbour, and higher up, nestling into the cliffs, another small solitary white-domed church. On the opposite side of the village in an even more precarious position, very nearly hanging over the sea, there was yet another. Into view came several large and impressive island houses with wooden shutters painted royal blue, black or a rich dove grey, whose floors and arched open loggias with large and small enclosed patches of courtyard, proffering hundreds of terracotta pots containing trees and bushes, climbed one above the other up the stony terrain. Chadwick could imagine summer flowers in bloom, bougainvillaea and trumpet vines draped over the white-washed walls surrounding them.

From that distance she could just make out the fishing boats at anchor in the crescent-shaped port, shop fronts on the quay, people lazily walking about, others sitting at café tables and dining in the sun.

The crew was now fully occupied with bringing the *Black Narcissus* into port, fast under full sail. The captain shouted to Chadwick, 'Our mooring.' Having caught her attention he pointed to a large, beautiful house, a hanging garden of tier upon tier dropping down the cliffs to a footpath. At the other side of the path the cliff plunged into the sea. 'I'm going to bring you home in style, Madam Chase.'

Chadwick knew very well what that meant. Captain Dimitri knew just how magnificent his schooner was, especially in full sail. He would bring her into dock by tacking across the harbour several times and dropping her sails at the very last minute to avoid crashing into the quay. No easy task but a thrilling show for the Livakians, and a test of skill and bravado for the captain and his crew. A gift to his passenger: an entrance into her new world that neither she nor anyone else would forget.

Dimitri had sounded the yacht's horn, several long and mournful blasts, before the yacht had rounded the point, signalling their arrival to Manoussos. Now he gave two more blasts to warn the boatmen to keep the harbour clear. The schooner started her first tack towards the harbour entrance. The sea was already flattening when the wind gave the *Black Narcissus* an extra burst of speed and the crew were hard at it, winching flat every sail. People rose from their chairs, left the shops, some came down from their houses or watched from them.

Most of the expatriates and several of their house guests, a few Greeks, some from Athens, and several Cretans who lived in Livakia, were lingering at a long table over the last of the Kavouria's house wine, empty platters and plates before them. It had not been any more or less amusing a lunch than usual but as always it had been interesting and fun. Fun was the operative word among the expatriate community: fun, interesting conversation, love affairs, passionate friendships, the hows and whys and wherefores of seeking their pleasures. For some like Mark Obermann, a modestly successful writer, Tom Plum, a famous painter, and Rachel al Hacq, a would-be poet, who were at the long table, it was their work, their ambitions and dreams, and above all seeking their pleasure, that kept them there. Others like Max de Bonn, D'Arcy Montesque and Laurence Hart, successful in their chosen work, were past striving. They played with what working life they had as they played with life in general: by living it to the full as and when it came. For them all Livakia was paradise, their home, the heart and hearth of their libertine lives, their pleasure seeking.

From the long table Elefherakis Khaliadakis watched the black schooner with its rust-coloured sails swoop into the harbour. He had sailed on the *Black Narcissus* with its owner and friends many times. Elefherakis was independently wealthy, a prominent Greek scholar, a handsome reprobate of a man of fifty-odd years, a dilettante who had spent his entire life reading and admiring beauty. An old Eton and Oxford man of utter charm and sophistication, he was a gentleman known for his generosity, wit and debauchery in his younger days; a libertine par excellence in his mature years. He remained famous in certain international social circles for his fascinating personality, brilliant intelligence, and especially because he was in all things subtle and discreet. He was, by his very nature, always the perfect host, entertaining the people he gathered around him in his large and beautiful house in Livakia.

The rich, famous and interesting from all walks of life who wanted to visit Crete and Livakia could usually be found staying there or in one of the other foreigner's houses because there was no hotel in the village, no *pension*, just a few Livakians who would let out a bed for a night or two. Mr Average Tourist rarely turned up in this coastal village which was too remote, difficult to get to, too closed a society, and very Cretan. This paradise and the people lounging round the table were lost to the package holiday visitor but graciously embraced any traveller on a voyage of discovery, poets and dreamers, and most especially if they were pleasure seekers ready to play for a few days. The residents of Livakia, both Cretan and foreign, by the very nature of the way they lived and loved, automatically dispelled any unwanted intruder.

The people sitting round that table were intrigued by the sight of the *Black Narcissus* sailing into port in all her glory. This was the quiet, lazy time of year when the more interesting travellers en route to Egypt and North Africa arrived for brief visits. And if the grand sight of her coming in was not enough to stir their hearts, the thought of someone new on board, put a sparkle in their eyes.

Mark Obermann was the first to speak up. 'Expecting guests, Elefherakis?'

Elefherakis told them, 'Not that I know of. One of your millionaire patrons or some art dealer on the hunt for a painting?' he asked Tom Plum.

'No, but you never can tell, only refuse the visit,' answered Tom, who was famed for guarding his privacy, receiving visitors on his terms only.

'It must be a friend of D'Arcy's or Max's. Damn, and they're not here, vanished as soon as they arrived the day before yesterday,' said Rachel, who immediately took out her compact and began repairing her face. New men were always desirable to the French coquette-cum-poetess.

Manoussos, who was sitting with them and whose eyes had not left the sight of the magnificent yacht tacking across the harbour, relit his cigar and listened with amusement to his friends. He too would have liked D'Arcy and Max to have been here for Chadwick's arrival.

People began to rise from their chairs and walk the few feet to the edge of the quay the better to see the *Black Narcissus*, still under full sail, make another impressive tack across the water. He rose from his chair and went to the cook Despina to order food for the lunch he had offered to buy Chadwick, captain and crew in celebration of their arrival. Then he went to stand next to Elefherakis and Mark.

'She's still coming in fast – impressive. That has to be Dimitri Cronos captaining. It's his style. I know, I've sailed with him several times.'

'It is,' Manoussos offered.

The two men turned to look at him. 'You've been expecting this yacht and you know who's on board?' said a surprised Mark.

Manoussos remained silent, his gaze still fixed on the yacht, now searching for his first sight of Chadwick. He was feeling incredibly happy but calm, in control in spite of his racing heart and lustful mind. She was here and she was his as she would never be any other man's again. The sex, the glorious sex they had revelled in! How well matched he and Chadwick were to make the erotic part of their life an adventure to love by. And then he saw her and his heart raced that little bit faster. How was it possible that she was even more ravishingly beautiful than he had remembered? It was then that he turned his gaze to the two men and told them, 'Yes, I have been expecting the *Black Narcissus*, and yes, I do know who is on board. She's called Chadwick Chase, come and meet her. And the captain? You were of course right, Eleflherakis. Dimitri Cronos is the man bringing in the yacht. I'm giving Chadwick, Dimitri and the crew lunch at the Kavouria.'

'You're in love!' piped up an astounded Rachel who had overheard the men.

Manoussos smiled at Rachel who had not the least idea

59

what love was. For her it began and ended with every glance at herself in the mirror. She was, of all his foreign friends in residence in Livakia, the least talented and most self-involved. She had raised her admiration of herself to such an art form that everyone accepted it and loved her for it. For Rachel, Rachel was as important as the very air she breathed. She was *the* flirt personified, who played the vestal virgin but had had every eligible man in Livakia and any other man she wanted a sexual liaison with. Rachel's idea of discretion in such matters was to plot and create elaborate charades where everyone had to play their part to sustain the illusion that she was hard to get. Petite and very pretty, she proffered a tiny waist and a large and luscious bosom, remarkable for its perfect, more often than not displayed cleavage, which she wore as if she were showing off the *croix de guerre*. Rachel was like a little doll one won as a prize at some game of skill at a country fair. Her saving grace was that her passion for herself was so amusing even she could laugh at it.

'Why don't you come too, Rachel? Actually I'd like you all to come and join us, pass the word around,' was his answer to her.

Manoussos gave nothing more away. He bent down and kissed Rachel on her pursed red lips and then started walking towards D'Arcy's garden and where he knew the boat would dock. By now people were lining the quay and edging the paths around the cliffs, watching the yacht criss-cross the harbour. Several joined him and jabbered in awe of the captain's courage in bringing in the yacht, when he should unfurl his sails, taking bets among themselves as to whether he would crash before he dropped anchor and set her dead still where he wanted her to be. Manoussos had no doubts Dimitri would dock the schooner exactly when and where he wanted her.

There are always moments of magic while sailing large schooners. Those who love the sea and the mastery of sailing, as did most of the people watching the *Black Narcissus*, were waiting for that moment. It came in a flash. In what seemed like a single instant all the sails plummeted to the deck. The three-masted schooner lost all its speed and seemed to stop dead in the water. The *Black Narcissus* was no more than fifteen feet from its mooring, just exactly where the captain wanted her to be. Admiring sounds rose all around the harbour.

Chadwick and Manoussos saw each other almost at the same time. They smiled and their lives linked together. With all the commotion of crew gathering up canvas, Dimitri guiding the *Black Narcissus* alongside the natural dock carved out of the cliffside, several Livakian men and boys calling for the mooring lines to be thrown to them, she seemed more goddess-like than ever in her stillness and beauty. Manoussos, who had only seen it before now, accepted that this solitary figure standing amidst all the chaos, this woman who had captured his heart, was an enigma. Instinct told him Chadwick was a woman who lived in a good deal of mystery. She had mysteries the way other people had family, friends and lovers. He was infatuated with a woman with a guarded personality who could never truly reveal herself, any more than she would easily give up her secrets.

It was here, in this place, at this time, that he realised their happiness was dependent on their living their love from moment to moment. He was not a man to question the gods or fate. He blew her a kiss from his hand, and their destiny was sealed.

Livakians loved their police chief in and out of uniform. They took pride in him as a law enforcer: his international fame as art detective supreme who made smuggling antique treasures out of Greece hazardous for thieves, his easygoing nature yet the ease with which he caught a murderer in their midst, and the manner in which he could defuse vendettas and potential crimes, demanded and received their respect.

Out of uniform, as he was now, they adored him as a good neighbour, one of them, who had been educated abroad and returned. Both men and women were admiring of his good looks and the many foreign women who fell in love with him. They had seen so many beauties come and go that his prowess as a lover was, as base as it seemed, a matter of village pride. As was his discretion *vis à vis* his promiscuity, the libertine private life he led. He had his reputation as police chief to maintain and so never flaunted his liaisons, in fact worked at playing them down, which only enhanced his fame. For years many a blind eye had been turned to his womanising together with that of his partner in this pastime, his best friend Max.

And Manoussos and D'Arcy? The Livakians loved D'Arcy, the foreigner they considered a Livakian, as Cretan as she was American. They had known her from the time she was a baby and living here with her mother and her mother's lovers. They had seen her and Manoussos as childhood friends, as adolescents in love, as on again, off again lovers in their adult life, and were romantic

about them. They liked and respected Manoussos for loving her in a romance they could only dream about. They were proud, so very proud, of their police chief's virility, something Cretans set great store by. It was exhibited to them by those many women who came and went, and they believed would always come and go in his life, until one day he would find a Cretan girl to settle down with and marry.

The men and boys standing close to Manoussos as Chadwick walked from the stern of the schooner grew suddenly silent. It was not her beauty alone that caught their interest but the look she had for no one, nothing at all, but Manoussos. They could sense the power and passion of this stranger who had made such an impressive arrival. Did they sense danger? Or could it be merely the overpowering sense of respect she seemed to inspire? Whatever it was, the moment she hopped on to the stony ground they stepped back and away, made a path for her, and she walked directly into Manoussos's arms.

They watched with awe as the lovers kissed and caressed each other, Manoussos opening her jacket and sliding it off her shoulders and arms until it fell to the ground. Now rid of the encumbrance he was closer to her flesh and he pressed her hard against his body, his hands fondling. They had never seen Manoussos so obviously seduced by a woman, so openly displaying his emotions, his lust for this stranger who had arrived from the sea. Still on board, taking some time to regain their energies, the crew watched with the same envy and appreciation as the Livakians what was happening to Chadwick and Manoussos, wrapped in a splendid, all-consuming embrace. It was one of the Livakian fisherman who finally broke the silence with an admiring and amusing remark about Aphrodite and how she had at last arrived in Livakia. It gave everyone a chance to laugh and dispel their amazement.

Manoussos regained himself and began to laugh too. Still holding her to him with an arm around her waist, he introduced by name everyone standing around them. The couple's happiness was infectious and very quickly a party atmosphere erupted followed by a good deal of affectionate teasing.

For them both there was a sense of ease and rightness to this reunion, and as they walked from the mooring along the path towards the port Chadwick volunteered, 'When the *Black Narcissus* rounded the headland and Livakia slowly came into view, something happened to me, Manoussos, something inexplicable. It was more than just seeing an amphitheatre of white houses basking in an afternoon sun. There was an aura of magic hovering over Livakia, a sense of time standing still, a place of no beginnings and no endings, just being. How much one has to live through to find this place! I don't intend to analyse what is happening to me, I don't care. Can you understand that?'

She stopped and stepped in front of him so he could go no further on the path. His answer was to take her in his arms and kiss her. They resumed their walk into the port, Manoussos telling her about the houses they passed and the people who lived in them, and Chadwick wondering where she had been and what she had done her whole life.

It was getting dark and the lights of Livakia were being turned on. Chadwick was seeing the old port transform itself. Siesta long since over, the shops were open again and the villagers were dressed for their evening walk, drifting into the coffee shops and the restaurants, gossiping in small groups near the water's edge about the arrival of the schooner, so majestic and intriguing. The sound of the water lapping against the *caiques*, the marvellous wooden boats undulating in a sea now dark and nearly vanishing in the dusky light; men playing backgammon, some drinking ouzo at small wooden tables set out on the cobblestoned quay, others smoking and talking of politics, the Greek national pastime.

The Cretans, always curious and anything but shy, sauntered past the long table to greet Manoussos, their way of begging an introduction to the stranger, the beauty, who had cast a spell on their chief of police.

The late lunch party was finally making ready to disperse, but not for long. They had agreed to meet again at ten o'clock, those who could sober up enough from the laughter and the wine, for dinner in the other restaurant in Livakia: Pasiphae's. That was at Elefherakis's invitation. He was completely intrigued by Chadwick.

A small boy was sent running to the restaurant set back from the port among a maze of narrow cobblestone lanes and white-washed walls, ruined houses and lost gardens. It had a pretty enclosed courtyard to dine in, though all agreed there was now too much of a nip in the air so they would dine inside. Andoni's task was to see if the temperamental chef was cooking that night, and if so to say that a dozen or more people would be arriving at ten. The boy's next stop was the musician's house with an invitation to join the dinner table. All were delighted when Andoni returned to the table unscathed and with a smile on his face. It had been more than likely he might have returned with a bruise from a flying pot. The Pasiphae's chef was not above such behaviour.

The news delighted everyone. Now they did begin to leave: the residents to do their evening errands or else return home to bathe and change, the crew to the *Black Narcissus* to secure their boat for the night and get ready for night life Livakian-style, and Manoussos and Chadwick to Manoussos's house to make love.

On the way home they were stopped every few paces by someone new to meet, and Chadwick was enchanted by it all. Arms round each other, she and Manoussos started their climb through the lanes up towards his house. They passed a string of donkeys, their bells echoing between the white-washed walls, their hooves clip-clopping on the cobblestones. They were coming down from the cliff top where there was a large terrace where the only road into Livakia ended. A mountain road that was hard core and dirt and rough riding, and the sea, were the only ways in and out of Livakia.

'They're marvellous, your friends, the Livakians and the foreigners. They're all so interesting, lead lives one only reads about. This is still the Greece of Katzanzakis novels and the music of Theodorakis. They seem to have got their lives right – well, their priorities anyway. They've left the rat race, whether social or work, behind them in order to live and laugh and pursue their pleasures. I'm as fascinated by them as much as I like them. Do I sound naive? Am I being naive?'

It had not taken more than an hour at that table for Manoussos to realise that Chadwick, for all her intelligence, beauty and incredible sensuality, was indeed naive, an innocent when it came to the harshness and the joys of real life. She had been a woman who had been cushioned and cared for. She had lived and loved and emotionally died in many and strange ways but always in a cocoon. It was at the table that he realised this odyssey she was on was probably the first time in her life she had struck out on her own. He loved her the more for it, too much to make her feel insecure by telling her he did believe she was naive about people and life. What he said was, 'Everybody at that table today takes each other at face value. No one really cares what their friends are or are not. In Livakia things are what they are, people will be what they will be. When that ceases to be then Livakia will lose its magic. This is a very egocentric place.'

Chadwick listened to his words, she more than listened, she really heard what Manoussos was saying and believed him. If only she had found out sooner that people could and did live like that; that hypocritical morality and guilt was no way to live.

She ran a few steps in front of Manoussos and turned to face him. She walking backwards, they advanced down the lane, their footsteps the only sound in the quiet of the early evening. She asked him, 'How much further to your house? I listened to Mark and was enthralled by his oratory and boyish good looks, flattered by his attention, but I wanted sex with you.' She opened her jacket and slowly, seductively, removed it and tossed it to Manoussos.

A crescent moon appeared overhead and shone white beams down the narrow lane. It lit Chadwick's face and reflected off the white-washed walls surrounding the houses and enclosing the cobblestone path. They continued walking and Chadwick told him, 'Elefherakis was charming. His manners, intelligence, the erotic aura around him, the way he looked at me as if he wanted to devour me in his lust ... but I could only think of the thrill of those hours of sex with you.'

Somewhere in the distance they heard a dog bark. The darkness of night descended further and suddenly the sky was peppered with millions of stars. Chadwick unwound the white silk scarf from around her neck and tossed that too to Manoussos who was mesmerised by her beauty in the moonlight, her seductive strip tease. She continued, 'I watched Rachel flirt and cock tease the crew, and became hot with lust to think that she would have them all, one at a time or altogether, but it was you I wanted to come with, not them.'

They were nearly at the end of the lane when Manoussos stopped before an ancient wooden door studded with antique bronze nails. Chadwick continued to walk backwards for several steps and then stopped. They were gazing at each other across the distance separating them. They had arrived at his house. Her heart filled with joy. She stripped off her jumper and now, naked to the waist, walked forward very slowly, continuing to speak. 'All through lunch, I saw Jane Plum watching us. I knew that you had had her by the look of envy in her eyes, and it didn't matter to me because you would never have her again. You will only love me in the way she wanted you to love her.'

Up close to him now, she unbuttoned her jeans. Anxious with desire, she pulled them open. He slipped his hand inside them and caressed her mound and her belly, her hips and her bottom, working his caresses up to her breasts. He was rough when he pulled her tight up

against him and, lowering his head, sucked on her erect nipples. She sighed, whimpered from the sheer sense of ecstasy overwhelming her as she came in a short and intense orgasm.

He opened the gate and swept her into his arms, carrying her through the courtyard and up several steps. His hands too busy, she managed the front-door latch and he kicked the door open. Up several more steps and into the sitting room where the moonlight was streaming through the windows. Not once since he had walked her through the courtyard had she stopped seducing him with lewd, base, hardcore sex-talk. Low, raunchy come-ons. No whore could have done better to excite lust, trigger depraved desires, and coming from a lady, a beautiful goddess of a woman whom he loved, it was even more thrilling, more wild.

This was inspired sexual seduction on Chadwick's part, played out to make them forget their egos and souls, love and the responsibility of relationships. Here was a woman who wanted to whip them both into anything goes sex. And she knew very well how to do it, Chadwick was a master at it. They were out of their clothes and over the edge sexually. Manoussos threw her face down on a carpet in front of the fireplace. The moonlight playing on her body only added to the mystery of Chadwick's sexual lust – oh, yes, there was definitely a mysterious and secretive quality about her sexuality. Manoussos used her white silk scarf to tie her wrists to the legs of a chair and held her down with one arm as he lit a match and tossed it into the fire laid in the hearth. It flared up at once and he turned his attention to Chadwick who was trying to turn herself over.

'No,' he told her firmly. She obeyed him and lay there quite still. He found a cushion and brought it back to her so she could rest her face upon it, stroked her hair and kissed the back of her neck, bit into it until she squirmed with pain. There were no caresses; no affection or foreplay would take place. One long and admiring look at her stunningly sexy body – the whiteness of the skin, the firmness and shapeliness of her flesh – was all he could manage. The heat of her desire to be possessed by him, her openness and vulnerability, he could refuse her nothing of what she wanted; she had manipulated him into her kind of lust, the sex she wanted. Now it was what he wanted, what he now demanded she accept.

He took his belt and used it across her bottom, not to give her pain but to awaken her lust further. Just a few strokes and she was trembling with anticipation of what was to come. He threw the belt across the room and laid his body over hers, rubbed himself up and down her several times, to feel her skin against his. He was madly, deeply, lustful for Chadwick. He raised her to her knees by her waist from behind and without ceremony, in one fell swoop, thrust as hard and as deep as was possible. She called out in a scream of passion and delight. He found his pace which was for her breathlessly quick and thrilling. At her instigation he took her wherever possible from behind and they had sex unfettered by fear and morality, became like animals in rut. They wallowed in their lust and depravity and both came several times until they collapsed in a heap of exhausted bliss.

Chadwick triggered a lust in them both that simply could not be sated. They bathed together and in the shower, after he came to her delivery of exquisite oral

sex, she made more demands that rendered him passive, on the receiving ends of her thrusts, under her control. Only lying in her arms and watching a dozing Chadwick did Manoussos come to understand that Chadwick Chase was the most dangerous thing that had ever entered his life and that for the time being he could do nothing about it, he had already thrown caution to the four winds. She had entrapped him in lust and love. He was as enslaved as he had ruthlessly enslaved so many women to him, for sex, a momentary love. He prayed this was not to be a case of poetic justice.

THE BACK WOODLANDS of TENNESSEE, NEW YORK, PALM BEACH

1972–1994

Chapter 4

It was oppressively warm and humid and there was a thick mauvy-pearl mist hovering in the trees. Chadwick could occasionally hear the rustle of some small animal in the underbrush, a larger one among the flowering plants: azalea, mountain laurel in an array of colours, rhododendron as large as small trees, and her favourite, dogwood, growing wild in the forest. From an unseen sun, streaks of brighter mist shone down at steep angles between the trunks of trees: ash, beech, elm, chestnut, the tulip poplar, pine, spruce.

Chadwick knew these woods as no one else. This was where she really lived. Here was where she played out her dreams, when she wasn't sitting in a tree willing her prince to come and take her away from the ugliness of her life, the lovelessness, poverty and hatred, the unbearable mental and physical cruelty she lived with every day, week after week, year in and year out.

Chadwick was drenched in perspiration. She raised the hem of her thin cotton dress and used its skirt to wipe her face, neck and arms. There was black bear in the woods – her father was the best bear hunter in the county – white-tailed deer – he excelled at that too – opossum, fox, but it was a rabbit that shot across her path now. She ran after it for several hundred yards but it vanished into the bushes. This was not running weather. She collapsed in a heap on the ground, laughing.

She didn't laugh much in the house or when she was anywhere near her family. Ed Chadwick, her father, was a killer who took enormous delight in killing whether it was animal, man, or laughter. Her father was a sadistic brute, an autocrat who ruled over and abused his children, a man people the entire county over, including the law, feared.

He ran two stills buried deep in the woods where he manufactured 100-proof alcohol. It was illegal but the law could never find them. He had shot several intruders on his land and a uniform would hardly deter Ed Chadwick, so they let him be. He feared only two people. One was the itinerant doctor who'd taken a gun to Ed's head and told him he would shoot him dead if Ed did not allow Chadwick to go to school, or if he ever found out that he was using her as he had used his other daughters and his sons. Chadwick, his incredibly beautiful, sensuous and courageous twelve-year-old daughter, was the other person. She was the only member of the family who stood up to him. She did, however, have to take her beatings for it.

Ed believed there was something of the same cold killer instinct in his youngest daughter as in him. It was something in her eyes, a certain look. He recognised that she would indeed kill him, which she had promised to do, if he ever forced an incestuous relationship on her. Nevertheless Chadwick was under constant threat from her father because he wanted her something fierce. So did most of the men who came to shoot with him. She was the prize beauty of the county, and had something more, something inscrutable, that drew the men to her.

The Chadwicks owned a small farm that just about kept the family self-sufficient, and some years didn't even do that. This was Tennessee's easternmost region, part of the Blue Ridge Mountain system. Most of the area was heavily forested and the soil thin and stony, yielding poor crops. The booze, and the hunting and fishing parties Ed Chadwick arranged, didn't make the family rich, merely kept them just above the poverty line. He used his wife and his children as slaves and married the girls off at the age of thirteen to other backwoods men like himself for money, and then only when he was through using them for his own sexual satisfaction.

Ed Chadwick was a mean, illiterate animal who believed that his farm and his land were his kingdom, places where he could do anything he wanted to do. He considered his wife and children to be his chattels, no more and no less than that. He not only believed he was above the law but lived that way so long as he was on his own land – one reason why he rarely left it and certainly never the county. Any trespassers were fair game to shoot, rob, or be disposed of as he saw fit.

Chadwick had turned the dense forest into a series of hideaways. They were her escape hatches from her prison of misery into the free world. On this particular day she was on her way up one of the lesser mountains they called Little Chickamauga where she had built a small lean-to to house her collection of American Indian relics, bits and pieces of artefacts she found on Little Chickamauga and in its surrounding forests.

The family had always called it Little Chickamauga because during the American Civil War a much smaller but equally fierce battle to the one that took place on the

Chickamauga battlefield had raged there. Five Chadwicks had fought and died there for the south.

Before Tennessee was settled several Indian tribes hunted and claimed portions of the area. After the Europeans arrived, the Shawnee, the Chickasaw and the Creek moved west, as did the Cherokee who claimed the central and eastern part, these very mountains and forests where the Chadwicks had settled more than a hundred years before and where they had remained. The first Chadwicks settled in with the Cherokee and even now there was a trace of Native American blood running through the veins of Ed Chadwick and his children though for generations the Chadwicks denied that while simply ignoring their inbreeding. Ed was proud of being considered white trash, backwoods, and feared.

Chadwick knew nothing of who and what she was and didn't much care. All she did know was that her school mates, whose backgrounds were not much different from her own and their poverty in some cases even worse, ignored and distrusted her. The rare times her father would collect her from school in his dilapidated, rusted, open Ford truck, they ran away in fear. Because of Ed, Chadwick's schooling was sporadic; because of him, her forays into the woods were not.

She did not have rich pickings for her collection but she did have a knack for finding odd Indian fragments. Throughout her childhood the few artefacts she did find were her only toys, her treasured possessions. They seemed to appear for her as if by magic, and sure enough today she spotted an arrow head, a very nearly perfect specimen. She dropped to her knees to search further in the undergrowth but was distracted. She thought she heard something farther up the mountain, then silence. She stood up and listened. Again, nothing. She strained her eyes, but visibility above six feet and more than twenty feet in front of her was obscured. By now she would have expected the sun to have burned off the heavy mist, but it hadn't, not a bit. She knew her forest well, if the heat, humidity and heavy mist had not broken by now they were in for several more days of this steamy weather. There seemed no point in going on because half the fun of being in the lean-to was that it had a spectacular view for miles around.

Chadwick turned to start for home but not before she buried her arrow head and marked the place with a broken branch of dogwood. She had only taken a few steps when she heard that same sound again. The cry of an eagle? No, it was more human than that. And again she heard it. She remained very still though she knew that whatever it was it was a good distance away; she knew how sound travelled through the forest. She waited for very nearly five minutes and heard nothing more. She waited a few minutes after that and then decided to make the climb to investigate.

She barely saw the wreckage of the plane until she was practically on top of it, that was how much more dense the mist was an hour's climb from where she had found her arrow head. The six-seater plane was cream-coloured and seemed to loom out of the mist like a ghost. It was up-ended, the wings and wreckage strewn around everywhere, the body broken in half, tail sticking nearly straight up in the air. The door was gone, the windows smashed out, two leather-covered seats on the ground. Two men had been flung from the plane, another was still sitting in the cockpit. He wasn't moving. The trees where the plane had swathed a path through them were sheared of their foliage and branches; once giants, they seemed to be lying around as if they were no more than toothpicks. Chadwick was for the moment traumatised by the sight. She merely stood there, taking it all in. One of the men lying on the ground opened his eyes. 'Good god, we're saved. It's a child.'

Chadwick, who'd thought they were all dead, was pulled out of her shock but frightened for a moment, thinking they were ghosts. She turned on her worn, ragged and laceless sneakers and started running away as fast as she could. 'Don't be frightened, for God's sake don't run away! We need your help. None of us is dead but we soon will be if you abandon us. We've been here more than two days.'

Chadwick stopped running and turned around. She did not move. It took some coaxing from the man in the cockpit who had raised his head off his chest and was now peering through what had once been a side window. 'My name is Hannibal Chase and I'm pinned in here. It's hard for me to breathe, even to talk. You see, I think I have broken ribs. That man with the broken leg is called Sam and the other man is Andrew. He's lost a great deal of blood from the gash in his leg, that's why he has a tourniquet tied on his thigh and can't move. We're very dehydrated, we need water and food and medical help and strong men to get us out of here. Can you understand that? Can you help us?'

Andrew, the one propped against the trunk of a tree and the oldest of the men, tried to stand up. He suddenly keeled sideways. Chadwick ran towards him to help. She managed to brace him against the tree. He called out in pain and quickly apologised. 'Sorry, I didn't mean to frighten you.'

'You're all sure in a mess. I'm not frightened. Best you

don't play brave and sit back down.' She went to the man with the broken leg and examined it thoughtfully. 'Well, Mr Sam, as I see it that's a pretty darn good splint. You do that, Mr Andrew?'

'Yes,' he told Chadwick.

She returned to Andrew Coggs and placed her small slender hand on his forehead. 'Mighty hot, and lordy, you're looking real white, sorta greenish-white and sickly.' She examined his wounded thigh, where his trouser leg had been torn away and the leg had been wrapped in cotton wadding and tied tight to staunch the blood. His shirt had been made into a bandage and wound into a rope through which a broken twig had been shoved which he kept twisted tightly. The open first aid kit lay on the ground. She looked briefly through it. 'Lucky you had this here Red Cross kit. I'd say all things considered, you men're not doing too badly. Except maybe this is the worse weather for an open wound.'

'You seem to know a lot,' said Andrew who had for the last twenty-four hours himself been worrying about gangrene.

'Have to, don't I? Doctors don't come easy round here. Now I'm coming up to assess the situation you're in, Mr Chase.'

The three looked at one another. Sam even managed a smile. All were in wonder over this strangely beautiful waif in her pathetically thin and worn printed cotton dress who seemed not only to have found them, but was calmly and collectedly taking them over. They watched in wonder as she climbed into the plane and struggled through the wreckage to the cockpit and Hannibal Chase.

She tossed out bits and pieces of debris to make room

for herself and then leaned against part of the fuselage, the part that had not pinned him to his seat. They looked intently at one another in silence for several minutes. Hannibal was quite stunned by her beauty, a certain aura. He had never seen a lovelier looking child. She seemed to him like the mysterious child-woman that every great artist past and present wants to paint. He smiled and asked, 'What's your name, child?'

'Chadwick.'

'Is that your first or your last name?'

She smiled at Hannibal Chase and, leaning forward, raised the printed scarf he had covered his head wound with and took a peek. He flinched. She then touched an open wound encrusted with coagulated blood on his cheek, another on his chin. He flinched again. He could move his arms and hands and raised one hand to remove hers gently from his face.

She gave him a smile and answered him. 'That's my only name. My pa says I can have the family name but no more. Don't deserve no more 'cause I think I'm somethin' and I act too clever by half, as if I'm better than him and my kin. So everybody calls me Nothing, 'cause that's what my pa says I am, or Hey, You, or Chadwick or Chad.'

'I'll call you Chadwick.'

'That'll do.'

'It would be nice to get out of here before dark, Chadwick. Do you think you can get your father to get help for us?'

'Have to, won't I?'

The look of relief on Hannibal Chase's face gave Chadwick a chance to assess this stranger who had crashed into her world. She had never met a strange man before.

82

All the men she ever met were relatives or neighbours who hunted with her father. Men with gruff voices and filthy manners who leered lustily and behaved like animals, cruel, mean and hard in their ruthlessness. Except for Dr Rudge.

Hannibal Chase was to the twelve-year-old child a beautiful man, the closest thing to the male glamour she had seen on the roadside billboards advertising Ronson razors, Marlboro cigarettes, and Chevrolet trucks. He had a grand voice. She liked his accent. It was Yankee but there was kindness in it, the same way as behind the pain and worry in his eyes there was something soft there, for her.

'Do you think you will be able to find us again?' asked Hannibal.

Chadwick laughed. 'I found you once, didn't I? Don't you fret. I can tell you one thing, Hannibal Chase, I know these mountains and backwoods well enough that I sure as hell itself woulda missed hitting Little Chickamauga like you done, even in this soupy mist. Two hours down, two hours back, at a good run, and two hours, maybe more, for me to find my Pa and him to round up some men. You won't see me before then.'

'The doctor, you won't forget the doctor?'

'Can't figure on a doctor comin' up here. Maybe at home. If we can get you home.'

'Water...'

'I was coming to that, Mr Chase. There's a good mountain stream half-hour from here. 'Fore I go down to fetch Pa, I'll go down to the stream.'

Amidst the debris Chadwick found canisters once filled with crisps and biscuits, peanuts, coffee, tea, and a piece of canvas luggage. She scraped up every last morsel of the scattered bar food and gave a handful to each of the men, loaded the torn but still usable canvas suitcase with the empty canisters, and with some clever innovations with Brooks Brothers shirts, turned it into a knapsack. Wasting little time she assured them, 'I'll be back as fast as I can with the best mountain stream water you ever did drink.'

She made the men as comfortable as she could and then she was off at a run for the stream. The men listened to the sound of rattling canisters as she vanished through the silent and dense underbrush, their hopes raised by a backwoods waif of unusual courage and charm. Good as her word, she was back before the hour was up and after handing out the precious canisters, and taking some time out to rest, she was off again, this time at a fast walk down Little Chickamauga to find Ed Chadwick.

Her father, who was sitting with two men on the front porch cleaning his rifle, paid no attention to his daughter as she ran breathlessly up the dirt road towards the rambling wooden house that looked half-drunk for the subsidence that took a toll on the Chadwick residence at about an inch a year. The two other men did. They teased Ed about Chadwick and his reluctance to marry her off. His answer was always the same, a nasty look and, 'When the price is right, that troublemaker is out of here like a shot. I just ain't found no one rich and mean enough to my liking to sell her to. And you, Benjie, ain't got three hundred dollars cash and a sow, so don't even think about it.'

'She's gonna have to be real sweet and clean for some man to pay that, and knowing you, Ed...' The glare Ed gave the man stopped him in mid-sentence. You could only tease Ed Chadwick so much then he started shooting, Benjie Stoner knew that.

Chadwick's heart sank at the sight of the two men. Benjie Stoner and Calumet Cherry were as low as you could get for men in this part of the county. Thieves who never worked a day in their lives, Calumet was a close sidekick of Ed's and together they were more of a terror than most people could cope with. She guessed they had been out at the still for supplies.

Chadwick never showed fear of the men but every time she saw them together she felt just a little bit sick in her stomach. It was the way they had of gawping at her. She was seven years old when she made up her mind she'd never be made dirty for the likes of a Benjie or a Calumet.

Up until she had this first sight of Ed, Benjie and Calumet on the porch it never occurred to her that the strangers were in as much danger being rescued by Ed as they were of dying where they lay. But there was nothing for it, they would have to take their chances. She was twenty feet from the porch and still running when she started shouting, 'Mama, Mama, there's trouble on Little Chickamauga.'

She was somewhat relieved when her mother opened the screen door, wiping her face on her apron. Paislee Chadwick was the only reason Chadwick didn't run away for good. Her mother's consumption was killing her slowly but at the same time protecting Chadwick to some degree. Dr Rudge's visits kept Ed only fractionally in line, but were enough to save Chadwick from an incestuous nightmare and had led to her being educated where the other children had missed out.

Chadwick collapsed on the porch floor near her father and breathlessly told him about the plane crash and the survivors. The first thing he did was stand up and pull her to her feet and slap her so hard across the face that she fell to the floor again. 'That's for runnin' round the woods when you're supposed to be doin' your chores.'

Chadwick never blinked an eye. The moment she had seen the men she'd expected to be beaten for something. Ed liked beating her in front of his cronies; he and they got some kind of sadistic pleasure from seeing him control her with violence. Her mother stood by passively. They both knew that was the easiest way out for Chadwick.

Ed pulled her up from the floor and dragged her to the wooden bench where he had been sitting, 'Now, girl, you tell it as it is,' he commanded.

A party of three men, four bloodhounds, two of Calumet's boys and three pack mules followed Chadwick in the rescue party. All the way up the mountain she listened to the men talk about the salvage and what a fair split was since Chadwick had been the one to find the crash. No doctor had been sent for and the food and jugs of water they did take with them were only because Ed was sure if the survivors were wealthy enough to be flying a private plane, they'd have enough money to buy the food. They also brought their hunting rifles.

Chadwick raced ahead, marking the trail. The closer she came to the crash victims, the more anxious she became for them. She didn't much like the way the men had ignored her talk of the survivors' injuries. She was fifteen minutes ahead of the rescue party. Seeing the crash victims once again, she realised what she had to do. The men seemed in an even more sorry state than when she had left them but greeted her with enthusiasm.

Hannibal Chase was horrified when he saw Chadwick. One side of her face was swollen and her eye was black and blue; the bruise raged down one whole side of it, even her lip was horridly disfigured by swelling and a cut across it. Andrew and Sam sensed her anxiety, the fear coming off her. She appeared to be a much less confident child than she had been when she had found them. 'What happened to you, Chadwick?' asked Andrew Coggs.

'The men, they're no more than fifteen minutes behind me. Please don't say nothing 'bout my face, it'll go worse for me if you do. That's the way my pa is. I don't want to scare you but they're mean old boys. They're talking salvage, not so much rescue. But they're bringing food and water and they'll expect money. Be careful. They're mountain men, backwoods people, and different than most folks. Mr Sam, Mr Andrew, you gotta work fast fore they get here. Hide them guns I saw you was protecting yourself from the animals with. They ask you got guns, say no. Money, say something like you got some but you be more grateful with money for the rescue when you can call home for someone to bring more. Long as they think you can get more for them, they'll be real good to you. It'll be all right, I promise, but you just got to be careful and a little smart 'cause they're really a lot dumb and life don't mean much to them.'

Andrew and Sam went into action while she climbed into the plane and made her way to Hannibal. The heat and the humidity were if anything even more unbearable there. Hannibal, wet with perspiration and extraordinarily weak from the heat and his injuries, did however manage a smile. 'It's because of us ... somehow I know that you took that beating because you found us. When this is over I promise you, Chadwick, your father will never lay a violent hand on you again.'

Chadwick, who never cried, wanted to burst into tears, but she fought them back and said, 'I hide in the woods and I pretend a lot that my prince will come and take me away on a white horse. Maybe I got my transportation wrong. Maybe he comes in a crashed plane.' She raised a corner of her skirt and wiped Hannibal Chase's face then she smiled. 'I know you mean well but it's best to say nothin' about me to my pa. You do and it'll be the worse for all of us. Most important thing, stand up to him like you're real important, like the President of the United States. And if trouble comes, don't worry. I got ways to help, secrets, ways to get away from him he never thought about.'

It didn't take the survivors long to realise how incredibly right and courageous the beautiful backwoods child who had found them was. As soon as the rescue party arrived Ed's barrage of questions began in a polite if obvious manner. The men soon gave themselves and their intentions away. It was not difficult to comprehend what these men were all about. No one examined their wounds, no one offered food or water, no one even unpinned Hannibal from his crash-imposed prison until a deal was struck, money promised for their safe delivery to the local hospital. They took the men's watches as deposit on the food and water, and a hundred and twenty-six dollars, supposedly all the money they had, for digging Hannibal Chase out of the cockpit, and all the salvage was theirs. The three survivors did as Chadwick had suggested. They played tough, hard negotiators for their lives and there was no doubt in any of the men striking the bargain that that was exactly what they were doing.

The first night of the rescue was spent on the site of the crash. The men cleared the area enough to make camp and build several fires, lighting kerosene lamps to work by in the cockpit. It took all the men, the boys and the mules towing away the fuselage seven hours to release Hannibal Chase. Calumet and Ed carried him from the wreckage. Miraculously his legs had not been damaged. His agony was as he had suspected from broken ribs pressing against his lungs, and he was black with bruises from his neck to his feet as well as festering cuts from flying glass. A corset of twigs and rope was made to keep him straight and after hot coffee laced with Ed's home brew and hot food, opossum and rabbit done on the open fire, he took charge of the situation with a great deal of authority, and even more diplomacy.

The most dangerous aspect of getting out of there for the crash victims was that the men kept constantly complaining about how much work this rescue entailed. It crossed Hannibal's mind several times that they might be happy to settle for the salvage, what money they had received and just shoot them; they were after all the laziest blackguards either Hannibal or his friends had ever come across. The mules were loaded not with men but with salvage, crutches were made for the men who would be carried or dragged along on make-shift chairs with runners rather than legs, an impossible idea because of the density of the underbrush. No pleading by the survivors could make Calumet, Benjie or Ed unload the mules and let them ride out of their misery. They ended up travelling on foot with the makeshift crutches and leaning on one another for support.

After three hours on the trail down the mountain they had not made much progress and tempers began to fray. Ed, Benjie and Calumet wanted to leave Andrew there and return for him because walking for him was the worst, his leg continued to bleed unless the pressure on the tourniquet was kept constant. Hannibal would not allow the party to be split up. He offered three hundred dollars for Andrew to ride the mule. Andrew was rough handled on top of the salvage and they continued on down the mountain.

The men were drinking too much. There were signs of danger: constant complaining about how much trouble this rescue was causing and even comments of, 'Hell, let 'em find their own way out or die. If they be men they ain't gonna die, and if they ain't men, well then they *should* die.' A great deal of laughter over that and looks of disdain for the crash victims. Was it a tease to frighten, and no more? Who could tell?

The injured men were exhausted. Clearly they couldn't go on without rest. The party stopped in a small natural clearing and ate some of the bread, cheese and smoked ham; drank from the jugs. Sam and Hannibal injected the last of the painkiller using the disposable syringes they had found in the First Aid kit. The rescuers looked angry, were tetchy.

'This is too hard, Pa. It's no more than half a mile outa the way to the Muchamanee. If you went and got Siddy Parton's boat we could take the rest of the way down by river.'

'Come here, girl!'

Everyone stopped talking and all eyes were on Ed Chadwick. Hannibal began to rise from the ground but Chadwick shot him a look and he forced himself to remain where he was and say nothing. She walked to stand in front of her father who was leaning against a tree. 'Did I speak to you?'

'No, Pa.'

'Miss Know-it-all.' He grabbed Chadwick by her thin bare arm and pinched it as hard as he could. She bit her lips for the pain but remained silent. 'Lucky for you, that's not so bad an idea 'cept that we ain't sharin' nothin' with Siddy Parton or no one else. The pie's cut too small already.' He pushed her hard and she fell against a tree trunk and steadied herself.

Benjie spoke up, 'What about that outboard o' yours, Ed? We could go an' get that. It'd take longer but you sure are right about not wanting to share any more o' this job. Just ain't worth it.'

It was Hannibal who spoke up next. 'I know that's extra work for you, Mr Chadwick, but I'm prepared to pay you another two hundred dollars if we go by boat.'

'How do I know I'm gonna be paid, that you even got that kind o' money? We're gettin' into lots o' money you'll be owing me now.'

They haggled and they haggled and finally, much to everyone's relief, Ed agreed to go for his boat. What was suspicious was his insistence that they all go so they could unload the mules and return with them for another load. It would mean another night in the woods for the survivors.

They were left the remaining food and water. Wood was gathered, a fire was laid for them to light to keep the animals away. When it was suggested that one of the boys or Chadwick be left to care for them, Ed laughed. 'Leave Chadwick! You city boys is just as horny and dirty as us fellas. Everybody wants Chadwick.' He smacked her on her bottom and then, grabbing her by the arm before she could run away, asked her, 'Make an auction, should I

91

missy? These city boys, maybe they'd buy you for more than Calumet here.'

He began to laugh and pushed her from him, telling her, 'You get ready, missy, 'cause you comin' with your pa. No city boys is gonna take that nice sweet cherry o' yours, nobody, not 'less I say so – and I ain't sayin' so unless it's for more money than yo' worth. And then maybe nobody's gonna get you at all. I might just keep you for me and the Lord.'

It was very nearly more than Sam could bear. He was about to say something but Hannibal headed him off by speaking up first. He asked for a rifle to be left with them for protection against bear and mountain lion. The three backwoodsmen actually laughed at him. It was then that Hannibal realised that they had been playing with him and his friends all along. The girl had been right. Dangling before them the promise of more money than they had ever seen at one time was the only hope of getting out of there.

Andrew, Sam and Hannibal watched Ed push Chadwick along by prodding her with his rifle butt several times while giving her instructions. 'Girl, you get those feet movin' for home, and fast. I'm hungry and dog tired and I want a hot meal when I come through that door. That's what you tell your ma.' She vanished into the bushes while they were still making ready to follow her.

It was almost a relief to hear and see the last of them. The vileness of man, his capacity for cruelty and loveless- ness gone, a kind of peace and serenity descended upon the wounded men though the shock of being involved with these aspects of life and these people still lingered.

'What scoundrels. Do you think they will come back?' asked Andrew.

'I honestly don't know. Frankly I think it's a matter of mood. If they're in the mood to work at getting us out, they will. For the money, of course,' answered Hannibal.

'That poor child. She seems way above her father, smart as a whip, courageous, kind. One thing is certain, she tried her best for us,' said Sam, taking his pistol from its hiding place under his shirt, shoved down his belt at the small of his back. Andrew took his from the pocket of the seersucker jacket he had been forced to wear in place of the shirt he had used for bandages.

The men closed their eyes and tried to sleep. No one said anything but the three were very much aware that if Ed and his friends returned within the next few hours, it very well might be to shoot them. The dozing men were certain to hear them coming through the undergrowth. Chances were, hunters or not, they would be less cautious than if they were stalking an animal because they did not suspect the city boys were on to them or that they had firearms. The trio were banking on that and ready to fight it out if it came to that.

They didn't have long to wait. No more than an hour later they heard a rustling in the undergrowth. The sun was still high in the sky but unable to burn through the still-lingering mists. It was steamy and jungle-like and very still except for the rustling. Sam Kane heard it first and poked Hannibal who shook Andrew awake. Before they could remove the safety catches from the pistols, much to everyone's relief Chadwick burst through a tangle of dogwood.

'Chadwick! You did give us a turn,' said Sam who looked as if he were about to faint.

She collapsed at their feet. Her hair was wet with

perspiration, she was scratched on her arms and legs from the bushes as she'd gone racing through them and she was panting, wanting a drink to quench her thirst. Finally she smiled and told them, 'They won't be back, not for hours and hours. But they will come back, looking for me. Only I won't be here and we'll all be safe. Well, safe till Pa finds me – and he will find me. He hates me too much to let me go. Now we got to get a move on.'

'Move on, how? Where to? What's happened? Why have you returned?' asked Hannibal.

'Oh, I guess it's best if I explain my plan.'

'Yes, I think you had better,' said Hannibal.

'Well, it's like the prince and the lady in distress game I'm always playing only it's turned round. I'm the prince and I'm saving three sorta ladies, if you get my meaning.' Her smile faded and she continued. 'Fact is, I know my pa. He's mean an' he's ornery an' he's a lazy dog of a man an' I just don't like the signs, so I lied. It's not half a mile to the Muchamanee River, it's 'bout quarter of a mile, maybe less. My pa is the best hunter round this county but he don't know these woods like me. He hunts where the game is and there's never been much good game in these woods so he don't come here as much as I do. And Siddy Parton's boat? Siddy'd never lend my pa that boat. He'd shoot him first and come for you himself *and* he'd take no money for his trouble, he's a learned man. Siddy's place is more than an hour downriver and another hour past him is Gingertown. I been there once and that's where Doc's got his office, in the hospital. It's got two nurses and six beds. But Pa'd never take you there. The law's office is in Ginger, and Pa stays clear of the law and the sheriff.'

'So you're saying we are going for the river. But my

darling, courageous and lovely child, what then?' asked Hannibal, trying to disguise the distress he was feeling for this child who was taking on the burden of saving them with so little thought for the consequences for herself.

'Why then, Mr Chase, we get in the canoe I got hidden there – I mean, I *have* hidden there – and we paddle down to Gingertown,' she answered him, mimicking his Harvard accent and diction perfectly. Her smile was strangely endearing for the cruel lopsidedness of it due to the swelling and bruising of her face and lips.

Chapter 5

Even now, lying between the roughest sheets Hannibal had ever slept in, he wondered how they could possibly have made it through to and down the Muchamanee. Three crippled men in a near-delirious state from broken bones, high fevers and infection, and a young girl with an iron will that they should survive. It had been the roughest terrain they had yet encountered, and the canoe, dented and with more and varied patches than its original skin, at first sight inspired thoughts of a watery grave. But it had been large and dry and the river swift-running with no rapids or falls. Manning it had been almost as difficult as getting to it: climbing in and out for the right distribution of weight, a modicum of comfort achieved for the men who must remain still for hours so as not to topple the vessel — certainly a possibility since it would be riding dangerously low in the water.

Every time Hannibal closed his eyes another vision of the three of them walking, dragging, at times even crawling any way they could through the dense wood, sometimes over huge jagged slab-like sheets of granite then stretches of loose shale to the river, made his eyes open again. At other times, while he listened to the constant whirr of the ceiling fan generating nothing more than moist warm air through the windowless, screened-in room Dr Rudge referred to as 'the ward', he would stare from his bed through the screens to the river. He could hear, as if it were happening at that very moment, the haunting melodic sound of Chadwick singing sad country music, ballads, as she paddled in a controlled and steady rhythm. It had been left to her and Sam, when he found the energy, using their makeshift paddles, to get them safely to Gingertown. Andrew's hands were busy with the tourniquet and Hannibal's own injuries hardly allowed for paddling.

He surveyed the small backwoods river town of twelve hundred people lazing in the heat. Hardly a dog moved, and only occasionally some person would cross the street to the general store-cum-post office-cum-barber shop and the screen door would swing noisily open and bang shut. The only real action in Gingertown was the sheriff's black and white police car, shining like a new penny, its silver star gleaming, the bar of red, white and blue lights on its roof flashing for ten seconds every time Bonner Gleason and his deputy turned on the ignition and shot out of town in a cloud of dust, or returned trailing one.

Sam cleared his throat. The sound drew Hannibal's attention back to the six-bed ward. It had been Sam who had had the worst of it for pain but aside from exhaustion, shock, and a hideous spiral fracture of his leg, he had ultimately fared the best because his injuries were straightforward. Andrew was fighting septicaemia, and up until that morning it had been touch and go; now he was winning. Hannibal was suffering from internal injuries that were not fatal but had needed immediate surgery. Now he was without a spleen and with his ribs tightly bound with a massive amount of adhesive tape. And Chadwick had got them here despite her own twisted ankle with a hairline crack in it. All in all the four of them occupying the ward was the most dramatic and exciting thing that had ever happened in Gingertown.

In the five days since they had been tended by Dr Rudge, a Johns Hopkins-trained surgeon who had given up a big city career to work as an itinerant backwoods doctor, when the survivors had not been sleeping or fighting their injuries with what energy they had left, they had been on the telephone to loved ones, the insurance company, their offices.

These were high-powered men. Hannibal, the most powerful of them, was indeed a president, not of the United States but of a number of companies. He was a man with connections: it took no more than a single call to a senator he knew. The right judge was found and a court order issued that Ed Chadwick was bound by law to stay within a half-mile's distance of his daughter, Chadwick, until further notice. It also gave temporary custody of Chadwick to Dr Rudge.

Chadwick was for the moment not in the ward. She had been sent with a nurse to the General Store to buy some clothes, as many dresses as she wanted, and shoes, a gift from her grateful friends. Hannibal slipped from his bed somewhat painfully and went to sit in the rocking chair between the two white metal-framed hospital beds where Sam and Andrew lay.

'It has to be addressed, what are we going to do for Chadwick after all she has done for us?' asked Andrew.

'Have you got something in mind?' asked Sam.

'An educational trust? A trust fund well invested that

will take care of her for the rest of her life? But that's hardly enough. Prosecute her father for assault, child abuse? That's about all we can get him on. Is that enough?'

'And thus speaks our legal mind,' said Hannibal, not facetiously but thoughtfully.

'And we have to catch the bastard first. No easy task according to Sheriff Gleason,' said Sam.

'I'm going to buy Chadwick from her father,' announced Hannibal.

Neither man lying in the beds to either side of him made any comment. They seemed neither surprised nor disgusted. It seemed to them at that moment just another idea about what to do with the child. Both had known and worked with Hannibal Chase for most of his life; they knew no kinder nor more philanthropic man. If he said he wanted to buy Chadwick, they knew that, as revolting an idea as it was, he had a plan brewing that would deliver her once and for all from the vile Ed Chadwick. They heard a car draw up to the hospital and watched through the screens as Dr Rudge approached.

'Can I have a word, Doctor?' called out Hannibal through the open screen window.

'Sure,' the doctor called back.

Dr Rudge's first words on entering the ward were to enquire where Chadwick was. None of the men missed the look of relief on the young doctor's face when he learned that she was only over at the General Store with Nurse Suelee. He walked from bed to bed checking pulses, examining Andrew's eyes, looking at his fingernails, inspecting the traction rope holding up Sam's leg, listening with a stethoscope to Hannibal's breathing. 'Full examinations later, gentlemen, if you want that 'copter picking you up tomorrow. Now what can I do for you, Mr Chase?' he asked as he drew up a chair and sat opposite him.

'I can't pretend to understand these backwoods ways or how one can deal with these people except on their own terms. Violence and death seem to me to be the only other options.'

'Now you *are* beginning to understand these people. Sorry, do go on,' Hal Rudge commented.

'Chadwick is an unusual, beautiful and courageous child, I cannot and will not return her to that ignorant, violent brute of a father of hers. I intend to adopt her, if she is willing for me to do so. Since her father would never understand a lawful procedure such as adoption or my motives, I intend to buy her off him. That he *will* understand. I feel that's the least I can do for her. In exchange for our lives, I want to give her a better one than she has ever known.'

'That's admirable, Mr Chase.'

'Hannibal will do, and Sam and Andrew, I think, Hal.'

'Yes, well, Hannibal, as I was saying that's an admirable, a fine gesture to make, and I'm all for it, as long as you know what you're getting into. Chadwick is an intelligent child but she has her secrets and a very mysterious soul. She's difficult to know in the deepest sense of the word. Love, kindness even ... she has not had much experience of such things. There have never been role models, no one to show her affection. Who and what she is, she has had to make up as she goes along. I don't know you from Adam or your friends and I would have to be assured that you will give her a good home.'

It was here that Andrew spoke up and explained that he was Hannibal's attorney and that several phone calls would assure Dr Hal Rudge just who Hannibal Chase was and what kind of a man was making this offer of a new life for the child. Sam added that had not Hannibal offered to adopt Chadwick, it had been on his mind to do so.

Hannibal was not a particularly emotional man but he was quite overcome by gratitude to his two friends for not only understanding how much it meant to him to save the girl, but for having similar sentiments. His reaction surprised him. Recovering himself, he rose from the rocker and went to Andrew, then Sam, and shook their hands and thanked them. He somehow needed their approval for allowing his heart to go out to this child.

He returned to his rocker and painfully, with the help of Hal, took his seat again. 'You will work with us on this, won't you, Hal? You see, I have a plan but without your co-operation, indeed your advice, and the sheriff's protection, I don't think I can make it work. I need you to help me with both father and daughter. Somehow you have found a way to handle them both. Despite all we three have gone through with that child, she is as remote from us as she was when she walked through the bushes and mist and found us – yet that remoteness and her beauty somehow enchanted us. However, enchantment is hardly a form of verbal communication, which is what is needed.'

The young doctor laughed. 'That's Chadwick, a child-woman enchantress, and the beauty of it is she doesn't even know it. What she does know is that she's despised by her family, beaten and abused by her father, what friends she might have made are afraid of her – and all because she's more intelligent, cleverer, prettier, courageous, and has a certain sensuality that makes her a cut above these backwoods people.

'What Chadwick has she holds tight for herself and will not allow to be beaten out of her. She makes her father crazy, causes him a great deal of trouble, because she won't lie down for him. He thinks that chances are when he does force her to, she will kill him. I'm the one that told him she was capable of it, a lie of course created by me to save her. Another lie I told: that I would shoot him if he didn't allow her to go to school, and that only worked with a pistol held and cocked against his temple. I know how you feel about saving Chadwick, gentlemen. To see a flower growing in the dust and not to transplant it is a crime. Of course I will help you.'

The four men shook hands and discussed how best to approach Ed Chadwick. The sheriff, Bonner Gleason, was sent for and sat in on the conference. He was all for throwing Ed Chadwick into prison to rot there for the rest of his life, but common sense and a true understanding of the man and the law told him that they would never get a conviction. Paislee Chadwick would never testify against her husband and she was the only witness to the assault on Chadwick other than Calumet and Benjie who would think nothing of perjuring themselves. Bonner had another problem to deal with: Ed was on the hunt for Chadwick, and he doubted she would get away with a beating this time. There was nothing else for it, the best way to keep the peace was to go with Hannibal Chase's plan.

Chadwick returned in a new canary yellow cotton dress patterned with tiny bright red and royal blue flowers, sizes too large for her and pathetically unpretty, while the men were working on their plan. She had on white ankle socks and sturdy shoes that looked too wide for her and under her arm she carried her old tattered things wrapped in a brown paper parcel. She seemed to Hannibal, even with her now only partially swollen face and a rainbow of fading bruises down one side of it, still to be the most enchantingly beautiful child.

She stood there, neither embarrassed nor overwhelmed, merely smiling as she turned round and the skirt flared out around her incredibly comely twelve-year-old legs. 'You look really pretty, Chadwick. You did buy more dresses?' asked Hannibal.

'No.'

'But we want you to have many more dresses and shoes and underthings,' said Sam.

'And a sun hat with a satin ribbon, if you like?' added Andrew.

A smile broke across Chadwick's lips. She tossed her head back and laughed and ran her fingers through her hair, pushing it off her face. 'Lordy, my pa would kill me for sure. I'll be lucky he doesn't burn the one I have bought.'

Hannibal couldn't bear for her to mention her father, and chose to ignore what she was telling them. 'And patent leather shoes. Do go back and see if they have patent leather shoes, white ones.'

Chadwick gave a girlish giggle and exclaimed, 'White shoes! Well, I never. I'm happy with what I gave me, and I have new undies with a bit of lace,' she whispered to the men in the ward.

Nurse Suelee shrugged her shoulders and told them, 'I tried to tell her she could have anything in the shop and lots of it but I don't think she's used to having much.'

Hannibal realised that for him it was a *fait accompli* that

Chadwick could have everything but as yet she didn't know or understand that. He called her to him and told her, 'You've done so much for us, Chadwick, how about one more thing – give us a party, a kind of celebration? You go with Nurse Suelee and get us some ice cream and cakes and chocolates. Nurse, take the wallet on my bedside table and spend all you have to, but allow Chadwick to do the choosing.'

By the time they returned with the brown paper bags the men had settled on their plan. And after a party of potato crisps, cherry soda, chocolate-covered vanilla ice cream sticks, Babe Ruth candy bars and a small bag of salted peanuts for each, the moment of truth came.

Dr Rudge called Chadwick over to him from where she had been presiding over the party, mostly in silence and with some wonder at the fun of it all. Conversation had been somewhat stilted but had had its moments, especially when Chadwick had teased the survivors about their lack of faith in her promise that she would save them and had cited specific incidents. There was added charm in the way she would slip back and forth from backwoods Tennessee English to a more cultivated accent taught to her at school or by mimicking Hannibal or Sam or Andrew.

Hannibal asked her to sit next to him, and hoisted her up on to the end of Andrew's bed. 'You know your pa has been looking for you, Chadwick?'

'I guessed as much. Does he know I'm here?' she answered, looking round the room at the faces of the men, aware that the party was over and something serious was happening.

'Yes.'

It was impossible to guess what she was thinking

because she showed nothing, internalised the news with not a change of expression, merely a sigh of resignation.

'Well, I guess I better be starting for home.'

'You don't have to.'

''Course I do. It'll be worse for me if he has to come for me.'

'No, it won't,' Andrew told her. 'There are things you don't know that I have to tell you. Mr Chase is a very important man and he has got the law to issue an order that your father cannot come within half a mile of you or he goes to prison. That's why he hasn't turned up in Gingertown so far.'

'You know my pa can't read, Dr Rudge. And if he could he'd pay no attention to no piece of paper.'

'Well, he will to this one. I went out to check on your mother and it was I who presented it to him, and explained that if he ever wanted to see the money these men owe him, he would have to abide by the writ issued.'

There was just a hint of a smile on Chadwick's lips when she said, 'He must have been hopping mad.'

'Oh, he was, he is.'

'That writ, Dr Rudge, is it forever?'

It was Andrew Coggs who, after telling her that he was a lawyer and knew all about these things, explained the legal aspects of the writ. Still unwell and weak, he had to pause before going on to explain as simply as he could about bringing a case of assault against Ed for the beating he had given Chadwick. He concluded sadly that in his legal opinion they could never get a conviction.

'So in essence what Andrew is saying, Chadwick, is you're safe from your father until we pay him the money we owe him, for a little time longer maybe,' added Sam.

'Then it's best I say goodbye now and get on with going home. It'll take the sting out of it if he sees I come home before he gets his money. I know pa, he'll think he's beat us all, got me and the money, and he didn't have to work to get you to hospital. Well, never mind, we sure did have some adventure, didn't we? And I think you learned a lot.'

'How would you like the adventure to go on forever, Chadwick?' asked Hannibal.

'Now you're talking fairy tales,' she said, very nearly giving him a smile.

'I'm a grown-up man, I no longer believe in fairy tales. I believe in new beginnings, a new life, in casting out the bad and never looking back. That's what I'm offering you.'

Now she did laugh and ran her hands through her hair again to push it off her face. 'Hannibal Chase, that *is* a fairy tale.'

Andrew struggled to sit up and take her hand. 'One that can come true if you want it to. Hannibal can make it come true. He wants to take you away to live with him as his daughter. Give you a life worth living, an education, and much happier adventures than the one we have just been on. And he can do it, within the law.'

Andrew then explained how adoption worked, that there were millions of people giving children a new home and family.

'And you would have a family: a grown-up sister Diana, she's twenty, and a brother Warren, he's twenty-three. You could be their little sister and my little girl,' added Hannibal.

'Have you asked your wife if she wants a backwoods twelve-year-old girl? My ma never wanted me, least that's

107

what she tells me all the time. Bred me for my pa, she says.
My ma, she likes me because I won't give myself to Pa's
ways like she and my sisters and brothers do, but she hates
me too because I won't and because I can read and write
and because I'm separate from them. I never want to go
again where I'm not wanted.'

None of this was said with self-pity, more a determined
facing up to reality. Chadwick was revealing more about
herself in those few words than she had in the entire time
she had been with the men, more than she had ever
revealed to Dr Rudge. Once she had finished saying what
she had to say she seemed once more to retreat into this
still, very still, mysteriously beautiful child. There was not
one man in that room who was not touched by her
inexplicable charm and sensibility.

It fell to the sheriff to say something to break the silence
left in the wake of her few words. 'Chadwick, Bonner
Gleason's here to tell you you are something else, little
gal.'

'Maybe so, maybe not, Sheriff. All I'm doing is the best
I can to be me and stay alive just like everybody else, so I'd
best go hide my canoe because if Pa finds it he'll burn it
right in front of my eyes. After that I'll be getting on with
goin' home.'

'Chadwick, come here,' invited Hannibal.

She went to him. He took both her hands in his and
asked her, 'How do you feel about me, Chadwick? Do you
like me, trust me?'

'Liked you from the minute I set eyes on you pinned in
your seat in the plane. For a minute there even thought you
were my handsome prince come to get me.'

Everyone laughed, including Chadwick and Hannibal,

and then she continued, 'Trust you? You and Sam and Andrew, you trusted me with your life. I guess that deserves fair exchange.'

'Chadwick, I have no wife, she died several years ago, and I do very much want to adopt you, give you my name, and a home, and a family who will love and respect you as a human being. You could be called Chadwick Chase, then you would have two names. You do deserve two names. But that would mean leaving your home and your family, never to return. Not that I wouldn't let you but because your father is an unforgiving, violent man.

'If you say yes, an agreement will be reached between your father and me, money will change hands and he will be made to sign a document that gives you up to me forever. But if you were ever to return home, I wouldn't trust your father not to hurt you, for no better reason than that you got away from him. He has what we would call an obsession about you, and not a healthy one.'

'It's a great deal to think about,' interceded Hal Rudge, who bent forward from his chair and turned her around to face him. He pressed his fingers lightly on the bruised side of her face to check the swelling. 'And not much time to do it in.'

'And so it turns out that my prince has come,' she said as she picked up a white three-legged stool and placed it next to Hannibal. She sat down on it and gazed directly into his eyes as she said, 'I'm very backwoods white trash, Hannibal. I don't think this is going to be easy, so best we both be warned.' Then she offered him her hand.

Two days later, Ed Chadwick, Calumet Cherry and Benjie Stoner arrived in Gingertown in Ed's pick-up truck and drove directly to the hospital. Bonner Gleason was there waiting with his deputy and four state troopers in obvious evidence round the hospital. The men were asked to leave their hunting rifles at the door. They made no protest. Chadwick was nowhere to be seen. A long table and chairs had been brought into the ward and Hannibal presided at one end, Dr Rudge at the other. The meeting was played low key, using the only spur that seemed to work with the likes of Ed, Calumet, and Benjie: money.

Incredibly the backwoods men asked for triple the amount agreed upon at the crash site. Their reasoning was that they did get the men to the hospital as promised. Chadwick after all did belong to the rescue party or rather Ed, number one justification for their claim. Number two: there wasn't as much salvageable from the plane as they had thought there would be. Hannibal hung tough. The unpleasantness nearly flared to exploding point until he reached into his briefcase and after withdrawing a huge wad of money, began counting out twenty-dollar bills and placing them in separate piles in front of himself. Greed calmed the volatile situation. They could actually see the men's anger recede as the stacks of money grew higher and higher. A sum was finally settled on for the rescue of the three men from the crash site.

Then began the bargaining for Chadwick. It opened with a demand from Ed for her return, went way past a sow and three hundred dollars and was concluded at a thousand dollars cash, two hogs and three sows. Hannibal, who had never in his life felt queasy and was in fact a hard man when dealing in business, felt quite sick to his stomach when Ed Chadwick banged his fist on the table and said, 'Sold! You overpaid for that bitch-child! Can't suck, never fucked, and you'll have some time teachin' her. I saw you lookin' at her, wantin' her just as fierce as Calumet here. Well, now you got her an' good riddance is all I say.'

Ed Chadwick and Hannibal Chase signed several documents drawn up hastily by Andrew, Ed's signature being no more than a crude, five-year-old's rendition of E. C. One of the men at the table was a judge flown in to Gingertown by helicopter from Memphis so that he could expedite the documents and return with them for registration in his courthouse. The meeting began and finished in thirty-six minutes.

The judge was the first to leave, barely able to restrain himself from charging Ed, Calumet and Benjie with a number of offences. The three backwoods men rose to leave only after they had haggled with each other and finally come to an agreement over the sharing of the money which was painstakingly counted out and handed over by Ed. Then, Calumet and Benjie still grumbling about how they had been cheated, all three left, but not before Ed told Hannibal: 'You tell that dirt Chadwick, so long as her pa's alive, she come on his land, she's dead meat an' I don't need no paper to say so. That's my country an' I'm the law.' The anger and hatred showed in his eyes as he emphasised his words by spitting a smelly stream laced with chewing tobacco in Hannibal's face. Hannibal knocked him out with one punch, screaming in pain as he did so.

Two hours later Chadwick boarded the helicopter with the three survivors, Dr Rudge in attendance. They transferred to an ambulance plane waiting for them on the nearest air strip and from there flew out of Tennessee never to return. It was all over: the crash, the ordeal of the three men and their rescue, Chadwick the heroine of the day. They became backwoods history.

Seeing the lights of New York City as the helicopter flew up the East River was the very first time that the survivors allowed themselves the luxury of giving in to pent-up emotion. They were back in their world, a civilisation they could understand and knew how to deal with. Sam covered his face with his hands and sobbed; Andrew wiped away the tears settling in the corner of his eyes; Hannibal held back tears of relief and gratitude for their survival, for Chadwick's sake. And Chadwick? She was so dazzled by seeing the city lights she went from window to window, clapping her hands.

Andrew went by one ambulance directly to hospital from the airport. Sam was met by his family and driven to his house in Greenwich, Connecticut. Hannibal went with his daughter and son, Chadwick by his side, in the second private ambulance to the family town house on East Sixty-seventh Street. The crash and their survival, saved by a backwoods child, did of course make all the papers but Hannibal managed to keep Chadwick not so much a secret as very nearly out of the press.

In those first few months in the house on East Sixty-seventh Street, Hannibal and his children, Warren and Diana, found in the charismatic child who had entered their life and their home a joy that had not been felt since the death of Hannibal's wife, their mother. It was not difficult to take her to their hearts. In New York she had that same mysterious beauty and quiet intelligence, the sense of a locked-up secret soul, that the survivors had found in the backwoods of Tennessee. Chadwick asked for nothing which made it so easy to give her everything: friendship, caring, affection, admiration, and fun as they fought to indulge the newest member of their family with material things. They wanted to spoil her but a part of their pleasure was that Chadwick was not and would never be a spoiled child.

For the first two months of Chadwick's new life, Hannibal, while recuperating from his injuries, remained at home with a nurse and his usual staff: houseman, cook, maid, cleaner, chauffeur, and a new addition, a private, live-in tutor for Chadwick. It was the time that was needed to create a unique closeness between Hannibal and Chadwick that neither had ever had in the past or would ever have in the future with another human being. They each of them had had in their own separate ways a near-death experience, and they had been saved by each other. It was during those first months that Hannibal and Chadwick became inextricably entwined and fell in love with each other.

Diana, who had always been a spoiled child and had grown up a spoiled young woman, found that Chadwick, rather than alienating her further from her father, eased whatever tensions there had been between them. She and her brother Warren maintained separate apartments around the corner from their family home in a building on Fifth Avenue. More often than not during those first few months of Chadwick's arrival in their family, both son and daughter, having had dinner with Hannibal, would stay the night in their old rooms. There was for once family unity, real affection, and three months after she had flown away from Tennessee, Chadwick had legally become Chadwick Chase.

Of all the wonders happening to Chadwick none would affect her more than that evening after a dinner party when they all withdrew to the garden: Hannibal, Diana and Warren, Chadwick's tutor Miss Cheevers, Sam and his wife, and Andrew and his.

It was an unusually warm end-of-September evening. The sky was clear and black and spattered with millions of twinkling stars. It was quiet except for the distant sound of New York evening traffic in the background. Akari, the houseman who had been with Hannibal for thirty years, walked from the house carrying a silver tray with crystal champagne flutes on it. He was followed by Telford the chauffeur carrying a baroque silver wine cooler with several open bottles of vintage Krug champagne, followed by Cook with a thin-layered chocolate cake decorated with small white butter cream birds, and a mass of small white candles all alight. Nurse, and the other household staff, slipped unobtrusively into the garden.

'A birthday party,' said Chadwick, looking excited at the prospect.

'A kind of birthday party, Chadwick,' said Hannibal.

Diana went to Chadwick. In her hand she had a paisley paper-covered box. She opened the lid and showed the contents to Chadwick. She lifted the first sheet of pale mauve-coloured note paper from the box and read aloud the engraved deep ruby red words at the top of the page: Chadwick Chase. She turned to look at Hannibal.

'I'm a man who always keeps my promises. You have always been a child worthy of a second name.'

Chadwick smiled at everyone gathered in the garden and then walked over to Hannibal and sat down next to him on the stone bench. He placed an arm round her shoulders and she leaned for a few seconds against him, resting her head against his heart. There had, as the months had gone by, been signs of affection from Chadwick to Hannibal but here was something more intimate. Not a person in the garden could help but be touched by the gesture, but what they did not know was that it was at that moment that Chadwick fell in love with Hannibal Chase.

Cook broke the spell by walking over to Chadwick and placing the cake on the table in front of her. Chadwick sat up and gazed at the array of tiny flames. Then, standing, she said, 'I'm going to make this my official birthday.'

'Well, that's a good thing because we all brought birthday presents,' said Warren.

For the first two years of Chadwick Chase's new life she remained at home studying with tutors who were teaching her academic subjects, elocution, piano, ballet, and the manners befitting a daughter of Hannibal Chase. She took everything in her stride, with enthusiasm and infinite joy. Chadwick was being educated and groomed so that she might be ready to go to Miss Porter's private school for wealthy society girls, not as a bumpkin from the back-woods but as, at the very least, an equal to her peers. That was where Diana had gone and her mother before her. Chadwick Chase was expected to finish her schooling and come out a debutante ready to take on society and the world – or so Diana and Warren and Hannibal's friends thought. But in both the child and Hannibal's hearts, though never spoken of, they were aware that Hannibal was grooming Chadwick not for the world but to become the perfect society beauty and companion of his life.

It was far from being all work and no play. There was

fun besides, happy times: in the city, shopping for clothes with Diana and even sometimes Hannibal. Incredibly, exposed to refined taste, Chadwick learned quickly what was beautiful and elegant, what was trashy and common, what best suited her unique kind of beauty. Warren took her to museums, and skating at Rockerfeller Centre. Hannibal took her with him to every social event where it was acceptable to take a child and that her schedule would allow. He was inordinately proud of his adoptive daughter and the affection between them was a joy for all to see.

There were concerts and operas, the theatre, and days and evenings at home, being quiet or attending one of Hannibal's dinner parties where there was always a place for her at table. Weekends were spent in the country house in upper state New York: an impeccably restored nineteenth-century mansion with stables, a pheasant shoot, and rolling grass fields down to the Hudson River. There were frequent house-parties there for friends of Hannibal's and his children. It was there that Chadwick learned to ride and shoot. But there were things that Hannibal would no longer do like walk for miles through the dense wood on the estate, though he didn't mind driving on the dirt roads cutting through it with Chadwick and a picnic by his side. Everyone said it was a matter of time, of getting over the trauma of his trek through the eastern Tennessee woods to save his life.

Strangely this new Chadwick who had loved the backwoods of Tennessee so much, like Hannibal had little interest in the beautiful woods surrounding Merrifields, and in running through them as a free spirit, none at all. What she had said in answer to Hannibal's questions about it was, 'That Chadwick never had anywhere else to go, she went there to stay alive. That Chadwick's gone forever. For Chadwick Chase everything is different. That other girl left the backwoods and her Indian relics, her canoe and a family who beat her, behind her.' At this point she slipped her arm through Hannibal's and stood on the tips of her toes to kiss him on the cheek, 'One day we'll take that walk through the woods together. Chadwick and Hannibal Chase.'

There were winter holidays in the Palm Beach house where the Chases were very much accepted among that small and closed upper crust society of the old New York Four Hundred. A group of socialites who even after so many generations were the descendants of those four hundred who were invited to the Vanderbilt Ball (no more would fit into the room, and that was the birth of American high society). Hannibal never entertained on a grand scale there. The beautiful mansion on the water was for family and close friends, of which there were many. Life was casual, and no matter what, he pursued his interests but never business. It was there in the winter sun that he would teach Chadwick all about society, high, low, *nouveau riche*, between sailing and swimming and deep sea fishing. And strangely it was there that he accepted the odd social invitation and kept up his obligations as one of the Four Hundred, seeing to it always that Chadwick was accepted by all as a Chase.

Even aged twelve Chadwick had caused men and women alike to be instantly interested in her, and they became more so as the years passed and she developed into a sensuously exciting, somewhat mysterious young woman with a haunting beauty and a certain charisma. Hannibal had finally to accept that he had been smitten by the mature

117

beauty and kindness and, yes, a certain sensuality about Chadwick from the very first time he had seen her. In his heart he had always known that he had bought Chadwick from her father as much for himself as he had for the child.

At sixteen it was difficult to ignore her stunning sexuality. Warren was besotted by it but restrained himself because she was his adopted sister. At Miss Porter's school she made friends and enjoyed them and had a stream of interested boyfriends from the time she was fifteen. She charmed and she teased them, not intentionally but by her sensual ways, her incredibly alluring secrecy, her kindness and intelligence which were never overbearing but if anything restrained.

Since the night when Chadwick had become Chadwick Chase she held back nothing of the deep affection she had for Hannibal. Everyone who saw it was charmed by her love for him; the way she would snuggle up to him and they would sit enfolded together as they read to each other in a deep leather chair by the fire, he sometimes petting and stroking her as if she were his favourite cat, she sometimes running her fingers through his hair. Diana, Warren and the staff thought it nothing out of the ordinary when they found Chadwick and Hannibal sitting in bed having breakfast together and reading the Sunday papers.

Their devotion to each other was total and Chadwick became enslaved by Hannibal's love for her. Her own love and gratitude for the life he created for her and her sexual attraction to Hannibal played its part. Yet they were not obsessed with each other. There were many women through the years in Hannibal's life. He had been forty-five years old at the time of the crash, a young and handsome, successful and very wealthy conservative widower of high society and old money. The women chased him; there were even several times when an engagement seemed imminent and all three children gave their approval. But he always sent the women away. Reserved and discreet, Hannibal had always had, would always have, a strong libido and an active and exciting sex life. His family and friends knew it, the gossips whispered about it.

When Chadwick was seventeen, her sexuality began to interest Hannibal. Quite simply, he wanted her in a new, intensely erotic way. But he kept those desires hidden from her; she was too precious to him to exploit. He took it upon himself to see that she was sexually educated but kept pure, unsullied by lust. He found exactly the right woman, a beautiful, discreet, two-thousand-dollar-a-night lady to tutor Chadwick in the ways of sexual pleasure.

The bond between Chadwick and Hannibal was so strong that they told each other everything and so he spoke to her about Lilana de Chernier and how and why he had chosen her to educate Chadwick in all things erotic, teach her about lust. 'I do know a lot,' was her answer to Hannibal.

'I am sure you do, dear, but wouldn't you like to know more, experience the adventurous side of all things erotic? If I didn't think you did, I would not have suggested you see Lilana.'

'You know me better even than I do, Hannibal.'

Chadwick had always called him by his first name, they had settled on that rather than Father or Dad, and never was he more happy about that than he was at this moment. Neither was she because the last thing she said to Hannibal as she walked from the room clutching Lilana de Chernier's calling card, excited but not showing it, was, 'I do hope that you can accept that you are doing this not for me but for us, Hannibal, because that's why I'll be going.'

Chapter 6

There had been boyfriends, and kisses, and petting. There had been expectations, even sensations that had stirred something in Chadwick. In that she was much the same as most of her girlfriends: sixteen-, seventeen-, eighteen-year-old girls hungry to find the man to turn the key that would open the door to their discovery of sensational sex and satisfaction.

Chadwick had been, in her younger years, exposed to the crudest of sexual antics by her father and his voracious appetite for sex. She had seen, had been made to observe sex in all its base raunchiness; it had become the norm, as much a part of her life as it was Ed's and in fact her entire family's. It was the environment she grew up in. She had wiped that out of her mind just as she had all else in her life that happened before she had found Hannibal and became Chadwick Chase.

Now, after several visits to Lilana, she had come to realise that from a very young age she had had strong sexual desires, albeit quiescent, and never fully understood. She had been too busy fighting off her father's advances even to contemplate them. As Lilana and she spoke about sex and sexuality she could understand how she had suppressed sexual desire, internalised it, turned sexual awakening into one of the many secrets that she kept to herself. Chadwick's secrets had always been important to her. They still were.

Lilana de Chernier was beautiful, sensuous, and with a very understated chic. A woman of thirty-five who looked more like twenty, she was intelligent, cultivated, incredibly glamorous, and kindness itself. Almost immediately a rapport developed between the seventeen-year-old Chadwick and Lilana. Chadwick was to learn from her every nuance of exciting sex: how thrilling the erotic could be in its many and varied forms, how to excite, to seduce a man; satisfy her own sexual inclinations; how to fire up desire – her own, a lover's.

The women talked of sex, erotic games and fantasies, over long, luxurious lunches in the small bay window of Lilana's flat that overlooked Central Park. After several weeks, Lilana recognised that Chadwick was hungry and ready to experience some of her sex education so they were joined at their luncheons by several different men. Handsome and sexy in the prime of their sexuality these men who ranged in age between twenty and thirty-five were only too delighted to dine with the glamorous and sensuous Lilana and her protégé to discuss sex, sexuality, the thrill of orgasm, how and what they delighted in sexually. It was very erotic for everyone concerned to fire up this very sexual seventeen-year-old with talk of their own sexual experiences.

Each time Lilana managed to leave Chadwick alone with their luncheon guest, not for too long, but long enough for the men to excite Chadwick with more than just words. It had been Jed Thomas who thrilled her with caresses, who sucked on her nipples, nibbled at her breasts, licked them with his tongue. Chadwick, for the first time, was able to feel the thrill of sexual heat that comes with passion, when erotic excitement sends shivers down the spine.

One afternoon Lilana had held her in her arms and stroked her hair, whispering in her ear the pleasures she was about to experience when she was left to Tom Fielding's lust. Lilana had known Tom for years and what an exciting lover he was: imaginative, thoughtful, a man who adored all forms of sex with young women. She had chosen Tom to ease Chadwick away from her virginity into love of a man for nothing more than the thrill of sex.

Tom was the first man with whom Chadwick experienced oral sex. Lilana had been a more than competent instructress and it was as pleasurable an experience for Chadwick as it was for Tom. However, never could Chadwick have imagined any sensation as thrilling as when Tom finally went down on her. She came in a wave of powerful orgasms and entered a world of sexual bliss. She knew from that moment on that this was a place where she wanted to dwell.

Tom was also the first man with whom she had sexual intercourse. That exquisite moment of pain when he broke her hymen was followed by slow and careful thrustings as Chadwick was possessed by his hard and throbbing penis. His kisses and caresses, his lust, made this important sexual experience pure pleasure and he instilled in her a love for the sexual side of her life and a man's erotic soul.

Once Chadwick was well versed in the experience of sex, and Lilana saw how ready she was to experiment with her erotic desires, more sexual adventures and games were played to excite, to take Chadwick one step further down the path that leads to erotic oblivion, that place she now craved to be in. She had, at first, been fearful and shy but now she enjoyed the many and varied sexual acts, sometime played out with two or as many as four men and women. For Chadwick it was sexual fun and adventure and it had to do with growing up sexually for the man she loved.

The more Chadwick developed this side of her nature, the more she wanted Hannibal for a lover, and the more he wanted her. The mere knowledge that Chadwick was experiencing sexual awakening without him began to prey on his mind. He and Chadwick had become such an integral part of each other's lives that as much as he thought he was prepared to let her go free, sexually, something more dark in his soul, erotic desire that knew no boundaries, ignored the morality he'd believed in all his life, was telling him he could not.

This man who had never been knowingly devious, who indeed despised deviousness in any form, was tortured by his own in relation to his sexual hunger for Chadwick. He fought it, made heroic efforts against it: once he had given Lilana de Chernier her brief to educate Chadwick in all things erotic, he never once discussed Chadwick or her sex life with Lilana. But that had been a small effort and accomplished only to assuage his guilt for wanting Chadwick sexually as he had never wanted any other woman before. His fantasies about sex with her were at first quite simple and then more complex and then more thrilling. They became the greatest pleasure of his life.

But as much as Hannibal lusted after Chadwick, he

loved her with the same intense passion. As the months of Chadwick's visits to Lilana passed, he came to terms with his love and lust for Chadwick, at least to some degree. He would never make a move on her for sex. Chadwick would have to approach him, theirs would have to be a mutual lust and love. Anything else would be unthinkable.

Often when they were together, and they were very much together as they had always been, he would wonder whether Chadwick had as yet been with men, what men, how those men might have enjoyed her, if she had enjoyed the sex with them? Strangely he felt no jealousy at the idea of her with handsome, powerfully sexual men. He did in fact quite enjoy the idea of her having sexual fulfilment, it became a part of his love for her.

And so life went on for them without tension or angst due to a mutual love that would not allow the changes in Chadwick's life to infringe on their joy in one another, their home life, the family. They still spent their Sunday mornings breakfasting in bed together, they still caressed and petted each other, they went almost everywhere together.

Hannibal sensed that the quiescent sexuality that Chadwick wore like a second skin was somehow not the same. It was not so much that it wasn't there as it had always been but more that her sexuality had been somehow transformed into one of those secrets about herself that she held so dear. It made her even more enigmatic, more intriguing.

It was a beautiful late-spring day, a Thursday, Hannibal was waiting for Chadwick to return from shopping and they were going to Merrifields for the weekend. For weeks, there had been great excitement in the house and the family. Chadwick had graduated from Miss Porter's with top grades and had had an acceptance from Yale University. Only Chadwick knew that as good as that was, for her the real joy was the flowering of her own sexuality, the realisation that one day all that Hannibal had groomed her for would be his, theirs, for she had made up her mind that there was nothing else for it: she would have to seduce Hannibal. Their relationship demanded that she make the first move. She didn't mind, it somehow seemed only fair to her.

All morning Hannibal had been testy. It had started the night before at a reception in the hall of the Metropolitan Opera House. He'd realised for the first time that Chadwick no longer looked like a young beauty but a sensuous, mysterious, stunningly perfect and delicious object of sexual desire. Not only he but very nearly every man who saw her took a second glance, and experienced an instant of wishful thinking. All evening, just being on his arm, standing next to him, the way she would look at him brought a burning heat to his loins.

Sitting in the darkness in their box during the performance of *Aida*, she caressed the inside of his thigh, never taking her eyes from the stage. It was a moment of exquisite pleasure for him rather than embarrassment. Just before the house lights went up Chadwick removed her hand, took one of his in hers and raised it to her lips to kiss his fingers. She turned his hand and licked his palm with the tip of her tongue, replaced the hand on his thigh before she put her own together and applauded the performance as she rose to her feet and called out, 'Bravo, bravo!'

He had risen from his chair, following suit, and glanced over at her. She turned to gaze into his eyes and he recognised, for the first time, lust in hers for him. His heart raced, he wanted to weep with joy; instead he smiled at this new woman dressed in a black silk taffeta strapless gown that barely covered her luscious breasts and whose bodice clung to her like a second skin above the many yards of deep amethyst-coloured taffeta swirling out from her narrow waist. Her voluptuous figure was accentuated even more by a belt of emerald green satin.

He held out the short jacket constructed completely of ruffle upon ruffle of black silk taffeta that buckled at the waist and she slipped into it. Neither could find the right words and so instead of speaking about what had passed, or themselves, they spoke about the opera. In the lobby they were joined by Andrew and his wife and son, Andrew Junior, and they all went on to dine at the Knickerbocker Club. After dinner, at home, Hannibal asked Chadwick to join him in the library where he poured himself an Armagnac and offered Chadwick a coffee liqueur, her favourite drink of the moment. She declined. There was not the least bit of tension between them, nothing awkward, they were as they had always been with each other.

Hannibal took a sip of his drink and watched her while she shrugged out of the ruffled sleeves of the pretty jacket to her dress. The long slim neck, her lovely naked shoulders, the swell of her breasts rising above the crisp black silk, were so young, so fresh, so delicious to behold. Hannibal and Chadwick were standing opposite each other and not too far apart. Hannibal placed his cut crystal tumbler on the mantelpiece and stepped closer to Chadwick. Very slowly, deliberately and with great finesse, he lowered the silk covering her breasts. He had seen her naked breasts many times before, had caressed them before, but not as he was doing now. Now there were sexual connotations to his touch. He kissed them but his kisses were no longer a teasing and quick peck, the affection of a man for a budding young girl. These kisses lingered, and he licked Chadwick's breasts with his warm moist tongue. With cupped hands he held them, caressed their luscious swell, felt the weight of them in his hands. He took her nipples between his fingers and teased them tenderly, pinched them with a light but decidedly erotic touch, enough to excite. Then he placed his lips upon first one and then the other and sucked.

Chadwick's eyes told him everything: how much she was enjoying his advances. Her sighs, the way she squirmed ever so slightly, a signal to him that she was ready to come or had already come in a small sweet rush of orgasm. Hannibal raised his face from between her breasts, he caressed them once more and then covered them with the top of her silk bodice. He stroked her hair and then kissed her first on one cheek and then the other. Her lips were trembling when he pressed his against them, not with the overwhelming passion he was feeling for Chadwick but with the deep and genuine love of a woman for a man.

Hannibal took both her hands in his and told her, 'In the box in the opera you were asking me something with your advances, my darling girl. Here, now, I have answered you with mine. You have to think quite hard about what's happening between us and all it entails. We both must. Tomorrow, you must give me your answer, or the day after, or the one after that. There is all the time in the world for you. I will never press you, merely ask you to say nothing tonight.'

Chadwick was ready, more than ready to answer him then and there, but for her Hannibal had always been right. It was quite natural for her to obey him, she always did in everything, almost without his having to ask. For the most part it was instinctive. Together, arm in arm, they walked from the library and up the long curved staircase to the floor above, Hannibal telling her how lovely she had looked at the opera and how she had turned all the men's heads. She smiled and laughed and before they started the next flight of stairs to the bedroom floor, she kissed him on the lips, a kiss to seduce, a kiss that promised the wonders of conjugal bliss, before tapping him teasingly on the end of his nose with the tip of her finger. Looking happier than Hannibal had ever seen her, she raised her voluminous skirts above her ankles and fled up the stairs to vanish behind her bedroom door.

The windows facing the street were open and the scent of daffodils and hyacinths from the planted window boxes were wafting through. Hannibal was standing by the window looking for Chadwick. He checked his watch. It was not like her to be late and he was anxious to get off to the country.

Once in bed the night before he had had Akari bring him another drink and had sipped it slowly, reliving the evening. Chadwick, this new Chadwick, was the most exciting and seductive creature any man could want – and she was his. He knew that in the very core of his being. He would wait for as long as it took to take sexual possession of her. He was the happiest of men. So happy that he had picked up the telephone and dialled Lilana's house.

She had answered the telephone and on hearing his

voice had said, 'My dear Hannibal, you do surprise me. I had expected you to call months ago. It does you much credit that you didn't.'

'I do now only to say thank you, Lilana. Tonight I saw for the first time what a magnificent erotic creature you have turned her into.'

'It wasn't difficult, Hannibal. If it happens for you, you must know you will be well matched. She has a strong sexual drive, as strong as yours, and she is courageous in her lust. She is also sexually free – adventurous eroticism will be that young woman's life. In that she is like yourself, only maybe more so. But, caution, Hannibal. You may one day possess her sexually – to be enslaved by lust is what she yearns for, she derives enormous pleasure from her sexuality, and, Hannibal, she wants you. However, that does not mean she will be easy to fathom. She's deep and mysterious and a law unto herself.'

'Lilana, I know Chadwick to the very marrow of her bones. We give each other everything.'

'How strange, those were her exact words about you.'

Now Hannibal could not help but smile as he remembered his conversation with Lilana. It confirmed what he had always sensed: Chadwick had saved his life to give him another. They had done that for each other, their lives had been cast together a long time ago. He heard the gate open and walked from the window to open the front door and watch the 1936 Rolls-Royce pull slowly off the street and on to the short horseshoe-shaped drive to the front door. The Chase house was one of only a few such town houses left in Manhattan to have the luxury of its own private drive.

Chadwick was riding in the rear seat. His intention was

to chastise her for being late but one look at her as she slid across the seat and opened the car door before Telford had a chance to get to it and he could think of nothing to say except, 'Where were you at breakfast?'

'It's a secret.' She smiled and very nearly sprang from the car to give Hannibal a kiss on the cheek.

'And why are you late?'

Once again a peck on the cheek. 'Another secret. And I'm not even sorry I'm late and neither will you be.' There it was, that unmistakable new seductive look just for him. He did and didn't like it, he wanted and didn't want it, but he couldn't help but smile at her, and she had excited his interest.

'I think we should leave immediately, I long to get out of town.'

'Me too.'

Telford drove them only a short distance, around the corner, to the building where Diana and Warren had their flats. Warren was waiting in front of the building. He sat down next to Chadwick, and Hannibal, amused and charmed now by her little game, said, 'Oh, I see you're part of this surprise, Warren.'

'No. I'm here to give Chadwick moral support, Dad.'

'Since when do you need moral support in anything, Chadwick?'

'Since I'm kidnapping you and we're going to the airport, and I don't want to give in when you tell Telford to turn the car around.'

'Then you're a party to this surprise, Warren?'

'Only in as much as I agreed to secure the company jet for the day for Chadwick. And there is no use asking me where you're going, or why, Dad. Chadwick refused to tell me or Diana, and you know she and Diana tell each other everything.' He laughed aloud before he continued, 'And Chadwick won't let us come along. In spite of that she talked me into helping because she said she hadn't the authority to arrange transportation for your getaway.'

All the way to the airport the two men indulged Chadwick in a game of guess where, after it was established that she thought Hannibal needed an adventure and she was determined to give him one. The guesses came fast and furious: safari, a tiger shoot in India, shooting the rapids on a river in Nepal, flying in a biplane through the Grand Canyon, sailing up the Nile in a felucca or down the Orinoco in a dugout, a day of shopping on Rodeo Drive, lunch in Rome, swimming with the dolphins in Baja California – all three of them letting their imaginations fly and suggesting what each of those adventures might entail.

Hannibal listened and played along with the game, enjoying himself enormously. Nor did Warren's interest in Chadwick go unnoticed by him; he was seeing his son's sexual attraction to her for the first time. It showed in his eyes, the way he touched her, spoke to her, it was somehow different. Lilana had indeed done her work well. She had been right when she'd said that Chadwick had that special kind of sensual attraction that only a very few women possess; that adventurous eroticism would be her life. What Lilana had not said was that a great many men would want Chadwick, never have her, suffer rejection, and the tortures of their lust for her. For the first time in five years Hannibal thought of the vile Ed Chadwick; he had been the first of such men and most surely would not be the last of Chadwick's victims.

It was not Africa or India, not even Nepal. But it was a

small private island just off the coast of Trinidad in the Caribbean. By the time the plane landed on the air strip running parallel to the sea, its waves gently lapping on one side of the beach, fringed on the other by a grove of coconut palms, a new life would already have begun for Hannibal and Chadwick. But this was still New York and as Hannibal was shaking hands with his son while bidding him farewell and was then following Chadwick up the few stairs and into the twelve seater Gulfstream Jet, he could not have imagined that was going to be the case.

They sat together buckled into the settee, facing the window, and waved goodbye to Warren as the plane taxied down the tarmac. 'This is a very extravagant surprise,' Hannibal told Chadwick, and gave her a gracious and winning smile.

Chadwick surveyed Hannibal's face, the face that she had fallen in love with as a child. He had aged well, in fact hardly at all. His hair was still dark brown and thick and worn on the long side to curl just above his coat collar. The sexy-looking square face had deep furrows in it and yet he remained young looking for a man of fifty. He had remained as slim as when she had met him and worked out so that his body was still taut and muscular. He was a big handsome man on whom all her girlfriends had a crush. She had often thought that possibly the uneasy relationship that Diana sometimes had with her father was because she too had a crush on Hannibal. His dark brown eyes had always been what Diana had called 'bedroom eyes', and she claimed that was why women fell in love with him. Chadwick tended to think that Diana was right. Now at the start of the runway, as the pilot was revving the engines making ready for take-off, she was fixated by his lips, his mouth. For weeks now when with Lilana discovering her sexuality, it was Hannibal's lips, his mouth, that she fantasised about while edging towards orgasm.

Chadwick had been several months with Lilana when she had finally confessed her sexual feelings for Hannibal to her mentor. And when Lilana understood that a sexual relationship, short- or long-lived, was inevitable for Chadwick and Hannibal, she made up her mind it would be the most erotic and sexually thrilling experience for them both. Anything else would be damaging to their relationship, one she was certain that neither Chadwick nor Hannibal could ever give up. Few would understand, as Lilana did, that she was privy to an unusual and most extraordinary love affair.

Taking all those things into consideration, she took it upon herself to educate and train Chadwick in how to enjoy the lustful life that Hannibal demanded of his women. She taught her not only how to develop an outstanding sexual life for Hannibal and herself, but explained about the demands he would make on her, even the psychology of his sexual appetites. She groomed Chadwick to be his sexual slave, a role that excited his sexual side and which she knew Chadwick herself would enjoy. Lilana went one step further; she taught her how she should periodically turn Hannibal into her own sexual slave and in such a subtle way that he would only realise it after the event, hate it, and redress the situation. Sex was more thrilling for Hannibal when power games were involved and love could be shunted aside.

Lilana could well understand how a man like Hannibal would want a woman like Chadwick in his life. She had a secret centre that would always be a challenge for a man.

Lilana fell just a little bit in love with her protégée herself. It was easy, they had many similar qualities and had something in common: they both loved and respected Hannibal who had kept Lilana de Chernier as a mistress years before he met Chadwick.

The friendship that grew between mentor and protégée made it easier for Lilana to express to Chadwick something a seventeen-year-old girl in love and sexually besotted might not want to hear: that she must be prepared for the possibility that though Hannibal might never want another woman once he had her, he might very well insist that she have other men, even other women. Lilana explained that it would ease his guilt over lusting after his adoptive daughter, over loving her as an erotic woman and keeping her as the companion of his life. Another reason: Hannibal genuinely loved Chadwick and would not want to deprive her of her chance of finding a younger, better love and sex life than he could offer.

When Chadwick told Lilana that she did understand Hannibal's and her own predicament, that she intended to obey him in all his wishes *vis à vis* their sexual and love life, Lilana knew that her protégée was ready for her heart's desire: a sexual liaison with the man of her life. Together they planned the seduction of Hannibal Chase.

The plane chased down the runway and took to the air at a steep angle. Chadwick, having at last stopped fixating over Hannibal's lips, smiled then sighed.

'You sound as if you've just ridden yourself of some tremendous weight,' said Hannibal.

'I have. We have,' she told him somewhat boldly, then ran her fingers through her hair and with a flick of her head shook it away from her face.

135

'I have?'

'You'll admit it to me later.'

'You seem very sure about that.'

'Oh, I am, I would stake my life on it.'

Just then a small light on the wall flashed, announcing they could if they wished undo their seat belts. They did and Hannibal began to rise from his chair. Chadwick stopped him. 'You were going to the cockpit to talk to Jim. Well, you're not allowed to. One of the ground rules. And that he is not allowed to come back here is another, not unless we invite him to. And you are not allowed to pilot the plane, not down to our destination or back from it.'

Hannibal was amused. 'That's a lot of ground rules.'

'There are more, but I'll tell you what they are as we go along.'

'You really have kidnapped me?'

'Not for a ransom,' she told him, gazing directly into his eyes.

They needed no words, their eyes were speaking for them. Hannibal's heart was racing. There had been so many women, beautiful, graceful and glamorous creatures, some even as young as Chadwick, but none had ever moved him to such fierce pangs of desire as she did now. He felt like a dying man, his life rushing past him, as if he had lived a whole lifetime just for this one moment. The ultimate expression of sex with undiminished love for the object of his desire.

Chadwick's heart was pounding, her hands trembling ever so slightly, he was hers as he had never been anyone else's. It shone in his eyes, and showed in the expression on his face. He was devouring her with lust. She placed one of her hands over her mouth and covered it with the other. Her breathing quickened and she closed her eyes for a moment. She came. The sensation was delicious, more thrilling than she had imagined it would be. She removed her hands from her mouth and ran her fingers through her hair before she slid from the seat and on to Hannibal's lap.

She leaned forward and kissed him, licking his lips. They parted, and passion rose between them in that first kiss. He had removed his jacket before take-off and loosened his tie. Now, slowly, she slid it from around his neck and dropped it on the floor. She kissed him again, and once more their kiss was deep and passionate as she ran her hands down his arms. The feel of him, his strength, through the fine white linen, ignited her desire for him even further. She opened the buttons of his shirt and pulled it away from his chest and out from under his belt.

How clever she was with her hands and her caresses. Hands so soft with fingers long and slender, pressing his flesh, pinching his already erect nipples. She lowered her lips to them and sucked on them, ran her tongue over his chest as her fingers worked the buttons on his cuffs. She slid his shirt from his shoulders and off his arms. Chadwick raised her face from his chest and rubbed her cheek against his and then licked his shoulder and bit hard into it while her arms slid around him and pulled him forward against her. Lust was taking her over, fierce sexual desire demanded of her that she dig her fingers and nails into his back.

Chadwick was now delivering light nibbling kisses on the flesh of his arms, stopping only long enough to lick his skin. She adored the scent and texture of his skin. Having worked her mouth down to his hands she took his fingers and placed them in her mouth and sucked on them. The feel of her teeth, used as lightly as if they were feathers, was erotic and teasing, as was the provocative, long and slow sucking. It put him on a sexual high note. He unbuckled the leather belt round his waist and Chadwick smiled at him and said, 'Oh, yes, please,' in a voice husky with lust. She removed his hands and took over sliding the belt from the loops of his jeans.

She was still on his lap, and while gazing into his eyes gently moved his legs apart, slipping round in such a way that she did not have to break her gaze. While facing him, she slipped from his lap to between his legs and on to her knees. That first feel of the swell of his erect penis against her body, even though it was still confined in his jeans, was outrageously sexy and glorious for Chadwick. Here was where all her attention focused now. She pressed it with the palms of her hands and then caressed the length of it and under it. She massaged it and his crotch and the inside of his thighs before she kissed the object of her desire through the faded blue denim.

Chadwick was bending over, slipping his shoes from his feet, removing his socks, when she felt his hands caressing the top of her head. She could hardly contain herself. Never had she dreamed that having sexual control of Hannibal could be so thrilling. She slid herself up his body and they kissed. She could feel his penis throbbing through the denim cloth and against her belly then her mound. She slid her hand under the jeans and caressed his hips and then slid down his body once more, this time sliding off his jeans as she went.

That first sweet yet acrid scent of warm and erect male genitalia was a natural perfume which sent her over the edge of erotic desire. It acted like a click in the head that switched her into over-drive: yearning to give and receive all things sexual, all acts, to reach the ultimate in erotic bliss. She caressed his penis with her lips and mouth, licked his scrotum and sucked the large and loose sac and its spherical contents into her mouth, playing with them with her tongue as she stroked his stunningly large penis and its handsome knob of a head with her hands.

Continuously stroking one hand after the other, so as to give him the greatest pleasure she could, she soon had him on the edge of orgasm. So was Chadwick, she was breathless with passion, they were past the point of no return. She could think of nothing else but the joy of feeling him burst forth with all the lust and come he could muster into her mouth. Desire, passion, need, they all played their part in Chadwick, wanting to feel his warm, sweet and salty life force trickle down her throat. Nothing less would do. Everything more could follow.

For Chadwick the taste of Hannibal's first orgasm was like nectar from the gods. She came in a copious, emotionally draining orgasm simultaneous with his. She had never had such an out-of-this-world experience, but that was what she did, for a few seconds, have. When she returned to the here and now, she released Hannibal who raised her from her knees to have her once again on his lap and hold her in his arms. He placed a long and passionate kiss upon her lips after which they slid from the settee on to the cabin floor. Clinging tight to each other, Hannibal kept whispering over and over again one or other of: 'My glorious dear girl', 'My heart', 'Chadwick, my love', between kisses that scorched their hearts, their very souls.

Chadwick had no sense of how long she slept or indeed whether she had slipped into a doze or had swooned from the sheer force of her many orgasms in such a short span of time. But once more she felt herself come alive to Hannibal's kisses, on her closed eyelids, on her lips. Her first words, issued barely above a whisper and even before she opened her eyes, were, 'Hannibal, I have always had, and will always have, a fever for you. Forgive me, please forgive me.'

She had shown Hannibal with her body and the passion of her soul, her lust, that she understood what was at stake by her actions. At last the moment was right for him to take on their sex life. It was what she wanted, what they both wanted. He kissed her and licked her lips, then as they lay gazing into each other's eyes, he told her, 'Chadwick, there is nothing to beg forgiveness for, there never will be, we'll work at there never having to be. You were magnificent, you are magnificent. Let your fever rage. Mine does for you, I'll prove it to you.'

Chadwick was still dressed as she had been when they had boarded the plane, except for her shoes which she had kicked off earlier. Now, lying on their sides facing each other, Hannibal raised her white crepe de chine blouse over her head and dropped it on the floor. The white wide linen trousers and her silk panties were soon dispensed with and she lay naked except for cream-coloured stockings held high on her comely thighs by a wide band of elasticised lace.

Now it was Hannibal's turn to seduce Chadwick to him. He intended to mark her forever with their first sublime sexual encounter and not leave a vestige of doubt as to how thrilling their sex life was going to be. He proceeded with caresses that excited her flesh, kisses, licking and sucking, nibbling, even biting into her flesh. How well he used her breasts to give her sexual pleasure and excite his own lust to taste her further.

He titillated Chadwick with his hunger to possess her and give her the ultimate in sexual pleasure by leaving not a morsel of her body free from his fondling. Still in his arms, he rolled her over and advanced his kisses down her back over the luscious full and firm orbs of her bottom. He caressed them and slapped them lovingly, and bit into the flesh of those cheeks, licked the deep crevice between them and what they hid.

She had come several times, short lazy orgasms, even before he placed his mouth over her most intimate and private place, her cunt, and began sucking the labia, penetrating her with a hungry tongue. Chadwick was crazed with lust, he was a master of cunnilingus. She came rapidly and often and felt as if her life's force was draining away – so much so she had to beg Hannibal to stop. An impossibility, at least until he had had his fill of the taste of her on his tongue, in his mouth.

She was unable to hold anything back from Hannibal; she whimpered with pleasure, sighed, actually moaned as she came. She trembled with excitement when he carried the silky smooth moisture from her on to his fingers, rubbed it on her lips and licked it off with his tongue.

He wanted her warm and wet, the easier for him to take her with one forceful thrust. His lust for her commanded that because he wanted Chadwick to feel the pain and pleasure of sex with him, to know his power and passion for all things sexual he wanted to experience with her, how divine total sexual submission could be for her, and most especially the very special bliss of fucking and coming together with someone you love.

Hannibal sensed that he would not have been her first fuck, he had never wanted that. He would not have been able to live with that. He was however certain he would be her first experience of sexual intercourse with a man who loved her and would do so to the death.

He held her down firmly with one arm across her chest, fondling her breast with his hand, pinching hard at her nipple, a calculated moment of distraction as he thrust as hard as he could. With his scrotum slapping against her, his sex took possession of her; there was no more me and you, they were as one body. Chadwick was feeling the force of his sex. Its throbbing awakened her flesh as if she had been scorched by fire. That act, those sensations, was so very raunchy as to drive them both into a frenzy. A scream roared in her throat. Hannibal stifled it with the palm of his free hand placed over her mouth and whispered in her ear, 'Chadwick, you are my majestic life, the most sweet and delicious of women, and so it begins for us.'

He then removed his hand and she called out. She gasped, panted, as unbound sexual pleasure, the savouring of Hannibal's throbbings within her own flesh, took possession of her life. Her voice was throaty with lust when she told him, 'Hannibal, you are so sublime, it feels too marvellous, more marvellous than my fantasies. The dark and lonely nights of desires, hopes and dreams, over at last!' Her heart pounded so hard she thought it might break open, and Hannibal, his hands on her waist, began his thrustings to a beat of passion and love.

They hardly spoke during the next few hours. Instead they experienced every inch of each other's bodies, used their lust to eat that much further into their souls. Lilana had made of Chadwick a sensual and sexual woman who was open and ready for an erotic life, with or without Hannibal. He understood that by the way she reacted to the sex they were experiencing. How gloriously exciting it was for Hannibal that she was so sexually free, so adventurous, without shame for her lust and the power of her sexual drives. Chadwick was a natural born libertine who had only been honed by Lilana.

They were dressed and sitting together as the plane taxied down the air strip. To watch the waves rush in and dissolve on the beach and the sway of the coconut palms as the jet rushed forward on its carpet of grass runway was to land in paradise. The sex that Hannibal and Chadwick had had on the plane had irrevocably changed their lives, but strangely not the way they were together. As they looked through the window of the plane Hannibal realised that they were the same two people who already loved each other in so many different ways. This was just another. They were merely adding to their lives. Chadwick issued several more ground rules which he happily obeyed and they left the plane for the speed boat waiting to take them to the small island they could see from the beach.

It was on that island, Lilana's private island, lent to Chadwick for this, her seduction of Hannibal, that they spent the next three days, making love, exploring each other's bodies and getting to know the boundaries of sex — or if indeed there were to be boundaries of sex for them. There were not, and that discovery was like a life-long aphrodisiac for the lovers. During those days and nights of erotic bliss they never discussed the future, they were too busy living in the moment, adjusting to the many surprises each was discovering about the other.

Ever since Hannibal had met Chadwick as a twelve-year-old child she had always produced intriguing surprises; there had never been anything obvious about her, what she thought, nor her feelings – quite the contrary. She had been always consistent in that, and here, now, on the island, in this the new phase of their relationship, she was as she had always been: experiencing everything to the fullest, expecting nothing and internalising everything, storing secrets to be treasured.

Her latest surprise for Hannibal was her ability to be, when they were not in a flagrant sexual assignation, both the seventeen-year-old Chadwick of a few days before and a mature, sophisticated, quite chic and sensuous older woman in love with a man almost three times her age. This, of course, was a most unbeatable combination in the seduction stakes, and she used it upon Hannibal until he was quite dizzy trying to separate these different Chadwicks. When he realised that it was an impossibility, he also realised that he was dealing with a dangerous woman, and that that was the excitement of Chadwick. He now understood that what she was demanding by her actions was that they would have a conventional life together for all the world to admire and that they should also have a tremendously erotic, even bizarre, sex life together. How clever she had been to understand that those were the things that would get him and keep him to the death. Could she sustain it? A better question might have been, could he?

A dozen times he would ask himself, Why me? He had seen the looks men gave Chadwick, always had even as a child. She had sexual charisma, could have any man she wanted. And always the same answer was there for him:

love chooses, fate shoots the arrow, they saved each other and so belonged together. They were hopelessly indebted to each other, were committed to make each other happy for the remainder of their lives. They were one body, one heart, one soul.

Chapter 7

As they stepped from the plane on to the tarmac almost exactly where their sexual odyssey had begun, Chadwick marvelled at how extraordinary a woman could feel having been sated by sex. Hannibal's wonder was that coming home had changed nothing. He felt happy, new life surging through his blood, and sensed that together things could only get better for them. He could visualise no clouds on the horizon, as he had expected there might be once they had returned home to New York. They were only a few steps from the plane when he grasped her hand. They stopped and faced each other; there was such happiness vibrating between them they could not help but smile.

'I was very good about your ground rules, was I not?'

'You were marvellous about obeying *all* my ground rules.'

'I would like us to stop off for a drink at the Carlisle before we go home. I think there are things to be said, and that it's my turn to establish some ground rules for us to live by.'

'So do I, Hannibal.'

'And you will obey them as I have obeyed yours?'

'Yes, Hannibal.'

That was the answer he had expected but the way she said it told him that he need not even have asked the question. Chadwick had made up her mind to submit to him in all things for as long as they loved and lusted after each other. He squeezed her hand, it seemed more rational than shouting out his delight with her for the world to hear.

In the Bemelmans Bar at the Carlisle Hotel they looked like well-dressed beachcombers among the smart Madison Avenue chic drinking their extra dry Martinis and Manhattans and listening to the sound of discreetly played piano music: Cole Porter, Rogers and Hart. Hannibal asked for a quiet corner table. His luck was holding, one was just being vacated. The Chase family frequented the bar, a blind eye could be turned to their dress for this one evening. It surprised and amused rather than annoyed the head waiter who hosted the bar.

'A bottle of my usual champagne,' ordered Hannibal.

'Not the Krug, Hannibal, the Cristal if you don't mind?' suggested Chadwick.

Hannibal corrected the order. Here was a subtle change: Chadwick quite firmly declaring her preference, and albeit politely demanding from him what she wanted without hesitation. Everyone, including Chadwick, knew his preferred champagne was vintage Krug. Not that she had not asked for things before; she had as a child, a young adult, but never as a woman relating to her lover, the man in her life. He could not help but take her hand in his and kiss her fingers as they gazed into each other's eyes. He liked her so very much in this, her new role.

Chadwick would never love Hannibal any more than

she did in that moment. She had expected as soon as they stepped off the plane that he would hide his feelings for her in public. All the way from the airport her confidence kept slipping at the very idea. The slide stopped here, now and forever with the touch of his lips upon her skin. She smiled as her heart sang.

'There is no question in your mind that I love you, and want you sexually in my life, is there, Chadwick?'

'No, none whatsoever.'

'Good, that's going to make our life together much easier to handle.' He smiled at her. Chadwick saw relief in his face, he even afforded her a smile.

The waiter arrived with the champagne cooler and opened the wine, filled their glasses and placed a plate of cheese straws on the table.

They sipped from their glasses and listened to the music. The Bemelmans Bar had always been a treat for Chadwick. Not only Hannibal but Warren and Diana often took her there with their friends. It seemed tonight to be no longer a treat but just the right place, at the right time, to be with Hannibal.

As if reading her mind he told her, 'It seemed somehow more right to come here and lay down *my* ground rules before we go home. It would be wonderful if there were no need for ground rules in this relationship, but by the very nature of who and what we are and have become to each other, I don't think I can handle this unless there are.'

'Should I be worried about this, Hannibal?'

'Not in the least worried but you may not like what I want for us. I don't, but I know we have to live with it. You are a seventeen-year-old, beautiful, intelligent and sexually exciting girl – maybe not my daughter in blood, but in spirit. For a man such as I, who has lived an impeccable, irreproachable life for himself and his family, and who has a solid moral code he has tried to abide by, to engage in an erotic affair with you is no easy thing. It will come as a shock to Warren and Diana, my friends, my business colleagues, the staff at home. Gossips will make a meal of us. I will be seen as a dirty old man who has used and abused you. Few will understand that a deep and abiding, most genuine love came first. That *we* lusted after each other.'

'Does it matter?'

'Not to you now possibly, but it might one day after I'm dead and gone from your life forever. Chadwick, I don't for the moment feel tortured because I'm going against what I believe is morally wrong, being sexually besotted with my adoptive daughter, but I might one day. I want to protect us from that. I want to make it as easy as possible for me as well as others to accept us. And most important of all, I want to be certain that I am, we are, what you want.'

'I am certain.'

Hannibal had sent the waiter away, saying he would tend to the wine. It was at that moment that he chose to do so. He refilled their glasses and took a deep swallow of his then topped the glass up once more before he spoke.

'I believe you are, but you are seventeen years old and with a lust for sex and men. I don't feel that at seventeen you can make a decision like giving up all men for me, loving, being infatuated, with me alone. Your never having lived outside my love for you is marvellous for me but is it enough for you? Saying yes to that now is a decision you might one day regret.'

'You don't want me?' The devastation could be heard in her voice.

'No, you have my word, I want you now and for always. Chadwick, you must never think otherwise. But I'm a man of more than fifty who has lived. I don't want to cheat you of your youth, and young men, and sex and passion, the flirtations that go along with being seventeen. The balls and house-parties and fun – and if it should happen, a love greater than ours. The father in me wants those things for you, though the lover will have at times to grapple with them.

'When you're away at Yale, I want you to go out with boys, have a sex life simultaneous with ours. I want you to make having other men a part of our sex life. That may seem strange to you now but it won't be, it will enhance our own erotic world. You are a clever woman – I don't think I can go on calling you a girl when you have shown me how much of an erotic woman you are – and it is that woman I appeal to now. Chadwick, I beg you to be discreet about what we feel and want from each other, very discreet, for the next two years.

'I don't want to, I will not, hide you in some back street, like a kept mistress. You deserve better than that. We deserve better than that. I want for us to unfold these new feelings we have for each other with caution, for our sake and the sake of others around us, until our sexual life becomes as natural for them to accept as it is for us to have.'

'You're thinking of Warren and Diana?'

'Yes, mainly.'

'Then discretion is one of your ground rules. A two-year test period is another. That I remain sexually active with other men is yet another. I do have that right, Hannibal?'

The tone of Chadwick's voice told Hannibal she was not happy with his ground rules. 'Correct, Chadwick.'

He took her hands in his and kissed them before he continued, this time unable to control his passion for her, the lust he felt in his loins at the very idea of the pleasure she would derive from men other than himself coming inside her. This fiery and yet still contained beauty who lusted after him and loved him with the fullest of hearts, moved him with her honesty. She had always been quick to understand, quick to meet her fate and grasp it with both hands. He had not the slightest doubt that she would accept and abide by his ground rules.

'If you still love me, feel the same intense sexual passion for me two years from now, I hope you will agree to marry me, Chadwick. Nothing would make me happier than for you to be acknowledged by the world as my wife.'

Ever since Chadwick had found the crashed plane in the woods and touched the cut on Hannibal's forehead with her hand, life had been a continuous stream running with chance, change and fate. So many lives found, so many lives left behind. She picked them up and lived them and became a master at never looking back, never looking forward. She had spent her entire existence expecting nothing and taking whatever she wanted from the life that had been dealt her. Hannibal's proposal had not been expected but she had no doubts that she would marry him in two years' time. They were too much each other's world for it to be otherwise. She leaned across the small table and kissed Hannibal on the cheek, grazed his lips with hers and then sat back and raised her glass and drank in a celebration of chance, change, and fate.

Diana and Warren loved Chadwick; they often discussed between themselves her many qualities, not the least of which was her unbelievable generosity of soul, her selflessness. Incredible from a backwoods child of twelve who had lived the life she had. What was as remarkable was that she remained all through her growing-up years the same, though she had been transformed from white trash to a pampered and privileged young woman by Hannibal, Warren and Diana.

At first her selflessness had shown in her attachment to Hannibal, but soon after getting to know Diana and Warren they too were considered before herself and in such a way that it took years for the family to realise it. Chadwick had many mysterious qualities that enchanted. She did however appear somewhat remote from people and events, appearing royal or goddess-like, and that was incredibly attractive. The family found Chadwick's self-lessness, and air of self-containment, admirable considering how spoiled she might otherwise have become. They had something by which to measure her qualities: both Diana and Warren were themselves spoiled and demanding, no matter how they tried not to be.

Diana found it easy to love Chadwick. Watching over her with pride came naturally, as did her enjoyment of Chadwick's happiness. The affection she had for her adoptive sister was without doubt an unexpectedly selfless side to her that surprised everyone.

During the months that Chadwick had been seeing Lilana, Diana became aware, very nearly without realising it, that the underlying sensual quality about Chadwick was developing into something more overt: sexual charisma. She was not at all jealous of it, but rather enjoyed the idea of Chadwick becoming a *femme fatale* and having a thrilling sex life. She enjoyed one herself.

Almost immediately on Hannibal's and Chadwick's return from the island, it became evident to Diana that both Warren and her father were reacting to this new sexual charisma of Chadwick's. Diana wanted to dislike, disapprove, make a scene, about the new way Hannibal looked and sometimes touched Chadwick in front of not only them but close friends. She somehow could not bring herself to. She loved them both too much, their happiness sang like the finest of birdsong, and they were terribly discreet, so much so there were times that Diana thought she imagined what she was seeing.

The night before Chadwick left for New Haven and Yale University the two women were in Chadwick's room packing before they went down to a family dinner: the Chases, Sam and his family and Andrew and his, who always shared the momentous occasions in Chadwick's life. Diana was feeling extremely emotional about Chadwick's leaving home. She realised that Chadwick had become an intimate part of her life, the loss would indeed be a tremendous wrench, and she wanted that never to happen. The realisation of what good friends the older and younger woman had become, and that Diana loved her, possibly even more than Hannibal or Warren, came as a surprise but one she appreciated.

It was those realisations that prompted Diana, apropos of nothing that had been said between them, to rise from the four-poster canopied bed where she was sitting to go to

Chadwick, hug her and ask with a good deal of urgency in her voice, 'You are just going off to school, aren't you? You won't ever really leave us, will you? You're family!'

It seemed the very best moment for Chadwick to speak up. 'No, Di, never. That is, if you can forgive me *anything*?'

Diana never knew whether it was intuition or that special enigmatic power that Chadwick possessed. Was it the way she could tell you everything with few words? It might even have been that strange magnetism of hers that drew one to her. Who was to tell and did it really matter? Diana somehow instantly got the message: Chadwick and Hannibal were lovers. She had to sit down, not so much from surprise or shock as the inevitability of the situation and the knowledge that now for certain they would always be a family. Chadwick sat down next to her but avoided looking directly at Diana. They sat there for a very long time, silent but somehow together, each of them contemplating their situation.

Finally it was Diana who made a move. She rose from the bed, sat down at Chadwick's dressing table and began packing bottles and jars, perfumes and powders, into Chadwick's open travelling case. She looked in the mirror, stopped what she was doing and studied first her own face and then for some time the reflection of Chadwick sitting on the bed. 'Would you like to wear my red chiffon?' she asked. A very selfless gesture since it was Diana's favourite dress and the one she had planned to wear to dinner.

For Warren, coming to terms with the new relationship between his father and Chadwick was far more complex. Firstly because he had seen it coming for a very long time, secondly because he was in love with Chadwick and, like his father, had been ever since that first time he saw her. He had wanted her sexually since her sixteenth birthday. Warren had been made aware of just how much only when his friends began to take notice of Chadwick as a young beauty with a difference: 'Your sister is a young woman without any artifice or games playing about her sensuality, and that excites lust,' they insisted on telling him.

There had never been the slightest possibility that Warren could ever express his true feelings about Chadwick to her or anyone else. Love for his father, being Hannibal's closest confidant, and watching his father and Chadwick together, made him understand long before she had kidnapped Hannibal to the island that Warren would have to accept Chadwick as the love of his father's life. He believed that as long as Hannibal was alive there could be no other man than him for Chadwick.

Warren had guessed, though he had not been expressly told, that the kidnap of Hannibal by Chadwick had been for seduction and sex. So the change of behaviour between Hannibal and Chadwick came as no surprise to him. He watched it and stood aside and bathed in the glow of the new light that came into the couple's lives, and the house, and consequently the family. He suppressed his lust for Chadwick and accepted the inevitable with the charm and grace befitting a gentleman of his class and upbringing.

Hannibal and Chadwick started out as they meant to go on, obeying Hannibal's ground rules and slowly easing Chadwick more and more into not only his private but his public life, until within the year she was seen to be the only woman he would take on his arm anywhere. To invite

Hannibal Chase was to invite Chadwick too. Strangely people hardly talked in any negative fashion about them, they had, of course, known her since she had been adopted into the family, and her dramatic rescue of Hannibal was truly romantic, to be savoured and never forgotten. It added a dignity to their relationship that New York society could accept. Hannibal's impeccable credentials as a moral and honourable man, a great philanthropist and part-time academic, helped, as did his and Chadwick's behaviour which was as intimates rather than lustful lovers. They became known as, if labelled anything, nothing more than 'an odd couple'.

Of course they were more than just that. They had an active sex life together that had to be considered, at the very least, as adventurous. Chadwick went to University, she obeyed Hannibal's wishes by having young, handsome studs for lovers, but they were in fact not her own wishes. As Hannibal had promised she learned first to accept the idea of other men, then to enjoy them for sex, even the odd flirtation. She acquiesced to his wishes even to the extent of trying to love one or two of her lovers but she never could enough to give up Hannibal. They travelled together to far and exciting places where erotic games entered their sex life. And always Chadwick obeyed Hannibal's every wish. And why not? They made her happier than she had been, his demands invariably enriching her life just as they always had.

Money and power, a good and well-respected name, a conservative out-of-the-limelight lifestyle, being high in that magic closed circle of American high society, and not least, the discreet behaviour of Hannibal and Chadwick, were responsible for a lesser scandal than might have been expected and the ease with which Chadwick slipped into the role of Mrs Hannibal Chase.

The wedding was private with only Warren and Diana, Sam and Helen, Andrew and Claudia, as witnesses. It took place on a bright sunny day in June in the interior of a small, dark, ancient church in Venice made bright by a thousand fat white candles and white flowers: lilies and roses in draped garlands and arrangements. A small boy sang like an angel, three flautists played Vivaldi on their silver flutes and the ceremony was performed by an Archbishop from Rome assisted by a Cardinal. The sounds rang like clear drops of crystal among the ancient stones and fourteenth-century frescoes. There was an air of profound happiness about the couple taking their vows, but there was too tremendous emotion for Hannibal, which he had not expected of himself.

When they had been declared man and wife until death do them part and kissed, Chadwick, screened by her wide-brimmed white organza hat with its one large and perfect white magnolia pinned against the crown, was able to hide from the guests the kisses that brushed away the tears from the corners of Hannibal's eyes.

They had not been easy for him, these last two years of waiting for this day, abiding by the ground rules *he* had set. Only now, in his happiness that Chadwick was by law and the church his, did he realise how he had suffered for loving and wanting Chadwick. Love, lust and guilt had been burning a small hole in his heart. As they left the church and their romantic wedding ceremony to step into the bright sunshine and walk the few paces to the waiting gondolas bedecked with more white flowers, everyone laughing and cheering and throwing rose petals, Hannibal wanted to shout to the gods his grateful thanks that at last his suffering was over. Chadwick had chosen to marry him and be his for always. That was, in fact, what he had said. Not 'Till death do us part', but 'For always'.

As for Chadwick, never had she looked lovelier, every inch the sophisticated, elegant beauty, as if she had been born and groomed to marry no one else but Hannibal Chase. For her this day and becoming Hannibal's wife was the continuation of a love and lust she had always had for the man who had saved her, her prince, and now that love, that lust, was sanctified. She was incredibly happy, in love, and knowing how happy Hannibal was doubled her pleasure. How lovely, she thought, that I can keep adding to his life, that the family will always stay together.

Chadwick stepped into her role as Mrs Hannibal Chase just as Hannibal had planned. She had, after all, been moulded for the part. She was to a great extent protected by Hannibal, Warren and Diana as she had always been. But slowly they began to depend on her as the female head of the family, a role which she took on happily and played with charm and a certain subtlety that was admirable. In addition to being Hannibal's wife, his lover, the mistress of his household and the confidant of his children, at Hannibal's insistence, during those first two years after their marriage, she finished Yale with a top degree.

It was then that Hannibal started cutting back on his workload so that he could spend most of his time with Chadwick. The most cultivated and interesting of men, he now had a companion to share his interests in the arts, history, philosophy and travel. Every year they were together was to the couple no more than a day. They had their public life: friends, society, charitable works, business for Hannibal. They had their family life: and it was by that they realised time; Warren married and fathered four children. It was not a happy marriage, his real happiness lay in being the right hand of his father in business and his confidant and friend, being close to Chadwick and loving her the only way possible. He saw a great deal of his father and Chadwick and on many occasions travelled with them, for their pleasure as well as his.

Chadwick saw Diana through several bad marriages and the birth of three children before she finally met and married the right man. She still idolised her father and was as obsessive about him as she had always been, and Hannibal and she still had an uneasy relationship. It was, as it had always been, Chadwick who was able to smooth out the problems that arose between them. Through all the years Chadwick had not changed in her feelings towards Diana; she still loved her, kept her on a pedestal, almost always took her side, and invariably helped her in her darkest moments. Chadwick had an enigmatic goodness that like so much about her was unfathomable.

The all-encompassing thing about Hannibal and Chadwick's life together was the support they gave one another. When and how that support turned into enslavement neither of them knew nor could they understand. In time it simply became one of the facts of their life together. That it existed was known only to them. Chadwick absorbed it, transformed it into one of her secrets. Hannibal only rarely thought about it and chose both to love and hate their condition and never to speak about it.

Their sexual life remained as it had begun: somewhat bizarre. They were each other's sexual slaves who still enjoyed driving themselves into a sexual frenzy. Their life as husband and wife, their genuine love for each other, their individual needs, the adventurous sex life they indulged in, over the years forged a deep and brooding, not always happy, and sometimes dark alliance that trained Chadwick to obey Hannibal's every wish. This dark side tortured Hannibal, but never troubled Chadwick. If she was ever unhappy it was because she sensed Hannibal's anxiety over the lengths he would go to to achieve the ultimate thrill and adventure in orgasm for them. He demanded that every man he watched fucking Chadwick must kiss and caress her breasts, and incite a wild passion in her with raunchy talk, come inside her, fill her with warm and thrilling sperm. Give her the vaginal orgasm he himself refused her.

More often than not he would come in her mouth at the same time as the other man filled her cunt. At those times, Chadwick felt crazed with excitement. Her madness was infectious for Hannibal and usually the stranger as well. Sex, such as this, was the ultimate for libertines such as Chadwick and Hannibal. More and more often the participants could not stop there; Chadwick would take on both men with oral sex until they were rampant and ready for more. The stranger and Hannibal would change positions and eventually take turns penetrating and thrusting.

Hannibal was imaginative in his sexual-game playing and sometimes dangerous: picking up strange men and women and bringing them to their bed, sometimes in discreet and not always elegant hotels. The dark side of sex was never brought into their own home. Part of Hannibal's liking was of the dirty backstreet aspect of sex and

Chadwick, too, found the danger and thrill of their libertine life seductive. But she was also aware that as dangerous as it might be, she was safe in Hannibal's arms, he would always protect her. It was therefore so easy for her to give her life to Hannibal and experience sex for sex's sake, to feed the libido.

Hannibal controlled her in many more ways and certainly one of those ways was to cultivate her in a sex life to satisfy both their lusty demands. Often he would create a sexual adventure for them that was too much even for them and so it was not repeated; as, when in Morocco at a friend's summer palace on the edge of the desert, Hannibal's host, who had frequently experienced sexual scenes with Hannibal and Chadwick, produced nine men for Chadwick. Two Nubian servants, big, strapping, handsome black men, two elegant Egyptian diplomats, Four Moroccan young bi-sexual beauties, and one Englishman. Hannibal had watched Chadwick consumed by passion as each excited lover had taken her in turn. For hours she had been enveloped by lust and sperm and kisses, licked all over and caressed with scented oils. She had imbibed glasses of champagne, been fed white chocolates and strawberries, tied with silk scarves and whipped with a slim leather belt. Anything and everything had been used to excite her lust, to keep her and her studs on the edge, always ready to go that very next bit more for another moment of sexual bliss. Hannibal had, one by one, replaced her lovers with himself. When he recognised that Chadwick was no longer aroused he took her in his arms and kissed her and carried her to his bed and told her, 'There are no other women in this world to match you in or out of your lust, I adore you.'

They lived in every moment of their life together for that moment and so the years seemed to fly by.

Hannibal had always combined his business acumen with his academic ambitions. Now, after many years he was getting international recognition for his rare appearances as a lecturer and as an author. They had come to Paris where he had been awarded a literary prize for his book *Existentialism in France and America*. That was how he and Chadwick happened to be sitting in the sunshine at the Café Flore.

The writing of the slim volume had been the culmination of a life-time of belief in a philosophy that he considered to be the most important of ideas in the history of twentieth-century thought. Though he most humbly accepted the prize he felt he was not very deserving of it. He had written the book for himself, to clarify the cultural differences in people's approaches to Existentialism and where and how he fitted into those differences. Hannibal had wanted a better understanding of his subject and his way of life, having embraced the philosophy as a young man and lived by it always. His peers had laughed when in his acceptance speech he had told them, 'For a man who has been considered a dilettante in the academic world and an academic in the business world, that I should win a prize for an anti-intellectualist philosophy of life that holds that man is free and responsible, based on the assumption that reality as existence can only be lived but can never become the object of thought, this is quite overwhelming.'

Those were the very words Hannibal was thinking about when the waiter brought him and Chadwick another Pernod. Hannibal added just the right amount of water to the yellow syrupy liquid in the bottom of the glass and then dropped in several cubes of ice. He did the same for Chadwick and then took a long and thoughtful gaze at her. How lovely she was in her cream coloured linen suit, the way the sunlight played on her fair skin and long silky hair. He watched people walking past them on the pavement and almost every one of them, man and woman alike, gave her a second glance. He delighted in people's admiration of Chadwick. He smiled at her and, taking her hand in his, lowered his head to kiss it. They had fulfilled each other's lives, the bright and dark side of their natures, because they had never allowed themselves to become objects of thought but had rather chosen to take every chance they could to live where their hearts and minds took them. It suddenly occurred to Hannibal that there would come a day when he would wake up and be obliged to pare down his life; that he would lose his freedom to be and would only be able to think about life as he wanted to live it. Age and infirmity would exact that. He was appalled by the thought and saw himself as nothing more than a walking corpse.

'Never!' he said aloud, most emphatically.

Chadwick, who knew her husband so well, heard something she had never heard before: a hardness, anger, bitterness, shimmering in that one word.

'Never what, Hannibal?'

He took a long draught of his drink. 'When it's over for me, when I am no longer capable of living, only thinking about living, when I can no longer take on the freedom and responsibility of my actions to you, Chadwick, I will no longer exist as the Hannibal I have always been, the man you love. I would hate to be otherwise. I want you to promise me that when the day comes that I no longer exist as the man I am now for you, for this glorious life we have lived all these years, you will put me out of my misery.'

'Hannibal!'

'Chadwick, you have lived practically your whole life for me, do you mean to tell me that you would not kill for me? That you would not grant me my last wish? I promise you it would be a mercy killing. Think, Chadwick, how many times we have died for each other in lust. The most cruel fate for me would be not to die when I was still riding high at the top of my life. You will have to do it, see me out, I would do no less for you.'

Chadwick began to laugh. 'You are being fanciful,' she chided him.

'About death? Hardly. Is it so wrong to want to go out of this life when I am still whole in myself, my mind clear, still desperately in love with my wife who loves me no less? What is so wrong about wanting to vanish on the crest of a wave, never to return, after a glorious meal, in a remote and romantic place, after a night of love and sex unbound with you, the other half of my soul? We both know anything less would begin to tear at the roots of this extraordinary love of ours. I won't have that, and I don't believe you could bear to see that happen either.'

For a very long time Chadwick sat there looking at Hannibal. He was as usual right. She would find it unbearable to see Hannibal less than the man he wanted to be, less than anything he wanted to be. She was acutely aware of how miserable he would be. She was thirty-three years old and he was sixty-six and they had been together since she was twelve. Did she not owe him his last wish? Indeed, owe both of them?

She was still and calm, looking remote and grand and

165

the loveliest of creatures. Hannibal told her in a voice now brimming with lust, as he slid his hand along her thigh and squeezed her knee under the small round table, 'Let's go back to the hotel for sex: a long and luscious stroll through an erotic landscape of rivers of come, mountains of passion, peaks of obscene acts of the flesh, valleys of warm sweet places to penetrate, a sky dark with promise and a bright moon to reach for. Would you like that?'

He could see it in her eyes, she would very much like that, and more. He knew she would rise to the sexual occasion he had just presented her with. She, however, was not so sure. She had lived so long under Hannibal's sexual domination. Her erotic enslavement was a rich and rewarding part of her life. She had no desire to be released from it. Whereas Chadwick had doubts as to what she would do, Hannibal knew that she would grant him his other wish. It suddenly occurred to him that he had trained her her entire life for his pleasure, their pleasure, but for one thing more as well: that she should be, when the time came, the one to say the last farewell and send him on his way.

ON THE ISLAND OF CRETE

1994

Chapter 8

Chadwick had been charmed by the life of the expatriate community in Livakia, the Livakians and their hospitality. Now as she walked along the cliffs among the first of the wild flowers and smelled the scent of rosemary and thyme, she gazed down to the white village clinging to the steep amphitheatre-shaped cliffs and the sheltered port with the open sea beyond. She marvelled that she was still, every single day, brimming with wonder at having found paradise and a new way to live.

Four months had passed since she had first seen Max, D'Arcy and Manoussos in that restaurant in Iraklion. She had seen them as lotus eaters addicted to being happy: free facile spirits, pleasure seekers. Now she, like Max and D'Arcy and the small group of other foreigners living in Livakia, was an expatriate living the good life, a pleasure seeker. She too was going down to the port early in the morning: waiting for the hot bread to come out of the oven, buying her fish off the boats when a catch came in, sitting on the quay drinking a coffee or a glass of wine, nibbling on *octopodi* fresh from the sea that had been beaten on the rocks to tenderise its tentacles, placed to roast over a ceramic dish of hot coals before being hacked up into bite-sized pieces and served on a worn, white plate, chipped to perfection.

Yes, there was that side to Livakia and island life: everything used, nothing thrown away, that she found just as enchanting. Worn, cracked, makeshift, old, new, perfection, existed next to 'never mind', 'it doesn't matter', as loving bedfellows. It was the simple life in this place where the donkey and the boat reigned as kings of transportation, even if you kept a jeep as Manoussos and Max did or a 2CV as D'Arcy did in the caves far up the cliffs to drive over the only road across the mountain range to Livakia which came to an abrupt end in the terrace. A steep donkey ride or walk from there was the only way down through the village to the port. The back-to-basics life allowed time and energy for the pleasure seekers to fulfil their heart's desires or, as the case may be, not fulfil them if it was easier not to and more fun thinking and talking about them.

Chadwick had edged her way into that simple but at times extravagant lifestyle: D'Arcy's walk-in larder like an Aladdin's cave filled with succulent foodstuffs, a mini Harrods Food Hall or Fortnum & Mason's grocery department. Jaunts on Max's plane, Elefherakis's hospitality and very grand house, the array of interesting and amusing people who dropped in for a few days of paradise and to visit one of the expatriates. The treats: caviar and champagne, steaks from Allen's in Mayfair, were rare but there, brought in after holidays abroad or when friends arrived for longer visits. Chadwick entertained her newfound friends and neighbours with cruises on board the *Black Narcissus*. Extravagance and generosity were never expected, always accepted, but most assuredly no one was ever trying to impress – and certainly not Chadwick.

In the expatriate community that was just not on, bad form, shunned, for hard times went with the good: money, love, creative problems for some. Commiseration was as big as sharing the fun and extravagance, the good times and even the boring ones when they rolled. Livakians, foreign or otherwise, clung together and yet respected privacy, another man's secrets, and always his dreams. That was how they came to live with everything as acceptable, no questions asked, and the perpetual gossip which was rife and almost always mundane: 'Manoussos is in love', 'Eleferhakis is infatuated with Chadwick', 'D'Arcy looks to be pregnant', 'Rachel gave a poem of love to a guest of Mark's', 'Tom sold a painting', 'Frances Pendenis's cake fell and she gave it as a gift anyway'.

Living on a Greek island did not, however, mean isolation, a dullness of the brain. Quite the contrary. With intelligent and interesting people, a smattering of success-ful men and women from the realms of arts and letters, interested in the world and its turnings, albeit more inquisitive from a distance and for the most part as voyeurs, there was always fascinating news to theorise on, stimulating conversation, amusement, clever banter that still, even all these months later, Chadwick found sparkling.

Here was a community that lived very much together yet very much apart, and most especially in the winter months when the weather kept them in their houses. Each of them managed to live private, uncomplicated lives inside and outside their own homes. The easy option, the fun option, the lazy option, socially speaking, was having lunch every day on local fare at the communal table at the Kavouria in the port or at Pasiphae's restaurant. Unless one preferred to dine alone or with a friend at a table close to the long table. Island sensibility did not consider that a slight.

Those lunches and dinners, the long table for food or drink, were not for sustenance alone. They had to do with camaraderie and were a social pastime for not only the foreign community but the Cretans as well. They were a very great part of the joy of living in an island village like the sun, the sea, the terrain, the attitude towards life in general. These were the real extravagances, this was the luxury for this odd group of foreigners who chose to drop out and make pleasure seeking and happiness, an elementary life, the only way to live. Livakia, Crete was the place they could live out their dreams and heal their other world, other life wounds, and many of her new friends were doing just that.

All this was there right before Chadwick's eyes to see and be part of but in truth she only lived on the edge of it. She had no dreams to live out, no wounds from another world and another life to heal, all that had died with Hannibal. She was here because she was, for the first time in her life, alone and free, had the wherewithal to live any sort of life she wanted to, *and* she had fallen in love at first sight with Manoussos. She remained in Livakia with him because they lusted after each other and being together seemed to be adding to their lives, or so everyone thought. The greater truth was, yes, she was there for that reason, but more importantly because every minute of every day she was creating a new Chadwick for herself. That was how those high climbs alone to the little church on the cliffs came about. The church became a haven for her, a place not to commune with God but with her new identity.

Chadwick placed the key in the lock of the church door and pushed it open. Coming into this tiny white-domed church with its dark interior, not very good frescoes and several very good icons, whose silver covers glistened by the light of candle offerings, had become part of Chadwick's Livakian life: like drinking her coffee with D'Arcy or Max, being amused by Rachel and her flirtations, listening to the fascist spoutings of Mark who could, when sober or drunk, which was a good deal of the time, mesmerise with his oratory, being Manoussos's woman.

She placed her offering, a box of beeswax candles, on the small table near the door then sat down on the lone rickety chair and allowed the aroma of years of beeswax and incense, silver polish and dusty dried flowers, the sea air that slipped in through the open door, to envelop her. It was here in this very quiet and spiritual place that her own spirit took flight. She imagined she was closer not to one god but all the gods, all the departed souls, and her own. Chadwick never went to the church in sadness or despair or looking for answers; she didn't have a sad spirit, quite the contrary. She always arrived there happy and left uplifted.

Manoussos was in his office, the upper floors of a two-hundred-year-old house facing the sea, and on the telephone when he heard the mournful sound of one single church bell echoing across the cliffs. It brought a smile to his lips. It always did when he knew that it was Chadwick ringing it. It meant that she would soon be running along the narrow footpath carved out of the cliffs that plunged dangerously down to the sea and then down through the village to meet him for lunch at the Kavouria.

Dimitrios, his deputy, was at the fax machine just tearing off a message from a friend and colleague of Manoussos's at Interpol. The fax sheet still in his hand, Dimitrios went to his chief and took the telephone from him; he too smiled at the thought of Chadwick racing along the cliffs. Not only was she courageous and a joy to watch but he always made money on Chadwick's run, something Manoussos knew nothing about, or so he thought. Dimitrios and the barber-cum-mayor had a running bet. They timed Chadwick's return.

'Go ahead, chief, I might just as well hold on for you until someone at the other end picks up the receiver. Oh, and take this. It's from Colin Templeton in London.'

Manoussos handed over the telephone and stepped out on to the narrow balcony into the sun. He shielded his eyes and looked across the harbour and up the cliffs. She was no more than a dot racing across the edge of the buff-coloured cliffs. Hardly any of the foreigners and very few Cretans had ever been to the white-washed church because of its perilous access; they were terrified of the footpath but proud of the church perched on its small precipice and believed that it was a blessing to have it guarding their village and harbour.

It had been built hundreds of years before as a memorial to a beloved dead father and remained always a private church though open to anyone who wanted to make the pilgrimage to it. One of the monks or the priests from the larger church in the village went there on occasion to ring the bell for those long gone whose spirits they wanted to call to order. At Easter and Christmas a procession of brave villagers led by the priest, impressive in his long black robes and tall black hat, heavy gold and silver crosses dangling from chains draped across his chest, and two visiting Mount Athos monks who seemed to be residing in the village, they had been in Livakia for so many years, would make the climb at dusk. One of the monks carried the village church's Greek Orthodox cross of silver on a staff, the other swung two incense burners from silver chains, everyone else carried white candles with paper cones wrapped around them to shield their flame from the wind. All the while they remained in the small candle-lit church on the precipice and prayed, a small boy rang the church's single bell. The echoing sound ringing off the cliffs then, as at all other times, was part of the fabric of life in Livakia.

Chadwick did not make the run from the church every day or even every week but she did do it often after that first time that Manoussos had taken her there in the Christmas procession. Several times he brought up the subject of her frequent visits to the church but though she was forthcoming about how exhilarating the walk to the church and the run back from it was, how much she enjoyed opening it up and bringing the odd offering, merely sitting there and enjoying the essence of faith, he actually had not the least idea what was behind those visits nor what she was telling him. And there was something. In the same way as there was always something unfathomable about Chadwick, this magnificently beautiful, enigmatic woman with whom Manoussos had fallen so deeply in love.

Dimitrios, the telephone against his ear, stepped out on the balcony and handed Manoussos a pair of powerful binoculars. It brought another smile to Manoussos's lips, and without taking his gaze from Chadwick, he took the glasses, placed them against his eyes and adjusting the focus said, 'Thanks.' Then asked because he could no longer resist teasing his deputy, 'What's the time she has to make today for you to win your bet, Dimitrios?'

'You know about the wagers!'

'And your winnings. The mayor is not a good loser, he always bitches when he loses. I don't much like a bad loser.'

Dimitrios could tell by the sound of the police chief's voice that Manoussos was more amused than annoyed though he would rather have read his boss's eyes than his voice. An impossibility because Manoussos still had the binoculars clamped against them.

'I should have known better than to think I could keep the wagers a secret. From you of all people, who have your fingers on the pulse of everything going on in town. I feel really embarrassed, chief,' said Dimitrios.

'You should be, that's what getting caught out is all about.'

'You're not angry are you?'

'No, not angry, disappointed. You're supposed to be, as a law enforcer, a good example to people. Taking a wager on a private person on a pilgrimage to a church shows a certain disrespect even though it is no big deal and certainly not against the law. Actually quite amusing. Something I might do myself if the woman in question were not such an important person in my life and I didn't feel so protective of her. How's Chadwick's time, are you winning?'

A nonplussed Dimitrios checked the stop watch mechanism on his wrist watch. 'So far I am.'

'Good! Win or lose you're joining Chadwick and me for lunch, and you're picking up the tab. You can think of it as your penance.'

Dimitrios could not afford such a fine and Manoussos knew it. He was quite stunned at the prospect not only of having to pay a financial penance for his misdeed but having to face it out over lunch. However, Cretan pride would not allow him to beg off. His silence caused Manoussos to lower the glasses and turn around to face his deputy who was flushed with embarrassment. Katzakis the grocer, who was sweeping the cobblestones in front of his shop, saw the two men on the balcony and called up, 'Dimitrios, it looks as if it will be your round of drinks tonight. Look!' And he pointed to Chadwick with the end of his broom. She was now halfway down the cliffs from the church.

'I would like to crawl into a hole,' said the deputy to his superior.

Manoussos could not help but laugh. 'My best policeman in a hole? No, I don't think so. There's Mark, Chadwick wanted to see him, I think I'll ask him to join us for lunch. That is all right, isn't it?'

Dimitrios had to swallow hard before answering, 'As you like.'

The telephone was still clamped to his ear and finally the man they had been trying to reach all morning was on the line. Dimitrios said a few words and then attempted to hand the telephone receiver over to Manoussos.

'I'll tell you what, Dimitrios, you take this call and get the information I want and that can be your penance. I'll buy the lunch.'

'I couldn't allow that,' said the deputy.

'Oh, yes, you can – so long as you give your winnings to the church.'

Dimitrios could not help but smile. A deal had been struck, and he had saved face. His admiration for his superior rose higher. A nod signalled his agreement and a much relieved deputy turned to go inside while he was already talking to Athens.

Manoussos tapped him on the shoulder and the deputy turned around. 'Dimitrios, don't do it again!' There was a harshness in Manoussos's voice, a firmness in his expression, and his eyes were as cold as stone. That was not a warning, it was an order.

That small, insignificant incident was a very good example of how Manoussos Stavrolakis, the chief of police of Livakia and its environs, the best art-theft detective in Greece, commanded order and respect from his men, his superiors, thieves, smugglers, murderers, and the more law-abiding citizens of his country. He could be as hard or as soft as a piece of jade, and with the same lustre. Yet another lesson on how to govern and keep the peace was learned by Dimitrios.

Once more Manoussos turned to gaze through the binoculars at Chadwick. The sun was playing on her dark hair, a warm breeze was blowing it away from her face and her red silk dress against her body. The jumper she had tied around her shoulders by its arms was flapping behind her. She looked like a free spirit, a voluptuous goddess, but somehow young, almost child-like, a quality in her that manifested itself in so many ways and enchanted him. This woman-child he loved, who was anything but child-like in her lust for sex and him, remained still, after so many months of their being together, a mystery to the police chief.

How he would have loved to have known her for all of her life: as the spoiled and privileged child she had been, with marvellous parents who had pampered and watched over her. And in her adolescent life, and through her marriage, had she been as mysterious and as enigmatic a creature then as she was now, a widow in Livakia? The little he knew of his lover's past had not been because she had sat down and said, 'Now here is my life, past tense,' and told her story to him. He had never asked questions, she had never volunteered a biography. Her life unfolded as bits and pieces of information gleaned from a word said here, another there, an anecdote told *en passant* at the long table after too much wine or when they were alone and being very much together.

Chadwick had taken to Livakia and his friends and settled in to the lifestyle as if here was the home, the paradise, the way of life she had been searching for all of her life. And his friends, those who were not in love or infatuated with her, as were Elefherakis, Mark, and Laurence, took to her. As did the locals, both men and women. They enjoyed her in the same way as they enjoyed D'Arcy; the only difference was they had known D'Arcy all her life, she having been brought up since a baby in the village and her mother being, even now, one of their heroines. Chadwick's beauty, her stillness, her generosity of spirit, their being able to communicate because of her skill in speaking their language, all the things they admired about her, did not stop them from whispering among themselves: 'Chadwick, she is deep, a woman with a secret, many secrets. Who knows her?'

Manousos was thinking about these whispers; a whisper in Livakia was always loud enough for him to hear. He took one last look at Chadwick's progress before he walked from the balcony pulling the fax sheet sent by Colin Templeton from his pocket. Placing the binoculars on his paper-strewn desk, he sat down and read it several times. Then he wrote the name 'Larry Snell' on a pad and, turning round to the computer, fired off a fax: 'Colin Templeton from Manoussos Stavrolakis. Fax understood, will be delighted to receive your friend and give him whatever he needs ... Manoussos.'

Chadwick was already sitting at the table with Rachel and Mark when Manoussos and Dimitrios arrived. Mark and Rachel were bickering friends. He wrote exquisite prose, she wrote flowery, *bad* poetry; the one thing they had in common was their self-centredness. They each suffered from a pathological case of it. Rachel was *petite* in every sense of the word: short, tiny waist, every feature on her face small except for her eyes which were enormous and beautiful and always made up, and her bosom which, for its size and weight, was a wonder in the face of gravity. She used her eyes and her breasts in the same way as she used her French accent and her sexuality: to flirt, to seduce, to pave her way.

She sexually teased and primped from the moment she opened her eyes, usually around eleven in the morning, until they closed – and that could be any time. She had had sex and shunned love with every eligible man in Livakia, and denied it, and then when caught out, denied that she'd enjoyed it. She played the reluctant sex kitten, protested constantly that she was not beautiful but was forever moving her chair out of the sun for fear of wrinkles or spots. She made such an extraordinary fuss about insisting on paying her share at the long table that almost always someone jumped up from their chair on her arrival and invited her as their guest before she sat down. Rachel found that acceptable if the invitation came before her bottom hit the chair. Her bargaining for a single drachma off a peach at Katzakis's was enough to turn the grocer into a babbling wreck. He preferred to give her the peach. She was one of the first to befriend Chadwick who had never met anyone like her and was naively amused by Rachel and her quest to suffer for her art's sake.

Chadwick, like everyone else who could afford to be, was generous to Rachel. For she did have to count her pennies, she was dependent on a monthly cheque from Mama in Paris, and borrowing from Elefherakis when she ran short of money. Chadwick learned after only a short period of time that in Livakia, and most particularly in the expatriate community, in one way or another everyone cared for everyone else; not much, just enough for it not to become burdensome.

From fifty feet away Manoussos could see that Rachel was flirting with both Chadwick and Mark, and Mark was flirting with Chadwick. He smiled to himself. It was going to be an amusing lunch. He almost laughed aloud when he glanced at his deputy. Dimitrios always went squiffy-eyed when he was near Rachel. Like most of the local Greek men, he found her the most glamorous and beautiful of creatures, a doll-like foreign girl, sexuality personified.

She raised hackles at the back of their necks and invariably a hand would fly to their crotch for a quick hitch of their trousers. He could almost hear Dimitrios's heart beating faster.

The two men joined the others at the table. Rachel was in top form, exclaiming about poetry, art, Crete, which she always got quite wrong and was screamingly mundane about, discussing her love life, attacking Mark for being a truly talented writer, and simultaneously seducing Dimitrios.

Manoussos was sitting across the table from Chadwick. She said so little. She was a woman who knew how to sit still, exude quietness in an intriguing, goddess-like way, yet her contribution seemed so large. What little she said was right and she was always amusing without ever trying. There was too that tremendous aura of sensuality that emanated from her and constantly drew everyone at the table to pay her attention, include her, seek her viewpoint.

During this lunch it was Mark on his soap box about the good side of Hitler and how it all went wrong. Rachel, a Parisian whose background made her a French-Iraqi Jewess, was jumping up and down from her chair, challenging Mark's dissertation. It was Frances Pendenis, who had only just joined the diners, a seventy-six-year-old English composer of classical music who had written but one opus in her life, and that in 1934, who finally changed the subject when she smacked Mark on the head with her handbag and said, 'Oh, dear boy, do give it a rest. You're sounding pathetic, very neo-Nazi, and impressing no one with your clap trap.' She poured him a glass of wine and started talking opera. The opera that she had been collaborating on with Mark for eleven years.

Rachel rolled her eyes. If they could have spoken they would have screamed, 'Not again,' when Mark and Frances suggested yet another evening at Chadwick's house where they would give a performance of the work in progress. Manoussos knew that Chadwick would say yes, from kindness, but he also knew that no one really wanted to hear it again. For Chadwick it was still something new and exciting, a creation in the making. For everyone else it was a ten-year-old bore which they tolerated.

Chadwick had kept the *Black Narcissus* moored in Livakia for two months after her arrival in the village. She and Manoussos had lived between the boat and Manoussos's house, and now they lived between his house and hers. They had always been utterly discreet when she was staying in Manoussos's place. His position in the community and as one of the more important law enforcers on the island demanded it. The Cretans were proud of their famous police chief, not only for his authority and his successes but for a certain morality which he possessed. It did also very much extend to his being a handsome, virile man known for his promiscuity, his love affairs with beautiful foreign women. But pride and whispers of admiration would not preclude criticism of a man in his position living in sin. And for Cretans, even in the nineties, living with a foreigner without a marriage blessed by the church was living in sin.

Always mindful of his position, though he travelled openly all over the island with Chadwick, they continued to keep separate his and hers houses which was somehow considered respectable among the Cretans because whispers had it that the police chief's position was no more than that of a man in love, having an affair – until the next beauty came along.

The reality was quite the opposite, Manoussos was as much in love with Chadwick as he had been from the moment of first seeing her. He knew that there would never be any other woman for him but Chadwick Chase. It was lust, there was no question about that, but it was more than that too. It was love as he had never known it before. It was two souls, two hearts that beat as one. It was something more than words could describe or even feelings express, and it was at that moment, when Chadwick was about to say yes to the table about a performance of the Frances-Mark opera at her house, that he spoke up.

He reached across the table, took Chadwick's hand in his and, smiling, said, 'No.'

All eyes were on Manoussos. It was unlike him to speak for Chadwick. Not at all in his character to do a take-over on the women in his life or anyone else for that matter. The surprise silenced everyone. Chadwick, her hands still in his, applied a little pressure in reassurance. 'Some other time. I have plans for us, Chadwick and I; they are undefined so it's best we keep our timetable loose, last-minute, go on as we have been, taking each day at a time.'

'What a good idea, what a relief!' said Rachel.

'Thanks, Rachel, you're such a little pig, so ungracious. If you didn't want to hear it you only had to say so, not be a bitch about it. I'll remember this attitude of yours when next you knock on my door looking for a sounding board for your latest poems.'

And Mark and Rachel were off again, bickering back and forth, until D'Arcy and Max arrived at the table and joined the group. They were still for Chadwick the most glamorous and adventurous couple, and so very nice and amusing with it. She had never met people like them before, such pleasure seekers, vital, so much fun to be with, so sensual – and their love story was so special. They were *the* beautiful people she had only read about: erotic libertines out in the world and for all the world to see, with no guilt. They were a constant reminder of what Chadwick's life with Hannibal had not been. Every day with Manoussos she was learning to love, lust, in a new and different way from any she had ever known. She felt the luckiest woman in the world to have had her life with Hannibal and to have found as thrilling but very different a love and life a second time around with Manoussos.

Ever since Chadwick's arrival in Manoussos's life he had been taking, every few weeks, his accumulated holiday time, and it was then that they had made use of the *Black Narcissus*. They had sailed to Alexandria and up the Nile to the ancient temples, to Turkey and followed its coastline as far as Syria, making excursions inland to see the ruins of ancient Greek cities. These had been luxurious house-party cruises and Chadwick had invited several of the expatriate community and Cretans as her guests. It was during those cruises when Max and D'Arcy were on board that Chadwick learned of the deep love and regard, the longtime, on again, off again affair that Manoussos had had with D'Arcy until she fell in love with Max and they declared themselves to each other. She quite liked the fact that Manoussos would always love D'Arcy in just the same way as she would always love Hannibal: love that would never go away but had run its course.

Now the *Black Narcissus* was no longer a part of their

lives and Chadwick lived in a house at the top of the village overlooking the harbour. She had rented it from Edgar Marion and Bill Withers who were on a round-the-world cruise, and it was here that she and Manoussos were able to get away from everyone and live in their very own private world.

The house had a certain seclusion as its closest neighbours were empty houses, romantic ruins. And it was perched in such a way against the cliffside as to give the most spectacular views. Chadwick and Manoussos were not quiet or sedate lovers; the seclusion of the Marion-Withers house suited their nights of adventurous sex. Often they would spend days together there doing nothing more than making love, stretching their erotic life to the farthest limits of ecstasy.

Lunch lingered on until most of Livakia was already home having a siesta. The laughter and arrival of more people including Elefherakis, who invited everyone from the table to his house for coffee and sweets before they dispersed, could do nothing to arrest Manoussos's urge to take Chadwick home for violent, passionate sex. However, though sex for Chadwick and Manoussos could be at times spontaneous or even instantaneous, anywhere, any place sort of sex, what was called for now was the other sort of erotic world they dwelt in: time-consuming, thrilling, dangerous sex. And they had left it too late. Manoussos was due back at the police station. He urged Chadwick to go with the others and said he would call for her at Elefherakis's house as soon as he was free. The gaze that passed between them confirmed to each of them that this evening it was to be home for them, lost in lust, giving themselves over to the god Eros.

The moment Manoussos walked into the building and up the stairs to his office he was acutely aware of a changed atmosphere: the phones were ringing and men were stomping around in heavy boots. Chadwick vanished from his mind. Manoussos was a policeman first, a man in love second. There was much excitement in the station house; several of Manoussos's men had arrived from the remote mountain villages where they had been conducting a surveillance operation for months. Manoussos and his men had been on the trail of a ring of art smugglers who were robbing the small Byzantine churches rich in rare icons, Minoan archaeological sites and museums for the much-coveted and sought after painted vases or *amphorae*, very large ceramic *pithos*, jewellery and coins, even the much prized mosaics.

Manoussos had deduced that the way the smugglers worked was systematically to rob specific sites and then bury or hide the objects in various places around the island for long periods of time, months, years even, before they moved them. These were not farmers digging up the odd relic for a few drachmas, these were very well-organised and wealthy, extremely knowledgeable smugglers thieving most likely to order for the rich antiquities dealers and collectors in London, Paris and New York. When the hunt for the missing treasures had cooled down, only then would they move them out, most likely by boat at night, on the first leg of their journey. This was no small operation and although Manoussos and his men had known for months some of the Cretans who were involved, they had never moved on them but bided their time. Manoussos wanted not the little men but the ring leaders, and to follow their route. When the art smugglers did finally make their move with the treasures in hand and had left the island, the police chief intended to nab them once he knew their destination and before they left Greece or its territorial waters.

It was dark when Manoussos's men left Livakia and that was only after he had treated them all to a meal at the Kavouria. They made their exit, having been briefed on the next stage of their investigation, riding on donkeys and guided by the donkey men, to the stony terrace at the top of the village. The men had not come by car: they were undercover agents pretending to be hunters and looked every bit the part with their game bags and shotguns slung over their shoulders, dressed in Cretan hunter's gear, white leather boots and all. The donkeys would take them a few miles down the very bad crushed stone and dirt road, the only one leading across the mountain range to Livakia, and from there they would walk the rest of the way by the bright white light of the waning moon. These were men who knew the mountains.

Manoussos had walked with them part of the way through the village and then turned back, intending to call for Chadwick, but he was joined on the path by Max. The two old friends decided to stop and have a drink together at Manoussos's house while Manoussos bathed and changed from his uniform. Dressed in a pair of cream-coloured cords and sitting on the bed putting on his socks and shoes, Manoussos laughed with Max about Mark and his fascist theorising.

'You would have thought he would have learned his lesson on how destructive his theories are, and downright lethal combined with his oratory. Melina is a case in point,' said Max.

There was an awkward silence. Max and Manoussos didn't often mention the young girl who had murdered their friend Arnold in Livakia only months before. Both men believed that she would never have killed their friend had she not been under Mark's influence. It had been a nasty and unhappy time that had torn the community apart for a short while and no one ever spoke of it now. Max's comment killed the moment of levity. But that soon passed and he changed the subject to Chadwick.

'You know, you really owe me for Chadwick, Manoussos.'

'You know, you really owe me for D'Arcy, Max.'

'Hell, what are good friends for if not to be generous and make each other happy?' quipped Max.

'I am going to marry her, Max.'

'And so, what else is new?'

'That's all you have to say?'

'She's well worth marrying. I find Chadwick as intriguing today, Manoussos, as I did that moment I walked into the restaurant and saw her for the first time. I can imagine she will be just as intriguing on your fiftieth anniversary. Have you told her yet?'

'No, but she knows it.'

'What are you waiting for?'

'She comes from a different world, a different culture. To marry a Cretan like me and live this life ... I want to make sure this is what she wants as much as I do.'

Max knew Manoussos very well. They had been friends for years and had seen each other through many love affairs and one night stands. They had womanised together, hunted together, Max had piloted his sea plane for Manoussos when he was on the hunt for smugglers, they had played poker every Thursday night when Max was in residence in Livakia for the last ten years. There was more to that statement than what was said. It was not that Manoussos was unsure of his love for Chadwick, it was more that something was wrong with his love for Chadwick.

As if Manoussos knew what Max was thinking, he looked up at his friend, rose from the bed and took the shirt that Max had chosen for him and began undoing the buttons.

'There are inconsistencies between what I know about Chadwick and her behaviour. She has a close-knit family apparently but has never made a phone call or received one from them. Not once in four months has she gone to the post office for her mail yet she claims they know where she is, and love her. She and her husband shared a great love, were sexually besotted with each other and had an adventurous, somewhat bizarre sex life, yet something she said in a moment of uncontrolled lust leads me to believe that her husband tortured her psychologically about their sexual excesses. He held back on her. She weeps with lust and passion when I come inside her. Each time it's as if she has been set free. For me it's bliss to be there like that, but for her it seems to be life itself as she has never known it.'

'Why don't you ask her what's going on?'

'Maybe because in my heart I think I'd better not know, *if* there is anything.'

'You could make enquiries elsewhere. Jesus, you're a policeman, you can manage that discreetly.'

'Wouldn't think of it, and don't you either. I want your word on that.'

'Done.'

'Besides, you won't believe this, Max, but I swear she is so enchanting that every time I see Chadwick or touch her, it's as if for the first time. She's always new and fresh and original and I never know what to expect. With a woman like that, what's to know?'

Max began to laugh and slapped Manoussos on the back. 'You've got it bad.'

'What?'

'Love. You're a fool in love, my friend. Join the club.'

Chapter 9

Elefherakis Khaliadakis was an erudite, fiftyish womaniser and his adoration of women was something they could rarely resist. Former lovers were constantly turning up at his door. Chadwick was no different from those women he had loved and sent away: she found him quite irresistible to be with. He was the best of company, and hospitable, his house a constant salon of changing faces from all walks of life, interesting people, never dull. He was a master at how to mix and match people: statesmen, former kings, minor royals and actors with young and beautiful travellers: back packers out to find themselves and the world. Famous artists, writers, philosophers and art historians rubbed shoulders with a range of clever beauties, lady intellects with pretty faces and stunning bodies, expensive ladies of the night, or rugged Cretan shepherds down from the mountains who talked Greek history with Oxford dons.

He was extremely sensual; there was always a scent of sex about Elefherakis. However, he was anything but obvious about the libertine life he led behind closed doors. He was more the Cretan aristocrat with the bearing of a duke whose invitations to house-parties were hard-won.

The several-hundred-year-old, very beautifully restored family house was large and behind walls, set on a precipice at the very end of the harbour. From the sea it was a breathtaking introduction to Livakia as you rounded the headland and it and its many small courtyards and gardens came into view. It was run like all great island houses by a large, mostly invisible staff of old retainers, many of whom had known Elefherakis since he was a child. An art historian and some-time writer, he spent a great deal of time reading when he wasn't playing at life or cooking. He was a brilliant chef. Chadwick and Manoussos had spoken about her attraction to him which was no more than her attraction to Max, normal for a woman who was a lustful creature. One of the exciting things about being in Elefherakis's house was the ambience. There was an air of cultivated decadence that teased the senses. Inhibitions vanished; one's secret desires were constantly tweaked.

No one had been at all surprised, in the late-afternoon while everyone who had lunched at the Kavouria was having coffee and cakes with Elefherakis at his house, when one of his old loves came knocking at his door. She had arrived in Livakia having hitched a ride on a fishing boat making its way down the coast to its home port of Sfakia. That was how just about everyone arrived in Livakia unless you knew the very loose timetable of the vessels that made their weekly stop off at the village with the post or supplies. It was either that, if you came by water, or hire a boat. She was received by everyone enthusiastically, except for Chadwick who had never met her before.

For those first few minutes after her arrival she described most amusingly what hell it had been getting from the airport at the Chania end of the island by taxi across the mountains to Skafidia Padromi and then the drama of finding a boat. Everyone gathered around her and listened as if they had never heard or experienced the same story dozens of times, which they had. They were so attentive to Astrid that it took more than several minutes before they realised she had arrived with a man.

Not so Chadwick. Her first sight of him was shortly after Astrid Hammunson had entered the room and was engulfed by her old friends. He just seemed to arrive and stand in the doorway to the large and very grand living room, eventually to lean against the door jamb and light a cigarette. He was attractive in a quintessentially English way. Sandy-coloured hair worn on the long side, very much the English public school/Oxbridge sort of haircut. His face was handsome, expressionless, yet his eyes, dark blue and bright, were not. Chadwick immediately saw them as observant eyes. He was a man who knew how to see things in the deeper meaning of instantly understand-ing. He had the same sort of understated sexuality as Laurence Hart, an Englishman and old love of D'Arcy's who lived in Livakia when he wasn't lecturing at Oxford had. There was something about the stranger's face, his body language, that was appealing and yet gave nothing away.

He was dressed oddly for travelling to Livakia, as if he had just stepped out of a taxi to enter his West End gentleman's club. A Savile Row-tailored black suit with a pencil thin stripe, a white shirt open at the collar; she guessed a black silk tie with a tiny white pattern in it had been removed and was now in his pocket. Casually slung over his shoulder was a Burberry raincoat which he would most assuredly have needed to keep warm on a sail down the coast of Crete in late-afternoon in early-spring. On the floor next to him was a small well-travelled leather case. Chadwick could glean nothing from his looks. He was inscrutable.

Possibly as much as ten minutes went by before Astrid remembered that he was there and introduced him to everyone. 'I am so sorry, I got carried away with seeing my old friends again,' she said to the man as she walked to the doorway and, taking him by the hand, ushered him into the room.

'Elefherakis, may I introduce you to Larry Snell? I met him in Skafidia Padromi. He too was looking for a ride down the coast. Amazingly he wanted to come here, so he actually gave me a ride.'

The two men shook hands and Elefherakis made the introductions with a short biography of each of the group: 'Most of the people here are long-time residents – Mark's a writer, Rachel a poet, I'm a sometime dilettante and an all-the-time lazy pleasure seeker as I am sure Astrid has already told you. How about a coffee and a sweet or would you rather have a scotch?'

Larry took the scotch whisky. He was well-spoken with an upper-class accent that went with his look and clothes. It was evident to everyone that if Astrid had returned to rekindle a romance with Elefherakis, she now had a second interest in tow. It was, however, difficult to tell just how interested Larry Snell was in the Swedish blonde. He gave little away. Chadwick was amused to see Rachel's compact of blusher materialise. She dusted her cheeks, wiped her tongue over her teeth to erase any trace of lipstick, and having kissed the air on either side of Astrid's cheeks, made a bee-line for Larry Snell.

Chadwick was sitting on a settee with Elefherakis and Larry, Rachel on a cushion on the floor at their feet. They were talking about Crete. Larry appeared to be very knowledgeable about the island though he confessed that he had never been there before this visit. It never occurred to anyone to ask what he was doing here, they all assumed he, as they were, was here on a getaway of one sort or another. It simply wasn't done to ask – expatriate courtesy, or was it traveller's protocol? Chadwick could never quite figure out which.

'Where are you staying?' asked Elefherakis.

'I'm not sure,' came the answer.

Chadwick had not missed the glance that passed between Astrid and Elefherakis. It was evident that she would have liked Elefherakis to invite Larry to stay with them but dare not ask. Chadwick picked something up that was happening between the three, Larry, Elefherakis and Astrid. A sex scene? Astrid wanted them both and both men knew it, liked it, and were considering it. There was something so very sexy and decadent about their intentions. Not a word had been said, hardly a look had passed between them to suggest such a thing ... and yet it was there, explicitly so. The very thought of Astrid's being held by one man as the other had her was thrilling. Chadwick had been there many times: two, sometimes three men at the same time had been part of her and Hannibal's sex life. His insistence on it had brought her untold pleasure, had satisfied his need to see her in lust and orgasm, and assuaged his guilt of depriving her of being awash with his seed, that vaginal orgasm she so craved to have with him and he had refused her. He had explained his sense of guilt so many times to her. His anxiety for lusting after his adopted daughter. But still his rejection pained her. Chadwick fantasised for a few seconds about the sex and outrageous lust that the three might generate for one another. It made her hot and bothered for Manoussos. He had no problems about brushing her womb with his come.

'You're welcome to stay here in the house with us,' invited Elefherakis.

And there it was. For the first time since Chadwick had seen Larry Snell standing in the door, a window into this man opened. Lust came into the steady, passive blue eyes but instead of training them on Astrid they focused on Chadwick. He answered Elefherakis but his words were for her. 'That's very generous of you but I have someone to see before I can accept. Why don't I do that now? May I leave my bag here? I won't be long.' Before anyone could say a word, Larry smiled and was on his feet and making for the door.

Chadwick was used to men wanting her. It sometimes excited her lust. Men lusting after her had always been a way of life for her. Sometimes she liked it more than other times; this was one of the more times. Manoussos knew some of her sexual history, he would understand – that is if she were to tell him.

It was dusk, very nearly dark, when Larry closed the gate to Elefherakis's house and walked down the steep path to the harbour. The port and the quay were busy getting ready for the evening: lights being turned on, tables laid at the Kavouria, coffee shops open and the tric-trac boards ready for play. The boats were secured for the night and a string of donkeys was waiting on the quay, their keepers sitting on rickety wooden chairs having a drink and talking politics. He walked along the quay, unable to get Chadwick Chase out of his mind.

Larry had recognised her at once from the many photographs he had seen of her, from the interviews he had had with Warren Chase and his sister Diana Chase Ogden, Andrew Coggs Senior and his son Andrew Junior. Dr Bill Ogden's, Diana's husband's, interview now came to mind because though the others insisted that they only wanted proof that Chadwick had had nothing to do with the sudden death of Hannibal Chase, it had been Dr Ogden who had declared outright he was against the investigation, that Chadwick was incapable of harming Hannibal but Hannibal was not incapable of harming her. He had strongly advised that Diana and Warren were opening a can of worms – the very private sex life that his children knew nothing about was better left sealed. His inference was that they might learn more than they might want to know.

Larry Snell rarely acted as an operative for his company. A case had really to attract his interest: a firm of strait-laced, ultra-conservative WASP American lawyers such as Chambers, Lodge, Dewy & Coggs hiring a private investigation firm to enquire into the death of Hannibal Chase and the movements of Chadwick Chase, his widow, whom the family believed might have murdered their father, had certainly been interesting. But it had been one brief glance at a close-up photograph of the suspect that had made it intriguing enough for Larry to take on the commission personally.

He stopped walking and leaned against a boatbuilder's workshop, slipped into his Burberry, lit a cigarette and watched the port coming alive with people drifting down from their houses. He thought of those interviews in New York, a world away from this place, and how the Chase brother and sister were forcing this investigation on two counts: to break the will their father had cut them out of, and to satisfy their belief that their father had not died a natural death. All that in spite of the fact that they had loved, admired and respected Chadwick Chase, their once adoptive sister, and though more than a decade younger than themselves, the step-mother they had admitted had been their best friend and who had loved their father utterly and faithfully.

Larry had conducted his interviews with his clients once as a group and then individually. It was his private interview with Bill Ogden that had fascinated him. It gave him a clue as to what had really happened to Hannibal Chase. Those interviews in New York had also painted a portrait of Chadwick Chase that had first teased his mind and then slowly drawn him towards her. Gathering a portfolio of information on Chadwick and her life with Hannibal had taken real sleuthing and proved to be time well spent. Bill Ogden had been right: the family were going to have some shocks about dear old dad to deal with.

Chadwick Chase . . . she had the answer as to what really happened, the how and why Hannibal had died so suddenly. Larry was in Livakia to spy on her so he could finish his report. It hadn't been all that difficult to track her down as having been living somewhere in Crete these last four months; exactly where had been marginally more difficult, at some point she'd begun covering her tracks. Why? He didn't much like playing the operative again, but he was so besotted by Chadwick and her life that more often than not it felt less like being a detective and more like chasing after an elusive creature you were out to snare for your own pleasure.

Astrid had been a find, a diversion. She had what a friend of his called a 'fuck me for fun, the ecstasy, the trip, and so long, big boy', attitude and that kind of sexual diversion was just what was needed. So he had gone along with her to Elefherakis's house, never expecting Chadwick to be very nearly the first person he would meet on landing in Livakia. The only thing that he did expect was that he would want to fuck Chadwick Chase. One look across a room and he knew his expectations were correct: she had a most unusual and provocative sexual charisma.

Larry Snell had been around, seen and done intriguing work for most of his life. He was a former MI5 man who left the service at the top of his career to form a specialist private detective agency with his American CIA equivalent. The partners were well matched in age, in their late forties, and personality. Their minds worked in the same way and they made excellent workmates, dealing with the top of the market in clandestine investigations for private individuals as well as governments.

Snell & Martin had offices in New York, London and Paris and was a powerful name in that very secret world such agencies worked in. The Chase investigation was not exactly their sort of case but Hank Martin felt obliged to take it on; his father-in-law was Alfred Chambers, a senior partner in the firm of Chambers, Lodge, Dewy & Coggs. He had been surprised and amused when going over the agency's case load, as the partners did once a month, to find that Larry had taken on the Chase file and wanted to handle it himself. He said he needed a change but Hank had known him for too long: Larry obviously liked the idea of a beautiful and mysterious murderess who would never come to trial or be punished if indeed she did do it. Scandal was always to be avoided with the old guard.

Larry Snell had no trouble finding the police station. He had found a man sitting in a coffee shop contemplating a backgammon board and drinking an ouzo. He asked the man if he might sit down and ordered a scotch for himself and one for the man at the table. The man was about fifty years old, and spoke English as if he came from Brooklyn New York.

'Greek-American?' inquired Larry.

'God forbid. Cretan from Livakia. I spent six years in New York, frying fish for my brother-in-law so I could come home and catch fish. Every Greek leaves his island so he can return to it. Andonis Lefrakakis. Can you play?' And he shoved out a rough and friendly hand for Larry to shake.

Larry lost both games and Andonis Lefrakakis bought the drinks and gave Larry directions to the police station and another set of directions to his sister's house. She did on occasion rent her front bedroom if she liked the person and they came recommended. Andonis had made the call from the coffee shop and the room was reserved. They had agreed on a price and had shaken hands on it. Larry told Andonis to tell his sister he would turn up but didn't know when because he was due back at Elefherakis Kaliadakis's house. A clucking sound of approval and a wink from Adonis, some flattering words and, 'I understand.'

On leaving the coffee house Larry realised that he had dropped two of the best names in town. All doors would easily be opened to him now. The end of a line of donkeys being managed by their keepers clip-clopped on the cobblestones past him; hunters, some walking, some riding, were singing as they vanished up a narrow street into the dark.

Larry found the long narrow staircase to the police station easily, climbed the stairs two at a time and entered the police station. Dimitrios was there and another policeman. Larry put out a hand. 'I'm a friend of Colin Templeton's. I think you had a fax from him that I was coming?'

Dimitrios sprang to his feet. 'Oh, yes.' He offered a handshake and kept pumping Larry's hand. Finally Larry managed to remove his hand from the deputy's. He looked around the room before he sat down and took a pack of cigarettes from his coat pocket. He offered one to Dimitrios and the other policeman in the room while introductions were being made.

'You want the chief, it's he who is expecting you. He'll be back shortly. Coffee, a drink?' offered Dimitrios.

'A coffee, thanks.'

While Dimitrios rang through to the coffee house Larry took stock of the room. He had seen and had had the co-operation of hundreds of provincial police precincts such as this one all over the world. Yet instinctively he thought he had better suss out the village and Manoussos Stavrolakis before he revealed too much of why he was in Livakia. That had not been Larry's intention before he had laid eyes on Chadwick Chase. Jesus, she's a dangerous woman. A few minutes with her and already I'm trying to protect her, was his reaction to that particular instinct, laughing at himself for having fallen for a suspect. By all he had heard from Colin, who had done everything to recruit Stavrolakis away from the Cretan police force and into Interpol, the district chief of police was a man who might not agree with the handling of the Chase affair.

He liked the deputy who asked a great many questions and revealed very little about Livakia and the people living there. Larry gathered from the few words he said about his police chief that he admired and respected him. His assessment: Dimitrios was a good policeman, would climb the law-enforcement ladder.

More than an hour later the officers and Larry heard footsteps on the stairs. 'Ah, that's my chief,' announced Dimitrios.

Two men entered the room and the deputy all but stood to attention when he made the introductions. 'Chief, this is Mr Snell, the friend of Colin Templeton. Mr Snell, meet Chief Manoussos Stavrolakis and Mr Max de Bonn.'

Though Larry had no preconceived idea what the police chief would be like he was nevertheless surprised at his good looks, the very smart cut of his tweed jacket, the very English cords and Turnbull & Asser shirt. That dark hair and very macho moustache, the open face ... he liked the bigness of the man, not only physically but his spirit, and the clever eyes. He took to him and his friend Max immediately, recognising them as men who liked men and were the devil with women.

'When did you arrive?' asked Manoussos.

'Several hours ago on a fishing boat on its way to Sfakia. My first trip to Crete, and when Colin heard I was coming he insisted I make a visit here to Livakia.'

'The spring – you couldn't have picked a better time. Do you play poker?' asked Max who was always looking for fresh blood for his Thursday night poker game.

'And bridge, chess and backgammon. I win at chess, sometimes at backgammon, but never against the Greeks, the Lebanese or Turks. They're too fast for me. Almost always at the poker table.' The two men looked at each other and then at Larry. Wry smiles broke out and they were all three friends.

'You're welcome to stay with me, if you like?' offered Manoussos.

'Thanks, but I think I'm already fixed up.'

The look that passed between Manoussos and Larry, the manner in which he said it, led Manoussos to understand that his invitation had not been a good idea. It also confirmed to him what he had instinctively thought when he had received the fax from Colin. This man was one of them, in the world of law enforcement. A member of Interpol? Something akin to it? And in Livakia on business?

'Where are you staying?' asked Max. A question Manoussos might have asked except for that look of Larry's that intimated, 'When we talk, it has to be in private.'

'I'm not sure, I think I might have a scene going.'

Max, always the lover of intrigue and gossip, most especially if it was sexual, asked admiringly, 'Who, what, where?'

'I stepped off the boat with Astrid Hammunson and she took me to Elefherakis Kaliadakis's house.'

'Astrid's back! Well, you might be right about a scene, Larry. You really landed on your feet there. She's a happy, sexy lady, who likes her men and no complications. Staying with Elefherakis is always fun. He's a brilliant host,' offered Max.

'I've reserved the front room of Andonis Lefrakakis's sister's house.'

'How did you manage that?' asked an amused Manoussos.

'It wasn't difficult, everyone likes an easy mark. I lost two games of backgammon to him,' answered Larry.

Larry Snell was proving to be a very interesting man. He had been in Livakia for two or three hours at the most and he had Astrid in tow, Elefherakis offering him a bed, and had managed to ingratiate himself to Andonis enough for Christina, Andonis's spinster sister, to give up her front room for him. All that and Manoussos was certain Larry had given nothing away about himself or why he was in Livakia.

Manoussos turned to his deputy and told him, 'Time to close up shop, Dimitrios, see you in the morning.' Then turning to Larry and Max, he said bluntly, 'Max, you'll be quite bored. I'm going to show Larry round the port. See you later.'

Max took the hint that he was not wanted and left the two men in the street. 'Maybe we'll see you later, Larry. If not, tomorrow night's Thursday night, poker at my house. See you then.' The two men shook hands and Max walked in one direction, they in the other.

'I'm starving,' Larry told Manoussos.

'Come to dinner with me and my lady.'

'I don't think I can wait.'

Just in front of the Kavouria the rotisserie was turning slowly round and round with skewers one above the other of lamb and small game birds, sheep's heads chin to chin, teeth glittering a strange pink from the light of the red hot coals, *cocoretsi* of all sorts of offal, wrapped in a sheep's intestine so that they resembléd enormous sausages. The smell of rosemary and roasting flesh, the aroma of spitting fat as it dripped on the hot coals and sent puffs of steam swirling up into the night air, confirmed to Larry that he most certainly could not wait. Manoussos ordered slices of *cocoretsi* from the man brushing the meats with olive oil and the two men entered the restaurant.

Frances Pendenis was sitting at a table alone reading *Time* magazine. Tom and Jane Plum were at another table; she looked bored, the famous painter looked content. Several Cretans greeted Manoussos: standing up, shaking his hand and offering him and his friend a chair. Manoussos made brief introductions and the two men sat down at a secluded table. A bottle of house wine and two chunky glasses were plunked down, and a plastic basket of bread. Not quite white thin paper napkins and cutlery dull and bent with age and wear were casually slung on the paper cloth. Larry broke into the bread just as a platter of the *cocoretsi* was placed in the middle of the table. Manoussos handed Larry a fork and a knife. He himself picked up a fork and the two men began eating off the platter since no dinner plates had as yet been produced.

'I like your Livakia,' offered Larry.

'You'll like it even better when I show you around. I'll be leaving tomorrow or the next day on a two-day tour of some of the mountain villages. I'll be taking my lady. Come along. You'll see marvellous things. Or are you not here to see marvellous things?'

Larry drank from his glass. 'I take it Colin was very discreet? So must I be, to a point. What I tell you I would like to be kept between ourselves. I'm the Snell from Snell & Martin – we're a very discreet detective agency. I run the London office, very rarely do fieldwork, but a case came across my desk that I found different, a small domestic investigation that fascinated me. Self-indulgently, I decided this was one I wanted to investigate myself.

'I've been four months gathering information on a couple. My firm's been hired by the family and their lawyers to investigate some very serious allegations. These are people whose lives are lived in a very different society from that of a Cretan coastal village. Big names in the conservative American corporate and philanthropic world. But I think it's here that I will find the real truth, the answers they seek.'

'That couple is here, in Livakia?'

'Only one of them is.'

'What are the allegations?'

'Murder for money.'

'Any proof?'

'That's what we're supposed to find. So far there is no proof that a court of law could convict on. Not that it would ever come to court: these are people who would never permit the scandal of a murder in the family. That's why they didn't go to the police. But they don't want a murderer in their midst either. If evidence is found that the woman in question is guilty, the family would punish her in their own way and keep her as a skeleton in the closet.'

'Her? And here in Livakia? Listen, Larry, I want this kept very quiet. The last thing Livakia, or Crete for that matter, needs is another murderess in their midst. Not six months ago, a young Cretan girl landed here in Livakia and was befriended by the foreign community. She was trouble, a sad case, a bad influence, but managed somehow to get a life together here and to some degree improve herself because she was influenced by an American writer who lives here, Mark Obermamn. She was an illiterate girl but wily, had a passion for Mark and listened avidly to everything he said and did. She was strongly influenced by him and developed an obsession to please him. This pathetic fifteen-year-old murdered in a crime of passion one of the expatriates living here, Arnold Topper. It tore the town apart, really traumatised the people living here to have a murderer in their midst. It divided the foreigners from the Cretans. All sorts of unpleasantness erupted. Arnold's body was found but it remained for some time a mystery why and by whom he was killed. I trapped the girl and got a confession out of her. And, believe me, the town is only just forgetting about it.'

'This is an odd coincidence. There are similarities between your case and mine. This is still only theory but I believe that the woman I'm after was involved in a crime of passion, killed, if she did, because she was under the influence of a man and a love that dominated both their lives. She was only the instrument of his will.'

'I have always believed that Melina was the instrument of Mark's will. That he was the real murderer only she conducted the act.'

More platters of food had been brought to the table but Larry only managed a few forkfuls because he got carried away with telling Manoussos the life story of the woman he was there in Livakia to investigate. Whereas the two men had forgotten the food they had not forgotten the wine and Manoussos kept topping up their glasses.

209

'When I took this case on, I will admit that I was attracted to the woman, the tremendous beauty and charisma she had to have had to have charmed and won her elderly husband and the hearts and minds of even the very people who are out to destroy her. Four months ago when I took this case on I was led to believe that the husband had been the victim. I no longer believe that. I believe that they were each other's victims. We're talking here about a most extraordinary love story, Manoussos, lived by a remarkable couple, the likes of which I think you and I would happily have laid down our lives for. If the woman killed him, she did it for love not for money, I would wager my life on that.'

'Love, a mercy killing? Larry, it's still murder to take another man's life, no matter how you qualify it.'

'And thus spake the law.'

'You're sure she's here in Livakia?'

'Oh, I'm sure. I walked into Elefherakis's house and there she was.'

'Chadwick!' Manoussos said in a whisper of disbelief.

He had not the slightest idea from what he had heard about the woman in question that it was Chadwick until the very moment Larry had said, 'And there she was.' There was something in Larry Snell's voice – an intonation? a quickening of his breathing? a look that came into his eyes, admiration, attraction, male lust – when he said those words. It was as if Larry had been waiting to find a woman such as Chadwick all his life. Manoussos recognised his own reactions whenever Chadwick appeared before him.

'You know her! Well, that's not surprising in a community as small as this.'

'She cannot be the same woman you're looking for.'

'I recognised her from photographs. Five minutes with her and I knew from the interviews I conducted in New York and Tennessee that she was the very woman I'm investigating.'

'I know this woman, Larry, her life bears no resemblance to that of the woman you described.'

'Then how do you explain that she's using the woman's name? I'm looking for Chadwick Chase, and she was introduced to me as Chadwick Chase.'

Manoussos put his hand to his forehead and began massaging it. He closed his eyes as if he were dizzy and trying to regain his balance. An uncomfortable silence descended on them. Larry Snell rose from his chair and left the table. Manoussos needed some space and Larry intended to give it to him. When he returned to the table it was with a bottle of scotch and two clean glasses. He poured an inch of scotch into each glass, handed one of them to Manoussos and sat down. Manoussos drank his down in one gulp.

'She's your lady! I had no idea.'

'How could you have?'

'Is it serious?'

'Marriage serious,' answered Manoussos.

'You mean, you're married?'

'I was going to ask her tonight.'

'Look, I'm not here to arrest her. I'm here to investigate her.'

'You are assuming she is the woman you're looking for, Larry. You had better reserve judgement on that. I have been living with Chadwick for four months and not one single fact of this other woman's life bears any resemblance to what my lady has told me about hers.'

'Manoussos, this is very awkward for us both. How do you want me to handle this?'

'How had you planned to handle this?'

'With discretion, keeping my identity a secret, surveying her and her lifestyle. Eventually, when I have gathered all the facts I can about her and her behaviour here, possibly confront her. If I can get her trust, I'll reveal my real identity and hope she will tell me the truth about what happened to her husband. The reason I'm here is because her husband's children want to know what happened the night their father died. Why, three weeks before his death, he changed his will in her favour and left her eighty million dollars and them a peppercorn each. They do not consider that normal behaviour on their father's part. They need to know to ease the pain of their loss, their being so utterly rejected by him. But as I told you before, so far they are not going to like what they hear about dear old dad.'

'Then I suggest you carry on your investigation but I would be grateful if you kept your findings to yourself and your clients. In fact, I would ask you for your word on that. I want no scandal, not a hint of it getting out here in Livakia. You will understand that if I offer you friendship and co-operation, it will have to be on the basis that I expect you to respect the life Chadwick and I have together as private and nothing to do with your investigation? You have a job to do, you do it.'

'And what about you and Chadwick?'

'That's some loaded question, Larry. What you really mean to ask me is what will I do if I discover that the Chadwick Chase I know and love does not exist, that she is a figment of the Chadwick Chase you are investigating's imagination? That I have fallen deeply in love with a

SECRET SOULS

beautiful, erotically tuned woman and a tissue of lies. A better question would have been that if you are proven right that my Chadwick is your Chadwick, how am I going to face being deceived by the only woman I ever wanted to marry?'

'Manoussos, I'm sorry about this. Hell, am I sorry.'

'So am I, Larry. It's all been said. Let's just get on with our lives and see where it leads us.'

Manoussos called for the bill but Larry insisted on paying and together the two men walked along the crescent-shaped port to Elefherakis's house, Manoussos giving Larry a colourful picture of the pleasure seekers of Livakia.

It was nearly eleven o'clock when the two men entered the room where Larry had first seen Chadwick Chase. *Borsolino* had been a New York Broadway musical some twenty years before and the beat of its music filled the room loudly. Several couples were dancing; Mark, Astrid, and Elefherakis alone but around each other. From the shadows the men watched Chadwick rise and hand a long-haired sleeping dog to someone before taking the floor. She moved to the music that seemed to reach down to her soul and as she danced. Something from the depth of her being seemed to rise and take her over. A very intimate, sensuous, inner life was there for all to see, and they did, and were mesmerised, seduced. One by one the others in the room stopped dancing and gravitated from the centre of the room to stand around and watch her. They saw Chadwick come alive as they had never seen her before. She displayed a beauty that left the room in wonder and admiration. She danced, oblivious to her surroundings. She was somewhere far away. Time stood still while she

213

danced and every person in that room sensed that they were watching that very special something that few women or men possess: pure lust for life.

It was very nearly midnight before Chadwick and Manoussos made the steep climb up to her house. This had not been how either of them had planned to spend the evening. But the easygoing life of Livakia made light of changing plans.

Larry Snell could attest to that. When he had started out for Livakia the last thing he was thinking about was a new erotic awakening. True, when he had met Astrid, who had a loose, free uncomplicated sexiness about her, he had felt an instant attraction to her. Her flirting with him was not only flattering but provocative. She promised much in the way she moved, in her husky voice, if not in words. She insinuated out-of-bounds sex games. He had anticipated most definitely great sex before the night was out.

As the evening progressed, it was difficult not to sense his assumption was correct. He understood very nearly at once that Elefherakis was in the equation: lust, a little depravity. The two men recognised that Astrid wanted them both, 'a threesome to fuck by,' she had whispered to each of them as they watched Chadwick dance.

It had been as simple as Chadwick's exquisite sexuality firing up lust, a tremendous hunger for raw unadulterated sex among the three of them. After the last guest had left and they were alone Elefherakis, Larry and Astrid linked arms and walked through the house to Elefherakis's bedroom discarding their clothes as they went.

Astrid and Elefherakis had a history of sex together,

they were attuned to each other's sexual fantasies and well versed in acting them out. They recognised in Larry unfulfilled sexual hunger and took him over. The long blonde-haired, blue-eyed, naked Astrid was a junoesque figure: the large, magnificent breasts, the dark nimbus around her long and fat nipples, the narrow waist and large hips, rounded bottom, she was made to fuck, suck and taste. Elefherakis was a virile hunk of masculinity, a libertine already erect, his eyes shone with desire for debauchery and all forms of the sexual experience.

Larry had been with two men and a woman before but not for many years. He had very nearly forgotten how thrilling it was to experience sex with both a man and a woman at the same time. The excitement of being devoured by both Astrid and Elefherakis, indeed of devouring them. A willing cunt wanting to be riven by two men who want the same woman and hold no fear of sharing the sexual experience with each other. To feel the full flow of their orgasms, a coming together where they would all three ascend into that moment of erotic bliss where for a few seconds infinity opened up for them, nothing else in the world seemed to matter.

Their first of many orgasms together that night set Larry free. The bliss of tasting and feeling Astrid's orgasms, Elefherakis's smooth silky come, watching his sexual playmates enjoying his own orgasms until they were all three steeped in exquisite debauchery such as he had never known before took over Larry's entire being.

How clever Astrid and Elefherakis were in their generosity and affection towards their guest. Before dawn he was a part of their sexual life and not at all a stranger, a friend who they had set free. He knew as they did that they had added to his life, changed it in a way for the better, a way he had never realised he had wanted so desperately.

Yes indeed, Livakia did make light of changing plans and, he realised, changing lives.

Chapter 10

'Tell me something about your husband.'

Chadwick was lying naked in Manoussos's arms. He had been stroking her hair and kissing her: light, sweet kisses on her cheeks, her lips, her chin. He surprised her with that particular request because Manoussos never asked such things, never, in fact, asked her anything much about her life before they met. Had she been naive believing he never would?

'Like what?'

'Anything you like.'

'Well, you know I loved him very much.'

'And he died in a car accident. I believe that's what you told Rachel?'

'Yes, he did.'

'Tell me something else about him?'

She sighed and lay back in his arms. 'He used to tell me, "You are the beat of my heart, I never want you to grow up; I want you to remain ageless, a goddess, a madonna, and only mine."'

'And were you only his?'

'Yes, until he died.'

'How old was your husband when he died, Chadwick?'

She pulled herself up against the pillows but remained

217

in Manoussos's arms. 'Why are we talking about my husband?'

'Maybe because I'm thinking of becoming a husband myself.'

'Manoussos!'

'You can't be surprised to hear that I love you more than life itself, that it is unbearable for me to think of not being with you forever? Ergo marriage, husband, wife. How old, Chadwick, you didn't say?'

'Thirty-three,' she answered him.

'Childhood sweethearts, I think you said?'

'Yes.'

'And it was a happy marriage?'

'The happiest.'

'Do you think, if I were to ask you to marry me, that I could make you as happy?'

'If this is a proposal of marriage, it's an odd one, Manoussos.'

'Why odd? I would think that before stepping into such a commitment, deciding whether I can make you happy is fundamental.'

'Not when you know you make me happy, that I never want to leave Crete or you, that my life here with you is a new kind of life for me.'

'And I'm a new kind of love.'

'Yes, like no other I have ever known. I feel newborn in your love for me, in my loving you. There are times I can hardly believe I lived any life at all until I met you and lost my heart and my soul in one glance,' she told him, emotion cracking in her voice, causing a tremor throughout the body in his arms that he so coveted.

Manoussos drew her closer to him and was choked with

emotion. That she should love him so much, this enigmatic beauty whom he knew was and would always be his one great love, simply overwhelmed him. They remained silent, clinging to each other.

The dawn light was just coming through the windows and the bedroom was beginning to take form. A mirror opposite the bed caught the light and Chadwick could see a reflection of them lying on the bed entwined in each other's arms. Mere shadows in the half-light.

Chadwick slipped on to her side, wanting to see her lover's face. How she loved his youthful good looks, the firm muscular flesh, his sexual hunger. She could taste the fruits of his lust in her mouth, could feel their orgasms caressing her womb. The very thought caused her to tighten. She wanted never to let that stream of sexual dreams flow away. She slipped her hand between his legs and caressed his semi-erect penis, lowered her mouth to it, to kiss it with first her lips and then her tongue.

Manoussos closed his eyes and sighed. How many times had they lived and died in lust together, taken sex and their erotic games and adventures to the brink of no return – and then gone beyond that to die the little death in orgasm, only to be born afresh? He had always known from the very moment he had set eyes on her that she was a dangerous woman. There had to be pitfalls to loving a woman who reached down not only to the bright but the darkest side of your soul and commanded: Give it to me, your life without boundaries. I want it all for love and the thrills, to go further, always one step further, or we have nothing. That had been her way with him, and could be his ruin. She was indeed the siren of Greek myth and her song was sweet and strong. It filled his ears and drew him to her. It was an odd proposal of marriage, but there it was, he had made it, and would marry her as soon as possible.

For a few minutes emotion had blinded him from seeing that Larry Snell would not go away. It had deafened him to that little voice within which told him: Listen with your ears, not your heart. He could have made it, put aside the doubts for the woman he loved if only she had remained silent. But she didn't.

Chadwick broke the hush that lay between them. 'I think you should know that when Hannibal died, our marriage died along with him and so did that long-time love. He wanted it that way.'

That was the first time ever she'd mentioned her husband's name. Manoussos felt sick; he was grateful for the half-light in the room. It gave him a cover of darkness to compose himself in. Hannibal was the name Larry Snell had given for the father of the Chase brother and sister calling for an investigation into their step-mother's life.

Some minutes passed, the two lovers still entwined in each other's arms, before Manoussos regained his composure enough to ask, 'And did you always give your husband what he wanted?'

'Always.'

Manoussos's mind was spinning. He would make her mention her husband's name again, that would be the moment to confront her, give her a chance to explain. 'Tell me something more about him? His name?'

His questions were making her panic. 'Alex, and you would have liked him and he would have liked you. Now can we leave it at that?'

Now he had caught her outright in a lie. It was his

moment but he couldn't take it. Didn't want to take it for fear of where it would lead them. Manoussos ignored her request and asked the first thing that came into his mind. 'When Alex died were you both still very much in love?'

There was a pause before Chadwick stammered, 'Utterly ... completely. Only his death killed our love for each other.'

'You never had children?'

'You know I have no children.'

'I want children.'

'And so do I. In fact...'

Manoussos interrupted her on two counts; trying to control his emotions at the very thought of their creating a baby. Until Chadwick, he had never thought about his unborn babies but she made him think about them all the time. His and Chadwick's progeny: a continuity to their love, their lives together. To think of not having them suddenly became unbearable to him. The second reason for his cutting her short was that he meant to know why she had never had any with her husband.

'A young couple, happily in love like you and your husband, which one of you didn't want children?'

Manoussos felt Chadwick grow tense in his arms. He had hit a nerve, something that really bothered her. But when she spoke there was no sign of anger in her voice; she sounded not at all disturbed by his question, merely firm in her reply. 'I don't really want to talk about my husband or my life with him, Manoussos. We loved, it died when it was still in its prime. That was as he wished it to be. To talk about it is to cheapen what we had and lost, and I have no intention of doing that. Please accept the subject of my husband and our relationship as closed.'

Manoussos was horrified. He had upset Chadwick. He found it very nearly unbearable that he should cause her the least anxiety. She did that not only to him but to everyone. Without asking, she engendered something very powerful that made men want to care for her. He had seen it manifest itself in Mark and Elefherakis. He even sensed that Larry Snell would do all he could to cushion things for her. And the husband, Hannibal, not the fictitious Alex – oh, yes, by now he could no long pretend that she was not Chadwick Chase, the widow of a sixty-six-year-old man called Hannibal who had left her eighty million dollars. A man who had spent his entire life caring for her, loving her, lusting after her, until that love ate away at him, at them, and all that remained was one life between them.

The same questions kept rolling over again and again through his mind. Why had she done it, entered his life and spun him a tissue of lies for them to live and love by? What had she to hide that made her create this new identity for him to fall in love with? A crime? Had she sensed that if her police chief lover had known about her life as he had heard it from Larry, and were to find out that she had perpetrated a crime, he would have to give her up? That his integrity, his entire life, would demand it? Manoussos realised that they had built up a magnificent romance on a foundation of lies. He felt destroyed by her deceit and, even worse, devastated that she might have had a hand in the death of her husband.

His position was untenable, he raged with despair. He gripped her harder in his arms and rolled them both over until he was on top of her, reached out and switched on the bedside lamp. The room sprang to life. He very nearly gasped. He wanted her to be ugly, twisted with immorality

222

and deceit. Instead she was radiantly beautiful, the sensuously erotic *femme fatale*-innocent child that tweaked his heart strings, sent an arrow straight to his lustful soul. She threw her arms back over her head and ran her fingers through her hair. It spread out across the pillows like a seductive, sensual fan, framing her face. His heart raced. Her eyes bored into him, spoke to him from her heart of her own lust and love for him.

He pulled her roughly from the pillows to crush her in his arms. Violent kisses, teeming with out-of-control passion, desperation. He sucked on her tongue and bit hard into her lips until he could taste a trickle of warm sweet blood. He could feel the tears smarting in his eyes, trickling down his cheeks. She led him on with her own lust, her own kisses, Chadwick bit into his flesh. Without uttering a word, she was begging for more of him, his lust, telling him she was there to receive him, all he was, all he was not, all he would ever be. While still lost in their kisses, he pulled a long white silk scarf she had had tied around her waist earlier in the evening from the table next to the bed and tied her wrists to the headboard of the bed.

She had come several times before he moved from her lips and her mouth to her breasts. Chadwick was not a quiet lover, she had the passion and lack of inhibitions that allowed her the freedom to express her feelings; expressions that had a tremendous raunchy appeal for her lovers, appeared to drive them on into sexual frenzy. There was sexual rage in Manoussos's fucking, and passion, and desperate love. Chadwick had experienced such lust for her before, innumerable times with Hannibal, several times with Manoussos; that was how she'd learned to understand it, make the most of it, extract the thrill of such fucking and use it for her own pleasure, her own inner rage and lust for the men in her life and sex unbound.

Manoussos was like a man possessed, he could not stop. The sex for them had always been, right from their first sexual encounter, thrilling, over-the-edge-of-reason sex, but this ... this was something else. They had died several deaths in orgasm and he would willingly have died the lasting death for the ecstasy that had been theirs. As he beat to a magnificent pace into Chadwick, while lost in the glory of this woman he loved beyond life itself, he was more alive than he had ever been at any time in his entire life. The sun was high in the sky when exhaustion finally took the lovers over. He only just managed to say, 'I love you, Chadwick,' before he fell asleep.

Manoussos stood over Chadwick for several minutes and watched her as she slept, not wanting to wake her but wanting to have one last look at her before he left the house. Ever so carefully he removed the thin white quilt covering her naked body. She lay as if she were a most gloriously refined and beautiful tossed down rag-doll: legs and arms all askew. Even in her sleep she appeared as a wanton seductress. Her body was so smooth and perfect, as if it had been hewn from cream-coloured alabaster in its every firm and fleshy curve: voluptuous for the full breasts, one of which had a violet-blue bruise upon it; a hip bore the marks of his fingers, lustrous in the morning light. He felt no shame for the tracks on her body, the silk scarf dangling loosely from the headboard of the bed. Indeed maybe he even felt a little pride, for the passion of his lovemaking and because he had never hurt her when he might have for her deceit.

He lowered his head to place his lips upon her bruised breast in a kiss and used his tongue to lick her nipple. She stirred. He pulled back. She didn't wake. Hers was a deep sleep, the sleep of an innocent child in the body of a libertine. Once more he lowered his head but this time to place his face upon her mound. He used his fingers delicately to part those more intimate of her lips and licked her cunt with pointed tongue and used his lips in a quick kiss. She moaned with pleasure but never climbed out of her dreams. He covered her once more with the quilt and walked noiselessly from the room.

Manoussos walked down to the port, aware of the warmth of the day, the scent of spring in the air. How blue and clear was the sky, the colour of the sea, how calm. On the cobblestones only a few feet in front of him, a light, warm breeze was playing with a crunched up ball of paper. It danced away, turned and tumbled down the steep steps to its own music, a delicate scratching sound. He felt suddenly more aware of every nuance of life than he had been for a very long time. It was as if his very existence depended on his not missing a single thing. He had no idea what had really happened to him deep down in the very core of his soul in the hours he had just spent in lust with Chadwick. Now, walking down to the port, he sensed that he had lost and found himself many times and had come through whole and possibly even a richer man for his sexual extremes with her, his despair in love. He knew what he had to do, what he would do.

Several people greeted him, he even stopped and chatted to Katzakis the grocer and strolled with him for part of the way round the port. All, paradise lazing in the brightness and warmth of the day, seemed as normal today as it had been yesterday, as it had been for all the days before that. Yet for Manoussos it was not. The sight of Larry Snell alone at a table on the edge of the quay having his breakfast in the sun was tangible proof of that.

He stopped a small boy passing him at a run by grabbing his arm and asked him to go to the coffee house and tell Phillipos the chief wanted his usual breakfast but with two orders of ham. He patted the child affectionately on the top of his head and the boy took off as fast as his feet would carry him. Manoussos picked up a wooden chair and walked towards Larry Snell.

Larry stood up as Manoussos placed his chair at the table. 'Do you mind?' he asked.

The two men shook hands and both sat down. 'How about some breakfast? asked Larry.

'I've ordered some. You seem to be doing all right. Not here even twenty-four hours and you've managed to find the best breakfast in Livakia. You continue, don't let those eggs get cold.'

'You know what it's like when you're working in the field. The first thing you suss out is where to eat, a safe place to sleep, the women. Once those priorities are in place, the work takes over.'

Manoussos reached into the bread basket. He broke the piece of coarse white bread in half and scraped some butter from the plate with the end of it then dipped it in the bowl of honey and popped it in his mouth. 'Oh, that's good, just what I needed. I don't know whether to ask how you found the accommodation at Christina's or was Astrid as delicious as ever?'

'Ah! You've been there, done that. Delicious, imaginative, fun. Elefherakis is a most unusual host.'

'Max will want details.'

'That doesn't mean he's going to get them from me.'

Manoussos began to laugh. 'He will, you know.'

Larry Snell liked Manoussos Stavrolakis and was much relieved to hear his laughter. It had a genuine ring to it and he sensed the man had come to terms with the inevitable realisation that his Chadwick and Larry's were one and the same woman. Larry handed him another piece of bread. This time he had spread butter on it and a thick slice of ham.

'Larry, I want to talk to you about Chadwick. There are things I have to know.'

'You're sure about this?'

'It doesn't seem to be a matter of choice any longer.'

Just then Phillipos arrived with a row of white plates balanced on his arm, a small boy carrying a large coffee pot and a cup and saucer running behind him: Manoussos's breakfast. Phillipos served the chief of police, sat down and poured the coffee, and while Manoussos cut into the perfectly fried eggs the man posed several questions to him. Some ten minutes later, satisfied with the answers, he left the two men to finish their breakfast.

Larry had been grateful for the distraction. He was curious as to what had changed Manoussos's mind that he now so readily accepted Chadwick had been deceiving him. He had almost asked him but that ten-minute interruption by Phillipos gave him time to think it over. Now he knew that he would not.

'Tell me some of the things people have said about Chadwick's character, Larry?' asked Manoussos.

227

A shrewd question for a policeman but not for a lover, thought Larry, who was aware that Manoussos was trying to build up a profile of Chadwick Chase, to see if she had the psychological make-up of a killer – the very same thing he himself was doing since there was no evidence to prove that she was.

'Diana, Hannibal's daughter, now believes that Chadwick had a native sassiness which she replaced with an acquired innocence. Before Hannibal's death she had never thought of Chadwick as having been cunning rather than intelligent, deceiving everyone by appearing to be naive about people as well as life in general. When she admitted that to me and that she had in fact thought quite the opposite until her father's sudden death, the will, Chadwick's strange behaviour subsequent to Hannibal's demise, I confronted her with her appraisal of Chadwick. I suggested to her that in the milieu Hannibal had thrust Chadwick into as a child of twelve and had kept her in until his death, her behaviour was rather a sign of someone brought up in wealth: only rich women are sheltered; only the overprotected ones unworldly, or in Chadwick's case allowed to be worldly only on Hannibal's terms. Maybe she had been right not to believe those things about Chadwick, and conceivably she was wrong now.'

'How did she take that?'

'Not very well at all.'

Larry wanted to ask Manoussos if he thought Diana's assessment was correct. He hesitated, and thought better of asking anything about the private life of the police chief and Chadwick; he had after all been asked not to. He would wait for things to develop.

He continued, 'Now Diana's husband, Bill Ogden, he

champions Chadwick. He thinks that she is the most brilliant orchestrator of image – a shrewd politician. He believes that Hannibal taught her those things, throughout her life, and to become a key participant in shaping the Hannibal Chase myth and securing a place in it for herself. He sees her as a perfectionist who knows exactly who she is and what she wants. And he believes that what she wanted was to be all things first and foremost to herself and then Hannibal. He believes that Hannibal and Chadwick loved each other unconditionally, that they could deny each other nothing because they were each of them living on borrowed time: he would have died in that crash had she not saved him and she would have died in the backwoods of Tennessee had he not saved her by never hesitating a minute to liberate her from the miserable and unhappy life she was leading there. They breathed new life into each other and never stopped until Hannibal took his last breath.'

'Did Chadwick tell Bill Ogden that?'

'Not in so many words. But Bill and Chadwick were good friends and they did talk and he had seen the way she was with her husband and her family. She was formidable, so was Hannibal, so was their marriage, but Bill Ogden – not being one of Hannibal's children except in law – was able to accept that there was a secret side to their marriage, something dark that they made light of and lived out. He sometimes thought it made Chadwick unhappy but she never gave him any proof of that. "She keeps her secrets," he told me. "They are in a strange way her life, her very private life, which she will never give up. If she had a hand in Hannibal's death she will never tell us, we will never find out, because Hannibal didn't want us to know."'

'Hannibal Chase? From all you told me about him and his relationship with the child he saved, how he groomed her to be his wife, the life they led, one minute I can get a grip on the character of the man, the next I lose it because I can't equate him with the man Chadwick described as her husband. It wasn't easy for me to face but I have: Chadwick has been deceiving me ever since that first day we met. It's been one lie after another. What is it about me that made her feel she had to do that? Was it out of a sense of guilt because she did have a hand in his death that she had to make up a fictitious life and husband for me to believe in? If not then what was it about Hannibal Chase that made her do that? These are haunting questions which will not leave me and will drive me away from the Chadwick I know and love because she was never really there.'

For several minutes the two men remained silent. Larry wanted to kick himself for having revealed the story of Chadwick and Hannibal to Manoussos without realising she was his woman, that they were in love. Had he been aware of that he would have handled the entire affair differently but now it was too late, there was no turning back.

'I have a theory.'

'As to whether Chadwick had a hand in Hannibal's death?'

'Yes.'

Larry watched Manoussos pale visibly. Here was a sharp and dedicated police officer. In love or not, he could not close his eyes or run away from the facts: he had been deceived, and there was a strong possibility that his lover was a criminal. Manoussos Stavrolakis, a man in love, was giving way to the man burned by lies, the Cretan, and not least, the detective.

'Well?' There was resignation in his voice when he uttered that one word but there was too a coldness in his eyes, a hardness in the expression on his face.

'I want your word that if I take you into my confidence you will consider whatever you learn from me to be out of your jurisdiction *vis à vis* the law? I have an obligation to the clients who have hired me to keep this a private matter. Unless I felt that it was safe to ask for your help, which I did because of what Colin had told me about you, I would never have been as indiscreet as I have been. Do I have your word?'

Larry picked up a moment of hesitation before Manoussos answered. 'Yes, you have my word. Look, Larry, for you it's business, for me it's private. My life with Chadwick is fast going down the tubes. I'm going to try and save it. Anything you can tell me might help.'

Larry pulled the pack of cigarettes from his pocket and, licking the end of one, placed it in his mouth and lit it. He took several draws on the cigarette. Then he spoke. 'OK, let me give you my impression of Hannibal. He was a very vital kind of man, handsome, conservative, a moral creature who fell in love with an unusually seductive child who saved his life. For the rest of his life he would suffer guilt for that, compounded by his lusting after her. But he was also a man who understood a great many things about himself and life in general. The entire foundation of his life was based on existentialist thinking: man is free and responsible only if he lives his reality and it never becomes mere thought. And what happens to Hannibal? He is saved by an extraordinary child who is by her very nature living out her life by the philosophy he is struggling to follow. He already knows by the time they meet that you learn whatever you can from every relationship – but that most aren't meant to last a lifetime and so you keep looking for one. There was nothing for it: once he and Chadwick saved each other, they were bound together and so he groomed her to last his lifetime. By all accounts that suited her very well. So they lived together in a good deal of mystery.

'Hannibal was an aristocrat in every sense of the word. But aristocrats are no more virtuous than ordinary people – what they have above all is courage, and after that taste and responsibility and a hell of a lot of endurance. He had those things in spades. Chadwick, backwoods white trash, had smidgeons of those traits when he met her. They overwhelmed him and he cultivated them in her for her and for himself. Of course he saw something else in her, that same thing you fell in love with and I find so seductive about her, what many men when they see Chadwick fall in love with: the image that is a mere thirty percent of the package. It's the other seventy percent, something much deeper than her astonishingly sensuous beauty, that sends men off the deep end.

'Hannibal's son Warren was his father's best friend and confidant and was close to Chadwick from the very first day Hannibal brought her home. He refused to reveal anything about their very private life but sent me on to a woman who did know about it. She was the woman Hannibal had hired to educate Chadwick sexually. Now *she* was fascinating and gave me a picture of them and their life together that explains a great deal.

'She saw them both, even though there was that vast difference in age between them, as equally matched sexually. Strong libido, sensuous, adventurous in sexual desire ... that was Hannibal Chase, and what he craved in his women. Lilana de Chernier taught Chadwick at the age of seventeen to understand and experience the thrill of those things and enjoy fully the ecstasy that can result from them. She groomed Chadwick to be a sexually free woman, and Hannibal, who had a profound depravity and a sexually deviant world he liked on occasion to dwell in, when Chadwick seduced him, was only too thrilled to find she had been taught how to luxuriate in his pleasures.

'Lilana says that Hannibal was a closet sybarite, one of those urbane and cynical people with an aversion to the strenuous and boring. He tried to compensate for being one through his philanthropic work, but was one nevertheless and pandered to his perversions. He considered that a flaw in his character, like his sexual libertinism, until he met and fell in lust and love with Chadwick. Whatever defects he had, he didn't have to hide them from her. She embraced them. She loved him totally and could accept and, yes, even revel in those things with him, which she did. They were a great part of their life together and became their secrets, their very private world. Even so, his demons did periodically cause him anxiety that made him sadistic in some ways to Chadwick. A guess made by Lilana and Bill Ogden. Only Chadwick will know if it's true.

'Lilana de Chernier knew them both very well. We know that kind of very special beauty Chadwick has. Well, she says that Hannibal worked on honing that beauty and taught Chadwick how to do the same from the moment he laid eyes on her. She believes that their relationship was indestructible, simple for Chadwick but complex for Hannibal. It was love and lust, total trust, loyalty that bound them together. Chadwick's beauty, her soul, was for him a moment of respite – redemption – for which he was constantly looking. He had in the past through beauty – a woman, a piece of art, a flower, a garden – found it, but very nearly as soon as it was found, like a breath it would evaporate. These were only signs of redemption and nothing more. But then Chadwick came into his life and here was beauty once found that stayed. He was redeemed, they were complete.

'Manoussos, we're not talking here of big egos and weak identities. Chadwick and Hannibal were both big egos with strong identities, two people who would lay down their lives for each other and did when they married, and I believe did once more when Hannibal died. My theory is that he died for *them*, not for him nor for her but for *them*. I don't quite know why. If Chadwick had a hand in it, it was not for money or power or to be rid of Hannibal Chase but because he asked her to.'

'But you have nothing to back up that theory?'

'Not yet.'

'But you expect to find something?'

'The more I learn about Chadwick, the more I believe there will never be evidence to prove my theory. Only Chadwick can tell us what really happened the night her husband died. Will she? Never to satisfy the family. Possibly for love, her love for you. But I wouldn't bank on that. That does not, however, mean that I won't confront her with what I know and ask her to tell me the truth about the death of Hannibal Chase. When and if I do challenge her it will be because it's my last shot at solving this case.'

'I hear everything you're telling me, I understand it and

still I have a problem believing that Chadwick, the Chadwick I wanted to make my wife, is no more than a fantasy produced for my benefit to fuck and love. Betrayal, deceit – for me! Why did she never deliver those same blows to Hannibal? What happened to love and lust, trust and loyalty for me? Those are burning questions.

'A fool in love, that's me, and that's why I closed my eyes and my ears. Right from the beginning I sensed danger, inconsistencies between her behaviour and how she portrayed herself. I realised she was a woman who kept her secrets. I had neither the need nor the desire to pry them from her. I did in fact respect her, love her, even more for those secrets, that life she lived for herself alone, that made her so enigmatic. Even now, if only she hadn't lied to me, I would have no reason or desire to demand an explanation. But unfortunately she *has* lied and betrayed my love and trust. There is little I can do but confront her with it. That's the situation you're in if you want to complete your investigation, and I'm in if I want the woman I love.'

'Why don't you just leave it alone, Manoussos? That is an option, you know.'

'No more for me than it is for you. Only in my case love, Cretan pride, sexual passion, demand to be assuaged.'

It was Larry who saw Chadwick approaching the table first. She was wearing a pair of wide navy blue linen trousers that moved seductively with every step she took; a white linen shirt that tied at her waist and had full, drop-shouldered sleeves buttoning tight to her wrists; a deep purple suede waistcoat. He was somehow mesmerised by the way her white sneakers kept popping out from under the trouser legs and would vanish again behind the blue linen, the sway of her hips. There was a fiery intimacy about her and yet a cool seductive beauty that made him want to lick his lips.

He only said what he did to Manoussos because he could not help himself. 'Men have jumped off cliffs for far less than the loss of love for a woman like Chadwick, who is as I speak approaching us. You're right, she is dangerous, but I would walk through fire to have what Hannibal had with her, what you do now, lies, deceit and all. Whatever you do, my newfound friend, think about it again before you do it.'

Manoussos turned in his chair. There seemed an extra special bloom about Chadwick's beauty this morning. It wrapped itself around him and almost broke his heart in two. He had thought she was his, they were each other's life for eternity. He loved her, he was possessed by her, he would give her another chance to make it right for them, to curtail the lies that they had built a life together on. If they were standing now on no more than a rickety foundation that was already toppling them over, then what hope was there for their survival in the future unless she made things right? He rose from his chair and walked the short distance separating them to place an arm round her shoulders and escort her back to the table.

Manoussos watched Larry and Chadwick from the window of his office for several minutes after he arrived there. He had ordered breakfast for her and, after suggesting she show Larry around the village and take him for a walk to the church in the cliffs and have a picnic there, had left them. He had wanted to confront her right then and there about the false persona she had created for herself but he had been frankly disarmed from doing so by her mere appearance. His love for her, memory of their sexual idyll the night before, had knocked him once more off kilter.

Mercifully he was called away from the window by an urgent phone call and then his day took off: there were signs that the art smugglers were on the move. He was momentarily relieved from the torture of loving her.

Two hours later, he and Dimitrios were climbing up through the village to the cave where he kept his World War II American jeep, and a message had been left in the hands of a boy who was to find Chadwick and deliver it to her. It told her where he was and that she should not expect him back that night. In fact he did not return until three days after he had left Livakia. And when he did it was in triumph. The operation had worked and he had snagged his smugglers.

Chapter 11

'Islands have a special kind of magic. I've been to many, in all parts of the world, but none has ever had the magic for me that the Greek islands do, and most particularly Patmos and Crete, especially on a hot day in early-spring, with a goddess by my side.'

Larry and Chadwick had been to the church and after that had found the remnants of an old goat track and followed it further up the cliff until they came to a natural formation that was, if not level, than graded enough to allow them to sit down and have their picnic. When he said those words they were sitting close together, catching their breath from the steep climb and shielding their eyes with hands placed like visors to their foreheads, gazing out across the sea. The blue of the sky was a blaze of white sunlight, the sea another kind of blue. Between them a nothingness that was ethereal and broken only by the jagged coastline of buff-coloured cliffs that lay upon the water like a ribbon fluttered down from the sky by some god who had felt generous and declared as he dropped it, 'Here's something for you mere mortals, a bit of paradise to live and love by.'

Larry began to laugh. Chadwick reached out and touched him and asked, 'Tell me, tell me.'

He raised her hand from his thigh and kissed it before he told her what he thought the gods had said and how Crete came into being.

'Larry Snell, you are a romantic, a pleasure seeker like we foreigners in Livakia, only I do believe you didn't know that until just now,' she teased.

As they spoke they stopped looking at the sea to gaze at each other and he was undone by his desire to take her in his arms. Reticent, he instead removed the cricket sweater he had tied around his waist and pulled his white shirt out from under the belt of his cricket whites, all the clothes he had brought with him other than the suit and Burberry he had arrived in from London. He undid the buttons on his cuffs and was rolling up his sleeves, and still they remained gazing into each other's eyes. He was hot from the heat of the sun, and exertion from the climb, but that was nothing to the heat that came with the fever of lust he had contracted for Chadwick.

Chadwick recognised his desire for her, how over-powering it was. She liked him for that, and because he was holding back from making an embarrassing move on her. She liked his fever for her. She had right from the first found him sexually attractive, and now in this deserted and most glorious and private place she wanted to show him how much she appreciated his body and acknowledged the chemistry going on between them. She leaned forward and removed her sneakers then shrugged out of her trousers, removed her waistcoat and lastly her shirt and lay down on her side, facing the now naked and reclining Larry Snell.

She was glorious in her nakedness, like every odalisque

that Ingres ever painted. She was Goya's Naked Maja, she was Hannibal's Chadwick, Manoussos's love, she was her own best creation that dazzled such men as they. Larry was burning with desire for her. It was sexual but it was much more than sexual and therein lay the danger.

She reached out and took his hand in hers, raised it to her lips and kissed it. 'I like your body, Larry, I like your sexiness, and I like your being in a fever for me.'

She edged closer to him and he placed a hand on the curve of her breast and ran it down over the contours of her body. She kissed his nipples and sucked on them; she ran her tongue over his skin and caressed him. He was erect and for Chadwick that was an added thing of beauty to be caressed, like the inside of his thighs, his legs, his feet. She kissed him now for the first time on his lips and licked them, but her kisses were filled with affection and admiration rather than passion and lust. She wrapped her arms around him and gently rolled him over on to his stomach and caressed him everywhere with lips and tongue and hands. No woman had ever seduced him as Chadwick was doing, no woman had ever been as adventurous with his body as she was.

There had been many women in Larry Snell's life: love affairs, one night stands, hookers from the most expensive down to the cheapest street walker, a divorced wife and at present a mistress, but none had ever made him feel as Chadwick Chase did — as if flayed, every nerve end exposed for her to enjoy. His heart raced. He wanted her to do whatever she wanted with him; to please her was to live at the top of life in thrilling excitement. Her wish was his every command.

She whispered in his ear, 'It's here and now for us, a moment of pure pleasure. My heart tells me this is all we are and will ever be and it's the best we can do.'

Larry knew she was right. He turned over and very gently laid her down on her back and made love to her, as she had him, with caresses and kisses. She came and came again, unashamed at the extent of the pleasure she derived from his adoration of her. Theirs was a celebration of unrequited lust and love. What might have been if they had been two different people in a different place at a different time in their lives? She had seduced him forever by what they had never had together. He could live with that and in gratitude for what she did deign to give him.

Naked, they lay side by side, holding hands, their faces up to the sun, bathing in the heat and the light for some time before Chadwick, after squeezing his hand and placing a quick kiss upon his cheek, began to dress. Larry watched her and understood for the first time what Chadwick's real power was over men. The obvious sensuality, beauty and grace which she possessed in abundance were invitations to men to meditate on themselves and their desires. A man alert for any sign of those things who found them in Chadwick was offered every joy and awakened at all moments to a news that is always arriving out of the silence of the soul. That was what Chadwick had in plenty: a deep silence of the soul that most human beings seek and never find.

Chadwick had sensed Larry had been seeking that which he had had no idea he was looking for until he was seduced by her into facing himself. Chadwick was master of her own bliss, a chemist of her own joy. She had all sorts of remedies at hand to elevate herself. She knew how to cheer herself, illuminate and inspire every breath she took, every movement she made. She was, and always would be, a spiritual practitioner: a person who lived in the presence of her own true self. Somehow she had found the springs and sources of profound inspiration and was able to use them continually while living truth passionately and that was what Hannibal recognised in her from that very first moment she spoke to him, what he had been seeking all his life. Having found it in her, he could never let her go. She existed apart from, not subject to, limitations. No wonder she was every man's dream. Discovering those things about Chadwick was a revelation for Larry.

They had their picnic there on the cliffs and talked about her life in Livakia, the people who had become her friends. Her sense of humour, like everything else about Chadwick Chase, was infectious and Larry found himself able to amuse her with his insights into the people he had met since his arrival. He skirted around talking about Manoussos and her love affair with him. She volunteered nothing. It was just as well because for the moment he was experiencing her and the magical place she had brought him to to the fullest, and wanted not to have to share it with even the thought of a man she loved more than him. Finally she rose from the stony ground and he followed.

They stood next to each other and gazed for several minutes in silence across the sea. Off in the distance they saw a speck of white, a sailing boat they assumed. 'I should warn you, the descent is more dangerous than the climb.'

He was certain Chadwick did not know that she had delivered a double entendre, but she had. She was speaking about making their way down the goat track to the church clinging to the cliffside and from there down the narrow footpath to the village. He understood what she meant *and* that he had to climb down from the few hours she had allowed him to love her.

'One kiss, a kiss to die by,' was what he asked for as he took her in his arms. Briefly she lost her composure. A shadow of sorts seemed to cross her face – fright? – as if someone had walked over her grave, and then it vanished as quickly as it had appeared. It was at that moment that Larry had the answer to the question haunting Diana and Warren, that burning question that had brought him to Livakia, that was destroying Manoussos's love for Chadwick. She did have something to do with Hannibal's death, he was certain of that now. He was neither shocked nor disappointed, merely accepting of what he believed. 'One kiss, a kiss to die by.' Had he imagined that momentary reaction of hers to his words? Had those been the very last words that Hannibal had said to Chadwick? Larry kissed her.

It was a long and sensuous kiss like no other he had ever had from any woman. It was an amorous kiss, as erotic as hell, but was at the same time the most pure of kisses, filled with affection and something as enigmatic as Chadwick herself. It was true; with one kiss from a woman such as Chadwick, death might come easier.

Larry stroked her hair, and she smiled at him and took his hand. 'A few hours like these we have just passed here on the cliffs under a Greek sun, above a Greek sea, on a magical spring day ... they're an experience to remember. I never take for granted such happenings,' she told him, and he understood they would never be together like this again.

Several hours later it was once again the long table at the Kavouria where Mark was presiding and Astrid was trying to rekindle a long-dead romance with Elefherakis, Rachel was flirting with Larry, and Max and D'Arcy, sitting on either side of Chadwick, were laughing about the many celebrities who had come, and gone from Livakia, at first being swept up by the place – the lifestyle, the people, sexual liaisons – and then running away. Terrified! The simple life of facing oneself alone with the sun and the sea, a night sky of white moon and winking stars, nature above the mayhem of another kind of life. Heady stuff, things that dreams are made of, and for some, too high a price to pay, the giving up of fame and applause.

Larry did not miss Chadwick's remark: 'I think the tragedy of my life would be if I had to move on from Manoussos and Livakia.'

'Are you so completely happy here, Chadwick?' Larry heard himself asking.

'Oh, yes.' There was no hesitation in her voice.

'Well, Manoussos will be glad to hear that, and so am I,' said D'Arcy.

Chadwick had found her place, her man, and tragedy was about to strike. Had Larry Snell not passed the day with her, had what had passed between them never happened on the cliffside, he might have been able to live with his infatuation with Chadwick, put in his report, and walk away from Livakia, leaving her to sort out her relationship with Manoussos. But the worst possible thing that can happen to a detective had happened to him: he cared about the subject of his investigation, he wanted to help and protect her. He wanted her never to have the tragedy of losing her place in the sun, the love that she now lived for. He would have to warn her of the vulnerable position she had put herself in *vis à vis* the family, *vis à vis* Manoussos.

Larry had earned his reputation for fieldwork. He had been in Livakia for forty-eight hours and had the measure of the place and the people, the lifestyle. He was more aware than ever that if he were to approach Chadwick in the hope of helping her, he had to be more than discreet, as she would have to be, to avoid suspicion of her real problems becoming public knowledge.

When he saw Max, D'Arcy and Chadwick rise from the table to leave, he went to her and asked, 'May I call on you in the morning?'

'That would be very nice but I'm flying off for the day with D'Arcy and Max. We'll be back by dark. See you here at dinner time.'

Larry watched Chadwick walk away. Rachel went to him and told him, 'I'll write a poem about her one day. She's the kind of woman that inspires all sorts of things in people. You want to make love to her.'

Larry turned to face Rachel. She smiled at him and continued, 'I can understand that, there's not a man in Livakia that doesn't want to have sex with Chadwick, and more than a few women if they were honest with themselves. I know I would, but I won't, wouldn't even think of making a pass at her. I'm not *very* clever, *chéri*, but smart enough to know that Chadwick's erotic life is only practised with whom she chooses, when she wants.

She calls the shots only she is clever enough to make men believe they do, that it's they who are seducing her. In that we are the same, Chadwick and I, except of course I never let love govern my sex life the way she does and you don't.'

Larry laughed and a smile crossed Rachel's lips. He had a penchant for frivolous pretty French girls, and ones with a sense of humour were rare. She distracted him from all thoughts of his work and dangerous infatuation with Chadwick. 'Are you making a pass at me, Rachel?'

'*Bien entendu*, are you not flattered?'

'Let's go then,' he told her, taking her arm.

He hated her room, the prissiness of it. She kept it neat and clean except for her dressing table which was like the cosmetics counter at Harrod's. Evidence of her vanity was everywhere: chiffon and silk scarves draped over chairs and lampshades, silk flowers attached to combs, wigs, dresses and swimsuits; tiny things, hung on wire hangers over curtain rails and from architraves. The carpet was strewn with shoes standing neatly together in pairs. The made-up bed had her nightdress, a diaphanous confection with satin ribbons, lying neatly across it. There was a decided absence of books and pencils and pens, the desk that one would have expected from any aspiring poetess.

Rachel had a sexual hunger that she covered very well with sexual teasing; an elaborate charade of unwillingness to submit to sex was the game she liked to play. It amused Larry but only to a point. She had the big breasts and tiny waist he liked, and all those creams and oils she enriched her skin with gave her a soft and smooth lustre he enjoyed, as he did her rounded and full bottom, so he played her game. Sex with Rachel was like following traffic signals: it's a green light, it's a red light, take a left, turn right, shift gears into high speed.

She was, as a body, a delicious fuck and so he gagged her with one of her chiffon scarves long enough to tell her that if she gave him one more sexual instruction he would tie her up and leave her there. When he removed the scarf she spluttered and coughed but never said another word to him until it was goodbye at half-past eleven the next morning.

Larry spent most of the remainder of the day asleep in the room he had rented in Christina's house. Walking down to the port in the late-afternoon he was amused at the thought of how he had flourished sexually since his arrival in Livakia: a sexual adventure with Elefherakis and Astrid, the bliss of a sensual day with Chadwick, and who would have expected Rachel to turn out to be such a firecracker between the sheets? But it was more than just the hot sex flourishing in Livakia that suited him. He liked the privacy and freedom that existed, the discretion that governed everyone's actions. It was somehow respectful of their community, their own self-esteem, this paradise they had landed in, and not least the mythical gods of Greece. No one liked to offend the gods and neither did he.

As the heat of the day ate into his bones, and he sat in the near deserted port where only a few fishermen were repairing nets, Katzakis the grocer was having a bottle of wine and reading the paper and there was not another foreigner about, Larry worked out how to close his investigation. Fortunately Alexandra, one of the cooks at the Kavouria, was still there and agreed to cook him some fresh fish caught only minutes before from the sea, reheat the rabbit *stiffado*, and allow him to fill his plate from several cooking pots simmering on the stove.

After his meal, he remained seated at the table set at the edge of the quay, reviewing the lives of the people involved in his investigation and considered how and if his findings would affect them. That was not his problem, and he was amazed to think that he had almost made it his dilemma. He was relieved that the professional in Larry Snell had won through.

That was not to say that the Hannibal Chase case had not changed his life, for it was doing just that. The love affair between Hannibal and Chadwick was a story that had opened his eyes to his own love relationships, his own sexual desires, his own ability to live in the moment. But more particularly it was Chadwick Chase, the glorious enigmatic Chadwick, whom he had, over the months of investigation, become infatuated with, and on finally meeting, fallen in love with. She was the real catalyst that was changing his life. She had shown him, that unlike her, he *thought* about living more than *living* without thought. He pondered as to when it was he had lost the courage that Chadwick had, to live life to the fullest and for the moment.

She had been right about him: he was a pleasure seeker like her, like her friends, only he had never understood that he was. He had come in search of her and found more than just Chadwick. Like the men whom she allowed to love her, Hannibal and Manoussos, and those many others who had crossed her path and wanted to love her, he had crashed out of his unfulfilled life on the rocks as he swam to her siren's song. Larry had at last cracked the riddle of Chadwick Chase: with her it was live *or* die in every sense of those words. She gave everything, she made men give everything. Her courage in living in the knowledge of that truth was admirable, so had Hannibal's been, and now so would his.

His first thought about Manoussos and what he was going to do about Chadwick was when Larry was halfway up the stairs to the police chief's office. Manoussos and Chadwick had a great deal to lose but he somehow had no fear for them. Each of them would do what they had to and get on with their life. He greeted the young officer left in charge and explained that he was there to use the fax and the telephone, demanded privacy, and got it. The young man was following instructions Manoussos had left to give Larry Snell every co-operation.

He was three hours typing out faxes, having conversations with his partner and Andrew Coggs, Junior and Senior, the Chase children and Bill Ogden. It was dark when he left the office and strolled into a port alive with lamplight and people, the smell of roasting meat and rosemary. The Kavouria was crowded with diners. Larry caught a glimpse of Chadwick sitting at a table with a dozen or so people. He went into Katzakis's shop and bought a bottle of whisky and went back to his room. He was drunk and asleep before midnight.

In the morning he woke early and, miraculously, without the slightest trace of a hangover. He felt marvellous and hummed a tune while he bathed and dressed, forgoing his cricket whites for his pinstripe double-breasted suit which he wore with the jacket unbuttoned, a clean white shirt open at the collar. But old habits die hard. He folded his tie neatly and placed it in his jacket pocket. His first stop was Rachel's room. She was, of course, fast asleep and tried to send him away. He would not be put off.

Larry sat on the end of her bed, lit a cigarette and watched her as she filled a coffee pot and placed it on an electric ring. He was quite riveted as she transformed herself at the dressing table into the pretty and amusing thing he had dallied with and one day hoped to dally with again.

Their eyes met in the mirror and it caused her to swivel round and face him. 'You're not falling in love with me, I hope?' she asked with a tone of pity for him in her voice.

'Why so worried? Because if I did it might interfere with your ambitions to be a great poet?'

'Precisely!'

'Ah, now that's what I want to talk to you about.'

'Poetry or love?'

'A little of both. The other night you were terrific, a very sexy lady, and I hope we can do that again some time, maybe even often – if it happens, it happens – and no, I'm not in love with you. I've come to say goodbye. I'll be leaving here in the next few days, and I wanted it to be a private goodbye since so much of life in Livakia is public.'

'I'm sorry you're leaving, Larry. Surprised. I thought you slipped into the life of Livakia so well that you would have been one of the people who might settle here. About the other night ... more of that would have been nice for me too, but you do understand about the poetry? I will win out on that score.'

'I have every hope that you will, Rachel. You were right about me and Livakia, I will settle here. It will take some time to accomplish that but before I leave I intend to ask Manoussos and Max to look out for a property for me. I mean to tell them that as long as you are respectful of it, and, if you should wish to, you may live in it until my return. I do understand about your burning desire to write, enough to want to give you two years to study at either Oxford or the Sorbonne, any place in fact that you can get on an excellent writing course. I'll be your patron, pay all your expenses, school fees, living expenses, and before you ask, you are under no obligation to me – and I mean that – not in any way.'

Rachel was overcome by this unexpected turn of events in her life. She paled and then after several seconds, when she was able to compose herself, in a voice cracking with more emotion than she had shown during their hours of lust together, she asked, 'Why are you doing this, Larry?'

'Because I can,' was the only answer he could give her.

After he had left a neatly typed out list of addresses and telephone numbers as to where he could be reached and a cheque for several hundred pounds, they parted on Rachel's words, 'They say you never lose the friends you make in Greece.' He found that to be a charming thank you, especially so because he hadn't been looking for one, nor expected the self-absorbed Rachel to issue one.

In the port there was an air of excitement, men talking in groups, some with a newspaper in their hand. Everyone seemed to be full of smiles and walking that little bit taller, the Cretan stride a good deal longer, heads held higher with ever more pride and arrogance. Larry approached a table where Max was having his breakfast with

Katzakis the grocer, the baker, and Elefherakis. 'What's all the excitement?'

'Manoussos has pulled it off, busted an international art-smuggling ring. Arrested them with the goods just before they were out of Greek territorial waters. It's in all the Greek papers,' Max told him.

Elefherakis continued translating from Greek into English. Larry took a seat, called for the waiter and ordered his breakfast. He listened. It seemed to the experienced Larry to have been a seriously big and dangerous game Manoussos had been playing and he had won out by not only catching his thieves but breaking the smuggling ring right to the top, with named ring leaders in London, Paris and New York. He marvelled at Manoussos Stavrolakis, how he had stalked his prey for months and months from Crete. The trap he had set had been brilliant. How Larry would have liked to have him at Martin & Snell!

'Chadwick, has she heard the news?'

'No one has seen her this morning. I can't believe Manoussos hasn't called her and told her. Will you give her a call and tell her, Larry? I have to rush off on an errand to Chania, a surprise for D'Arcy.'

'I'll do better than that. Tell me how to get to her house and I'll go and tell her and take a newspaper.'

'Great idea.'

Max gave explicit instructions after which Larry asked if he could walk with him round the cliffs to the bay where Max kept his plane. It was during that walk that he asked Max to find him a property to buy in Livakia. They discussed it at length and Larry appreciated Max's enthusiasm over his decision to settle in Livakia. The men shook hands and a new kind of excitement, the reality of his decision, caused Larry a new kind of happiness with himself.

Half an hour later he was knocking at the gate of Edgar Marion and Bill Withers's house where Chadwick was living. He was still breathless from the steep climb and leaning against the white-washed wall surrounding the house when she opened the gate. He wondered as he looked at her standing there, the sun behind her, showing the outline of her body through the cream-coloured silk sarong wrapped around her, if his heart would always race at the sight of her. He thought it would until the end of his days.

'You're a surprise!' she told him with a welcoming smile.

'And very out of breath.'

'Come in,' she laughed, and the sound of bells in her laughter made him adore her even more than he already did, though it did nothing to deter his resolve.

'I've come with the newspapers, they're about Manoussos. Have you heard?'

'He called me at about two in the morning – isn't it thrilling? I should be seeing him in time for a late lunch. He was of course short on the details but clearly thrilled at the success of the operation. It's strange that you should have made the climb to tell me about the capture of those men because Manoussos suggested I see you this morning, spend some time with you before we met. That we get a boat to take us to Sfakia where he will meet us for a celebration feast. You will come?'

Chadwick had her arm through Larry's. They walked up the terraces to a table and chairs where she sat him down. 'You will?' she repeated as she took the paper from his hands and sat opposite him and began reading.

It was several minutes before she realised he had not answered her. She put the paper down and gazed into his eyes. He imagined she had realised that something was not quite right. 'Yes, of course I will. Could I have a drink of something cool and not alcoholic?' he asked.

He could see the relief come into her eyes, the glimmer of a smile cross her lips. She stood up. 'How very stupid of me, of course.'

When she returned it was with a glass jug of iced pomegranate juice, sweetened with honey. It looked incredibly cool and refreshing with sprigs of bright green mint sprouting from the jug. She poured him a glass and placed a plate of slim vanilla wafers in front of him.

Chadwick caught him off guard when she didn't pick up the paper again and asked nothing of what he had heard in the village about the arrest of the smugglers, but instead remarked, 'You have your business suit on. You arrived in that suit and a Burberry slung casually over one shoulder.'

It sounded very nearly like an accusation, at the very least showed that she understood that something was amiss. All he could manage was, 'Yes.'

Chadwick rose from her chair and walked to a retaining wall at the end of the terrace. She sat on its ledge and looked out across the water. It was several minutes before he carried his drink over to the wall and sat down facing her. She had her face tilted up to the sun, her eyes closed. The sarong had opened and one long, tanned leg and a good deal of succulent thigh was exposed. He caressed her knee and she opened her eyes.

'Aren't you going to ask me something?' he pressed.

'What shall I ask you? Larry, why aren't you wearing your cricket whites?'

'Is that all you want to know about me?' he asked, irritated with himself and not even knowing why that was.

'I sense that if I do there will be things I don't particularly want to hear.'

She gently removed his glass from his hand and drank from it. She handed it back to him and he placed it on the wall, stood up, and taking her hand, drew her from the wall to stand in front of him. He ran his fingers through her hair, caressed her naked shoulders and then kissed her full on the lips before he walked with her through the garden to sit with her on a bench under a large spreading fig tree.

'I am the co-owner of a private detective firm called Martin & Snell. We almost never take on domestic cases, we're big and very discreet. Chambers, Lodge, Dewy & Coggs hired us on behalf of their clients Diana Chase Ogden and Warren Chase to investigate you, the life you led with your husband Hannibal and the circumstances of his death, the life you are leading now. I know it all, Chadwick.'

Larry did not know what he had expected but it had been some reaction. There was none. 'Don't you have anything to say?' he asked.

'No.'

'Nothing?'

'What do you want me to say, Larry? That I expected this, yes, expected the children were not ready to give up? That I'm shocked it's you snooping into my private life?

Well, I'm not. You had a job to do, you've done it. You say you know it all. I don't know how true that is or is not, and does it matter anyway? Whatever you know it will not change my life, only Warren's and Diana's, and only then if they allow it to.'

Neither of them spoke for several minutes and then Larry did. He asked, 'Chadwick, I have been on this case for nearly five months. I want to close it and I can't do that without an interview with you. Grant me that interview. Here, now, please?'

'And why should I do that?'

'So I can fill in the missing pieces, close the case, and maybe together we can find a way to get the family off your back once and for all. Unless you do, this thing may haunt you for the rest of your life. Please.'

'Is that why Manoussos asked me to see you this morning?'

'I don't know, I can only suspect so.'

'How much does he know?'

'Everything that I know.'

'That wasn't worthy of you, Larry.'

'I didn't know you even knew each other at the time I told him about the case I was working on, about the woman I was looking for.'

'How long has he known?'

'Since the night of my arrival here in Livakia. He didn't believe you were the same Chadwick Chase I was looking for. He refused to believe it because of the fantasy persona you created for yourself. Then you made an error in your story and he had to believe you were Hannibal Chase's wife.'

'That explains his behaviour the night we spent together before he was called away.'

'I don't want to get involved in your private life with Manoussos, Chadwick, but grant me this interview and maybe we can achieve something that will help you make it right for you and him.'

'You are assuming there is something wrong. Is there something you know that I don't?'

Chadwick's life in Livakia and with Manoussos was crumbling, surely she was not blind to that, and yet she was as centred and calm as if nothing was changing for them. It was Larry who was feeling unnerved, off balance, frightened for her. Recognising that, he put those things aside immediately and rather than answering her, asked, 'Whyever did you lie to him, make up a life that never existed, deny who and what you really are? Did you honestly think he would never find out, that you could keep up this charade? Why the lies, the deceit, for a man who loves you and whom you love and want to build a life with? What were you trying to hide?'

Chadwick, ignoring his questions, told him, 'I'll grant you your interview, Larry, in Sfakia. But now I must go in and change for our voyage. How apt it would be if we sailed out on a boat called the *Discovery*. I think I prefer you in your cricket whites.' Then rising from her seat she walked past him, as beautiful and regal as ever.

Once in the house Chadwick felt suddenly quite queasy. She actually leaned against the wall and closed her eyes for a few minutes. It was Hannibal she was thinking about. Hannibal, her beloved Hannibal, of what seemed now to be a life time ago. What did he and her past life have to do with the new life she wanted to live in

Livakia? And what did he have to do with a new and fresh love, the passion and excitement of a sensual life with a young Greek chief of police? Nothing. Hannibal would have understood that, and why, with his death, she had left him and their life together behind her. He would have applauded her for getting on with her life on her terms and in the manner she had chosen to do it.

She felt less queasy, in fact it had passed, and she took a deep breath. Her feeling of well-being was restored. Cream, yes, she would wear cream-coloured linen. Of all colours, Manoussos liked her best in cream.

Chapter 12

Manoussos was already in Sfakia. He was sitting with a few men at a table close to the water, half a dozen or so other men and boys standing around them. The table was littered with wine bottles, some still with wine in them, glasses, newspapers. Chadwick's heart took a momentary turn at the sight of her handsome lover, sitting in his shirt sleeves and smoking a very large Havana cigar. He looked very happy listening to Dimitrios giving the men an account of the spectacular arrest he had made. She was assuming that that was what had all the men so enthralled because Andonis Lefrakakis's boat was still too far from the beach for them to hear anything.

Chadwick pulled the cord of the fishing boat's horn with one hand while she removed her wide-brimmed straw hat from her head and waved it to announce their arrival. She watched Manoussos at once rise from his chair and wave back at her, a smile breaking across his face. He shook a few hands and began walking along the beach to the rickety wooden dock where he signalled for Andonis to drop anchor.

She turned to Larry. 'Whenever I arrive somewhere on Crete it's always as if for the first time, always an adventure, always a bit of magic for the romantic soul.'

'I know exactly how you feel,' Larry told her.

'Yes, of course you must, or you wouldn't be planning to set down roots in Livakia.'

All the way from Livakia they had spoken about his major decision to buy a house there, of the quality of life he expected to find in Livakia, of the car he would buy, the old fishing *caique* he wanted Andonis to find for him. Every time he made an attempt to talk to Chadwick on any subject pertaining to her she would only answer him with, 'In Sfakia, you will get your interview in Sfakia.' Well, now they were in Sfakia.

Larry watched Manoussos take Chadwick in his arms. They kissed, a long and lingering kiss. He stroked her hair and told her how lovely she looked. He caressed her face several times with the back of his hand and his love for her shone in his eyes. Then quite suddenly that look vanished. There was a decidedly awkward moment of silence before he smiled at Larry and shook his hand. Andonis greeted him with a slap on the back and congratulated him. Larry complimented him with, 'No wonder Colin is always trying to recruit you for Interpol. I would make a try for you for Martin & Snell if I thought there was the remotest chance that you would leave Crete.'

'All very flattering,' Manoussos said. Then turning to Chadwick, he asked, 'Did you bring my things?'

She had brought him a pair of blue jeans, a white linen shirt, his old Panama hat as he had requested. He went to the stern of the boat and changed into them.

When he returned he suggested that they walk along the coastal path which they did until they came to a cafe, nothing more than a thatched lean-to with three tables and several chairs before a spectacular view. They were the only people there and after ordering coffee Manoussos raised Chadwick's hand and kissed it before he asked, 'Have you and Larry sorted things out? Does he have the answers he's looking for, Chadwick?'

'You know, Manoussos, that is one of the very few personal questions you have ever asked me. I take it that you have a vested interest in this much sought-after interview?'

'Well, of course I have, Chadwick.'

'I thought as much, and though I take umbrage at that, that's why I have put off the interview until now.'

There was no anger in Chadwick's tone of voice, nor did Larry think that she had said what she did to embarrass Manoussos. There was none when she declared, 'I want you both to understand that I am not on trial here. The way I see it Larry has a job to do, and you, Manoussos, may be the one being tested here. That said, let's get on with it.'

'Chadwick, all I want is for us to get on with our lives. Deceit, lies, a detective with leading questions, accusations of murder or at the very least strange circumstances surrounding the death of a husband – and not even the fantasy husband I thought you had – and *I* am the one being tested here! What for? Loyalty, love? You have those things from me or I wouldn't be sitting here now. You want to keep them? Answers to Larry's leading questions might help.'

'"Might help" implies something is already lost. How sad for us both that the policeman and the man turn out to be not two separate men but just a policeman who can't follow his heart.'

There was genuine sadness in her voice that could not be missed. This was one of Chadwick's truths that delivered a blow to Manoussos so hard he had to turn his eyes away from her to gaze out to sea. Larry spoke up, began his interview to break the sad silence that can come with dying love.

'Chadwick, what happened the night that Hannibal died?'

'You've read the police report. That is exactly what happened.'

'You both went for a moonlight swim, you found it too cold and so returned to the house. You never saw Hannibal again and his body was washed up on shore two days later. It was more than nine hours before you reported him missing. You claim that you bathed after you came in from the sea and went to your room where you read for a short time before you fell asleep. When you wakened it was morning and Hannibal was nowhere to be found in the house. There were no signs that he had ever returned from his swim. All that I read and know to be true because I checked out every detail of the story. But I don't believe it is the entire story.'

'But you have no proof that it isn't, and I would therefore ask you what you think happened that night?' asked Chadwick.

'Cards on the table? OK. The fact is, Chadwick, that I am a very thorough investigator and it's best that you know what *I* think is based on evidence that I have unearthed. I know more about your life and Hannibal's than any other human being. Certainly more than Warren and Diana know, or Bill Ogden suspects. Though Warren knows a great deal more than he admits even to himself. The poor bastard has spent a lifetime forgetting the lustful and sometimes dark side of a father he adored, admired as a human being, loved as a son, because he is and has always been in love with you.

'What happened that night began a long time ago, when you and Hannibal fell in love and he groomed you to be his life's companion. I have a file full of testimonies to how happy your life was together, what a good wife you were to him, how you took your place in society next to him and won the hearts of everyone who had said your marriage would never last. Your devotion to his children and grandchildren, what a hostess you were. It was far more difficult to find men who would talk about their participation in or knowledge of the sexual and guilty side of Hannibal Chase and how well you learned to live with it, not out of necessity but from love and passion for him. I can thank Lilana de Chernier for putting me in touch with the right people who gave me that very private but important insight into your lives. It wasn't easy to get her to help me, but she wanted your name cleared. You see, it was she who convinced me that in your love for him you could never do anything to harm Hannibal Chase. She also claimed that he loved you too much ever to live with you except at the top of his life. You were each other's prime of life. Only he was sixty-six years old and you were thirty-three.'

Manoussos actually closed his eyes and placed his hands over his face for several seconds. But he was not fast enough for Chadwick not to catch the revulsion in his eyes. It had been the age difference. He was imagining her life with an old man because that was of course how Manoussos would consider Hannibal. She realised only now how weak she had been, how disloyal not to Manoussos but to Hannibal for not telling him her husband had been an old man, though she had not created a new persona for herself for that reason.

'Hannibal Chase was not a man to settle for less than the best of himself, isn't that true, Chadwick?'

'Yes, I think you could say that.'

'He had spent his entire life, ever since the day he took you away from Tennessee, giving you nothing less than the best of himself that he could. That too is true, isn't it, Chadwick?'

'What's your point, Larry?' asked Manoussos, who then snapped his fingers for the proprietor's attention and asked for a bottle of wine.

The break caused by a small boy arriving at the table to clear cups and saucers and run back and forth with glasses and the bottle of wine gave Chadwick a chance to rise from her chair and walk away from the table for a moment of space which she sorely needed. Manoussos joined her and took her hand, stroked her hair, but could find no words. He was angry with her for the life she had lived and lied about, for not being the woman she had portrayed herself as. Yet he was disarmed by her beauty, his own yearning for her hungry, sensual soul. Could she make it right for them?

They returned to the table where Larry had already poured the wine. Manoussos and Larry drank from their glasses, Chadwick left hers untouched.

'Chadwick, I've sieved through the many clues I've collected to reach a conclusion about what happened that night. For a man like Hannibal, when it came to a love such as you had together, if he could not sustain the quality of the life he was living with you, and that love, that lust, he would not want to exist any longer. You told each other everything, so I believe he told you that, and more. That if he, a happy and healthy man in his prime, had the courage to leave you then you must have the courage to be happy for him, kiss him farewell, and get on with a new and fresh life.'

Larry paused but never took his gaze from Chadwick's eyes. He expected some reaction. There was none. If anything she looked more serene than ever. 'You're not going to help me out here, are you?' he asked.

'No,' she answered.

'Hannibal was a clever and cautious man who plotted everything. That was how he was able to live the life he wanted and create another life and image for the world to admire. You were his partner in everything, it stands to reason that he made you his partner in his final adventure. Months, possibly weeks, but I think it was months before the event, he told you he intended to die in his prime. He never left anything to chance, he was subtly preparing you both for the time when *he* chose the day and *he* the manner in which he planned to part from you. It would be at the perfect psychological moment, when he was ready to go and you were used to the idea of beginning another life without him.

'That night in Palm Beach you went to a glittering dinner party but left early to go down to the dock at the bottom of your garden where Hannibal's yacht was moored. The steward served you a bottle of champagne and then left at Hannibal's request. I can only suppose that you spent several hours together. You then changed into swimsuits and swam together for a good distance. My guess is until he asked you for, "A kiss to die by."'

Chadwick jumped up from her chair, upsetting her

wineglass. The red stain spread across the white paper cloth covering the table. No one moved or said a word. She sat down and they watched the boy who had rushed over with a fresh cloth and a wet rag to mop up the table.

'You gave him that kiss and he swam away from you until he vanished in the darkness of night and between the swell of the waves. You swam back to shore and went not to the boat but to the house, bathed, and went to bed. And there is not one shred of real evidence that would hold up in a court of law to prove that I am right or even near right. It's all clues, a case built up out of investigation into your lives and based on your deep and profound love for Hannibal, that was sustained by your joy in obeying every demand he made on you.'

'Do you expect me to comment on your suppositions, Larry?'

'If you did I would be surprised and sorely disappointed in you. You see, before my arrival in Livakia I didn't have a complete picture of you and your character, only bits and pieces that still kept me guessing as to whether you were or were not capable of the things the family accused you of.

'No, of course you will not comment on my interpretation of that night or reveal to anyone what really happened. You can't. To do so would be a betrayal of Hannibal's trust and you could never do that. To tell the truth about that night would indicate that he committed suicide and you did nothing to stop him because you felt, as he did, that as a free man of sound mind he had the right to live and die how and when he chose to. That would have tarnished his image and yours, which Hannibal wanted you to protect at all costs. To live as a grieving widow, which would have satisfied Diana and Warren's grief, would have betrayed his trust that you would leave the past firmly in the past and begin a new life so you did nothing to defend yourself against their accusations. Whatever the price you must pay to keep your secrets, you will pay it.

'Hannibal had planned it that way and as always it was easy for you to follow his plans because your thinking was and still is very much the same as his. Ever since you were a child you held your secrets close to you, all for yourself; they were your private world where you lived how you wanted to live. Hannibal understood that and respected it because he too enjoyed his secrets. Warren and Diana can't even begin to understand that side of your and Hannibal's life – not many people would. They saw your silence and your behaviour as something dark and sinister and so went on the attack.

'After the funeral, an entire life was over for you. You were dumped into the world at the age of thirty-three with a past that vanished overnight, an innocent with eighty million dollars in a world without Hannibal, having to learn how to live, love, and protect yourself all over again. Only you were not *just* all innocent. You were a woman who knew herself and her worth, and one who lived in truth. And there was one thing more: you were joyful, had always been a joyful soul. Life had always been an adventure for you, Chadwick, so you set out for new horizons, leaving Diana and Warren, Hannibal's grandchildren, all your extended family, whom you had loved and been devoted to, behind you. Not abandoned, just left behind. Let Diana and Warren sort themselves out, come to their senses about you, that would be the time to bring them into your new life. Was that what you thought, maybe even still think?'

Larry closed his eyes and drew in a long, deep breath, held it for several seconds, and when he opened them it was with a sigh. He felt tremendous relief, incredible happiness. It was over, he had cracked the case. He knew it. Manoussos knew it. Larry could see that by the expression on his face. And it was the lack of expression on Chadwick's face, just a hint of a smile in her eyes, the manner in which she raised her chin and flicked her hair back with a quick snap of her head, that confirmed to him just how right he was.

'Well, Larry, what's the next step? My guess is New York, that the Martin & Snell agency will make its findings and assumptions available to Chambers, Lodge, Dewy & Coggs, who will then make them available to Warren and Diana?' she challenged.

'The meeting is already set up for three days hence.'

'Chadwick, is that all you have to say? Larry has created a scenario that puts you square in the picture of colluding with your husband, acting as an accessory to the death of a human being in full mental and physical health. For God's sake, if he's got it wrong this is the time to stand up and say what really happened. And if nothing other than what you claimed at the time of Hannibal's death happened, then at the very least tell Larry he has got it all wrong. Your silence condemns you.'

'It's not my silence that condemns me but you, Manoussos, and that does surprise me. You listened to Larry. How sad for us that you really didn't hear what he was saying.'

'Don't patronise me, Chadwick, I don't deserve it.'

Larry rose from his chair and said, 'Clearly you two

have things to work out. I'll walk ahead and meet you at the boat. Take your time.'

Chadwick reached across the table and took Manoussos's hand in hers. She kissed it and her voice had a tremor of emotion in it when she told him, 'I didn't mean to be patronising.'

'Then what did you mean, Chadwick?' asked Manoussos, his anger dissolving, his heart warming towards her for the sadness in her voice, for the love for him so evident in her eyes.

'I love you very much and the life I have living with you. We fell in love at first sight. It was not a one-sided thing that happened to us nor was it just one kind of love. It was sexual and still is sexual, was and is, on my part, for the total being, the very heart and soul of everything you are and have ever been. I know you had and have those very same feelings for me. Ours has been a love lived totally in the moment, from moment to moment, thrilling for the adventure of constantly discovering something new and fresh to add to this life we're living together. The past, other lives and experiences before we met, they moulded us, made us what we are and what we are is what we fell in love with, not the stories of our lives, dead and gone forever.'

Tears were brimming in Chadwick's eyes. Manoussos thought his heart would break for the love for her that was tearing it apart. He placed several bank notes on the table and rose from his chair. His hand still in hers, he drew her up and into his arms.

Together they walked several paces from the coffee shop before they stopped and Manoussos caressed her face. He kissed her eyes and licked a tear from the corner of one then kissed her on the lips. His mind was spinning with fragments of Larry's summary of Chadwick's life with Hannibal, of his conclusions as to what had really happened the night her husband died. Their kiss deepened and his love rose above his anger at what he had perceived as deceit and lies, and drove it away for what he realised had to be forever.

'Then you were never running away from anything?'

'Just refusing to carry the baggage of the past into the present.'

'Something that Warren and Diana couldn't do but you had every faith that they would one day be able to do?'

'I've always been strong on faith.'

They walked the coast road back to the port in silence, seemingly wrapped up in the heat and beauty of the day, the scent of wild flowers pushing up through the barren landscape, the perfume of the sea. Manoussos was severely shaken by the realisation that in the four months he had been living with Chadwick he had been happier than he had ever been in his life because *he* had not carried the baggage of his past into their relationship. Yet he had expected her to, and furthermore for him to approve or disapprove of.

He stopped and took her arm, turning her to face him. He took a long look at her, this beautiful and remarkable woman who loved him. This was the moment of truth for him. He must embrace her faith, her profound belief that living in total freedom in every breath she took was the only truth, that the past was an illusion in the same way as the future is. She lived in the here and now, in the moment, and he knew that she was right to do so.

'I don't think I can live without you, Chadwick.'

'Well then, it's a good thing you don't have to.'

'Oh, thank God. I thought you might no longer want me.'

'I don't give up my happiness so easily, and I thank all the gods that you don't either.'

Epilogue

Livakia was making ready for a christening. That, in itself, was not unusual but the sheer size of this particular event was the cause of great excitement. The child's parents, who had deprived themselves of a large and lavish wedding, were not stinting on this occasion. People started to arrive on the Thursday before the Sunday of the christening. Very nearly every house in the village was being used to accommodate guests from the surrounding mountain villages, from the towns and hamlets of Crete, from Athens and various other places in Greece as well as housing a set of international friends belonging to Chadwick and Manoussos.

Several yachts were already anchored in the bay, their owners and guests kept going to and from the harbour to the port in small motor launches decked with blue and white silk flags and bunting. People remarked that there had never been such a happy occasion on such a grand scale in Livakia.

D'Arcy and Max had taken it upon themselves to make arrangements for the flowers in the church as well as at the port, where the reception after the church service was being held: a sit down luncheon for the entire village and other guests. Max was flying in and out of the port with flowers and trees and several different groups of musicians who were there to play at the many private lunches and dinner parties given in honour of baby Alexandrine Marianna Stavrolakis, the first born of Chadwick and Manoussos.

Overland from Chania and Iraklion came the food and wine and several chefs who had agreed a truce with those of the Kavouria and Pasiphae in order to work together to create a luncheon never to be forgotten. The champagne arrived, cases of it, by boat; vintage Bollinger was Elefherakis's gift. Mark was in charge of organising the many Greeks who wanted to participate in the after-dinner speeches and he declared that he would recite one of the epic Cretan poems. Rachel wrote a poem for the parents, Alexandrine and the event. No one had the heart to ask her not to recite it.

Chadwick had written to Andrew Coggs and Sam, those good men who she had saved and who, in return, had sought to save her. She invited them to the christening to share in this new life she was now living. The invitation had also been issued to some of the many friends she and Hannibal had spent so many years with. They had all accepted and had now been enjoying themselves in Livakia for two days. Diana and Warren, who after Larry Snell's report had abandoned any thought of proceeding against Chadwick but who had not been in contact with her, were asked, along with Larry Snell and Max, to be god parents to Alexandrine. Larry and Max had accepted but neither Diana nor Warren had even given her the courtesy of a reply.

Chadwick had left the excitement and fun going on in the port to climb to the church on the cliffs to dress the small interior with white tulips and lilacs and to light a few candles, to meditate in the peace and beauty of the place she had grown to love so very much. This place was where she felt closer to god and godliness. As she was about to leave she took one last look into the dark interior shimmering in the afternoon sunlight that streamed in through the door. She felt Hannibal's presence as close as if he were standing next to her. Something grazed her cheek, she touched it with her hand, and sensed his kiss, his love for her was still as strong as ever. Whether it was a kiss of the spirit or the imagination she didn't know, but she knew that he loved her and blessed her. 'Hannibal,' she whispered.

A warm breeze caressed her, enveloped her and for a few seconds she bathed in it. Tears came to her eyes and she became engulfed in a sense of love and well-being. The tears vanished and she closed the door, locked it and placed the key in its hiding place. She looked out to sea and it was at that moment that the *Black Narcissus* came round the headland in full sail, the sound of her ship's horn echoing against the cliffs.

Chadwick's heart skipped a beat, she felt that special surge of happiness that she always felt when she knew she was about to see Manoussos. He was on board having left in the early hours of the morning to go and meet the *Black Narcissus* who was bringing in several more friends, whom Chadwick had never met, and Alexandrine's godfather-to-be Larry Snell. For one brief moment she felt a pang of regret for her other family; Diana, Warren, their children, Bill Ogden, who couldn't bring themselves to love her without Hannibal. That was the only flaw to this happy occasion.

She waved to those on board the *Black Narcissus*, aware

that they might not even spot her there among the cliffs, then she hitched up her long white linen skirt into the narrow white snakeskin belt of her backless sun dress and started to run down the cliff path to the port. She would be standing on the quay where the schooner would dock as it dropped anchor.

She had timed it perfectly. The sails were down and she heard the anchor splash into the water and saw Manoussos and Larry at the prow. Chadwick rushed on board and hugged Larry first and then gave Manoussos with a long passionate kiss. He placed his arm round her and she asked, 'Where are your friends? Oh no, have they not come?'

'They have, they're below. Close your eyes, they want to surprise you.'

The happiness in both Manoussos and Larry's face was infectious, she felt as if her heart was singing and closed her eyes.

Footsteps on the deck and muffled giggles and laughter. 'Now! Open your eyes,' ordered Manoussos. She did and Diana, tears in her eyes, rushed forward into Chadwick's arms.

'I knew you'd forgiven us when you asked Warren and I to be god parents. All we have to do now is forgive ourselves.'

The two women hugged each other. Hannibal's grandchildren rushed forward before Warren could get to her, and more kisses and hugs followed. When he did reach her, they clasped each other and kissed and he said, 'Even when lost in our madness we never stopped loving you, we just never knew how to cope with the loss of our father. Thank God you did.'